Twins

Part Two

Books 4 – 6

Katrina Kahler

Table of Contents

Book 4

Consequences

CHAPTER ONE
Ali

Today was crazier than I ever expected. Although it was a huge relief to be myself again, it was strange at the same time. After pretending to be Casey for some many days, I was becoming mixed up with which name I should respond to. I had to keep reminding myself I was Ali again. It was so confusing. Then the Jake thing happened.

Jake had asked me to go out with him.

Jake had actually asked me out!

As I waited for my dad to arrive, I watched all the kids run to their school buses or the cars in the parking lot, and the words were on constant rewind in my head.

Jake asked me out!

Repeating that in my mind still didn't make it real. The best looking boy in our grade was actually interested in me.

As much as I didn't want to admit my crush, it was a little exciting. For a moment, I imagined Jake and me at the movies or just hanging out together. I'd never been out on a date with a boy before, and Jake would make a perfect first one. We had so much in common and got along so well.

But I quickly pushed away those thoughts. It was absolutely not going to happen. I could never do that to Casey. Especially since we did this swap so that she could be with Jake. That had been the whole point. And she would never forgive me.

Or would she?

I shook my head. No, she wouldn't! I tried to picture myself in her shoes and I was certain that I wouldn't be okay with Casey going out with someone I liked first. Especially someone I'd had a crush on long before she arrived. She'd known him for much longer than me and had even told me right away that she liked him. It wasn't until I hung out with him while I was pretending to be her that my feelings grew.

Jake's handsome face flashed through my mind. His brown eyes stared dreamily back at me as I pictured the scene in the hallway only ten minutes earlier.

"Hey, Ali, I was thinking we could do something together this week. Just the two of us," Jake had said. I saw him adjust the straps of his backpack as if he was the one who was nervous.

But I was practically shaking. "Like a date?" I had blurted.

Then he gave me the most amazing smile I'd seen. It was a mix of a cheeky grin and a shy one. That smile had made my stomach flip-flop in a way it had never done before.

"Yeah, like a date." The words had come from his mouth, but I could still hardly believe he'd said them.

It had been so much fun hanging out with him and his friends at school as myself instead of Casey, but I never expected him to ask me out. I even stood there in the hallway for a few seconds, trying to figure out if he thought I was Casey or not. It was obvious that he meant me since he'd said my name, but I still couldn't believe it.

"Oh, um…" I stammered, stalling for words.

When my eyes drifted away from him I saw Casey and Brie down the hallway. They hadn't seen us yet but I didn't want Casey to get the wrong impression. My whole body tingled at that moment but not in a good way. And when I looked back at Jake, he was still only looking at me, waiting for my response.

"Hey, Jake!" Holly and Ronnie had said in unison, breaking the awkward silence between me and Jake.

"Hey, Ali," Ronnie had said. Then she winked at me.

Oh no, had she heard Jake asking me out? Ronnie and Holly were big gossipers. What if they told the whole school? If Casey found out, she would not be happy with me at all. While I hoped they hadn't heard anything, I was happy they'd interrupted us. That had given me a chance to escape.

"Um, Jake, I have to go meet my dad. See you tomorrow." Then, without another word, I had rushed down the hallway.

I heard him calling after me but I didn't dare turn around. If those eyes looked at me once more I might not have had the courage to refuse.

I blinked a few times, holding my overwhelmed emotions in check. The more distance I put between Jake and me, the better I felt. But when I stopped at the curb, my dad's car was nowhere in sight. That was strange in itself. Dad was always on time. So, where could he be?

I took my phone out of my bag and turned it on. Maybe he'd texted to say he was running late. A terrible thought crossed my mind. What if something had happened to Mom? When the phone screen turned on, I didn't have any texts from him. He definitely would have sent me something if there had been an issue. Right?

I held my phone in my fist then crossed my arms. I wanted to be as far away from school as possible. And I wanted to see my parents again. It had been a whole week since I'd seen them last.

I gazed around, and when the figure of someone approaching me appeared in the corner of my eye I turned in that direction.

Jake was coming down the front steps, waving at me. *Oh no!*

I turned quickly back towards the road, a shiver moving down my spine. Leaning closer to the curb, I looked for my dad's car. Of all days for him to be late, I could not believe it had to be this one!

I couldn't deal with Jake right now. The whole situation was awkward. He was supposed to be asking Casey out! He'd had such a good time with "her" this weekend. Even though it was really me, he didn't know that. He thought he was with the real Casey the whole time, so why the sudden interest in me?

While I was thrilled with the idea of going out with Jake as myself, it was something I could not do to Casey.

I glanced over my shoulder again and was surprised to come face to face with my twin. My eyes widened. Would she be able to tell through our psychic connection what had happened?

Casey and Brie stopped next to me. I turned around and smiled at them.

Casey didn't smile back. My stomach churned.

Jake was only a few feet away from us. Would he try and ask me out again with Casey standing right there? I certainly hoped he wouldn't. At the same time, I suspected she already knew that he'd asked me.

"Ali, I want to talk to you about something that I heard," Casey said.

I chewed on my bottom lip. "Sure."

Just as she opened her mouth to speak, a car rolled up beside us.

Turning towards the vehicle in front of me, I looked at the driver who was staring out the window, his eyes wide with surprise.

OMG, it was Dad!

CHAPTER TWO
Casey

As I stood in front of the bathroom mirror, staring at the confused expression on my face, Holly's voice filled my mind. A few minutes earlier, Brie and I had been standing by our lockers in the hallway, when Holly ran to us with the latest news.

Jake asked Ali out. Ali! Not me. How was that possible? What was going on? This wasn't supposed to happen. At camp, Ali hadn't been interested in Jake. She was the one to push him in my direction while pretending to be me. Had she lied? Did she pretend not to like him in front of me, but underneath she really did?

Tears pinched at my eyes. Was this all a plan? Did she know this would happen when we swapped back to our true identities? From the first day she arrived at school, Jake had liked Ali's outgoing and fun personality, just like everyone else. Had Ali planned this all along? Had she used that personality to fool me too?

I had a hard time believing that Ali would intentionally do this to me. She was my sister. My twin! Even though we'd just met a short time ago, we'd developed such a strong bond already.

My mind drifted to the other side of the argument. Was Ali really the person she made herself out to be? Or was she really the spoiled, rich girl that I thought when I first met her? She'd kept the secret of her mother's illness hidden, what other secrets did she have?

I hated feeling that way about her. If this was what it meant to have a sister, then perhaps I would have been better not knowing her at all.

"Casey," Brie said, breaking through my thoughts, "talk to me."

"I don't think Ali would go out with Jake," I said, trying to stop my tears from falling.

"Well, according to Holly, he asked her out."

"I know. I'm just confused about all of this." It was nice to have Brie to talk to. As much as she wasn't good at keeping secrets, she had kept this one, and was firmly on my side.

"I need to talk to Ali," I said. "I have to know if what Holly said was true."

"And if it is?" she asked.

"Then I'll give Ali a chance to explain herself."

"What do you think she'll say?"

"I don't know," I said.

And I really didn't. I hoped that if the rumor was true then she would have said no to Jake. But he was so adorable and so nice. What girl could turn that down?

Brie nodded and we walked out of the bathroom together.

My head was spinning as we made our way to the buses in front of the school. My mind whirled with thoughts of Ali lying to me, and being together with Jake behind my back. When I got home I planned to call her and ask her straight out if Jake had actually asked her out. I'd give her a chance to explain herself. I just hoped she had a good excuse for why Jake would be interested in her. After all, she was supposed to be playing me all weekend each time they saw each other.

"Do you want me to come over later when you call her?" Brie asked.

"I'm not sure," I said. "I'm going to have to talk to my family about this weekend, since Ali spilled the beans."

Thinking about it all, I wondered when I'd get a chance to talk to Ali. I was certain she'd be busy catching up with her family when she arrived home. That part made me wary of her too. I understood it had been hard to keep the secret of our swap, but it seemed that she didn't take it seriously enough. Was it her plan to get my family, as well as the boy I was interested in, to like her more than me?

Brie sucked in a quick breath.

"What is it?" I asked.

"Ali's over there," she said.

I looked in the direction she was indicating and saw Ali waiting by the curb for her dad. This was even better than calling her. My bus hadn't arrived yet, so I'd be able to ask her to her face before going home. Then I'd be able to see for myself if she was telling the truth. Everything right then seemed to be falling into place for once. At least if I got this part out of the way, I'd be able to give all my attention to Mom and Grandma Ann when I got home. I was sure they had questions for me, probably as many as I did for them.

Each step I took toward, the sight of Ali made my stomach churn. I didn't want to think she'd lied to me, but I had to know. She didn't even see us coming until we were right next to her.

Brie crossed her arms and I felt a strength inside me at having my best friend by my side. In that moment, I felt like the lucky one.

"Ali, I want to talk to you about something I just heard," I said.

"Sure," Ali said, looking uncomfortable.

Just as I opened my mouth to speak, a familiar car stopped next to us.

Ali glanced at the car while I side-stepped until I was behind Brie. Ali turned and gave me a look, but I grabbed Brie's arms and tried to hide behind her. Although as Brie was so much smaller than me, it was difficult to stay out of view. But this wasn't the time or the place to tell Ali's dad that we were twins.

He leaned over and looked out the window. He smiled at Ali and it was then that he spotted me. He seemed to stare for a moment. I watched fearfully as his thick eyebrows drew together and his eyes darted between Ali and me. I should have thought this through. I should have known this was a possibility since Ali was picked up by her father each afternoon.

I tilted my head and shook my hair forward so it partly covered my face. It helped that Ali and I didn't dress alike, but after all, we were twins. And he knew what his daughter looked like with her hair down. Would he recognize me as Ali's twin? I looked over at Ali who had the same expression of concern that I did.

CHAPTER THREE
Ali

Dad looked at me and Casey a few times before I snapped into action. I rushed to the car and opened the door.

"Hi Dad," I said a little breathlessly, and jumped into my seat. I sat forward and turned towards him, blocking his view of Casey.

"Um, hi, Ali." He tried to glance around me, but I moved whenever he did. He looked right into my eyes and then settled into his seat.

I took a quick peek back at Casey who was frozen on the curb, her body shaded slightly by Brie.

I waved for them to get moving so my dad wouldn't realize there was a girl at my school who looked exactly like me. This wasn't the time or place for Dad to know what was going on.

"How come you were late?" I asked.

His eyes were narrowed as he focused on the steering wheel in front of him, then he turned to look out the window again. I needed to distract him. I leaned forward until I was almost in his face. "How are you? How was your day? How's Mom? Let's go home now, I want to see her. I was worried all day."

Dad blinked and then looked at me, settling into his seat once again. He shook his head and put the car into drive.

"You seem very chatty this afternoon." He stared at the rearview mirror as we pulled away from the curb. His eyes darted from side to side as he took in the view behind us. I just hoped that Casey was far enough away not to have him suspect anything.

"Yeah, I um…" I tried to think of an excuse. "I had two cookies at lunch today. I think they hyped me up or something." I tried to make a joke of it but he didn't find it at all amusing.

Frowning, he asked, "Who was that girl standing with you on the curb?"

I made a show of turning around. Casey and Brie were walking toward their buses with their backs to us. Even if Dad looked behind us again, neither of them would resemble me from that distance. I let out a breath.

"Which girl? Oh, you mean Brie?" I turned back in my seat, "She's one of my new friends. She's really nice. She was at that slumber party I went to. Her little brother is obsessed with Harry Potter. Brie and I became really close at camp."

Dad cleared his throat as we turned out of the lot. He wasn't even listening to me.

"So how's Mom feeling today?" My distraction attempts weren't working, but I had to keep trying, I needed him to think he was wrong in seeing a girl who looked exactly like me. Why had Casey chosen that moment to talk to me? She knew my dad picked me up. It would have been smart of her to realize that he would probably arrive at any minute. Though he had pulled up rather suddenly. And if my fears were correct, she might already know about Jake asking me out. It was all such a mess.

Dad opened his mouth to speak but I interrupted him with more questions.

"It's so good to see you, Dad. How was work? And Mom? Is she feeling okay today? I think that tie is my favorite of yours, it really brings out your eyes. When did you get that shirt? You look so handsome when you wear it!"

He smirked. “What's with you today? We only saw each other this morning. I was wearing this same shirt and tie. You're acting like you haven't seen me for days.”

I let out a forced laugh. And then I smiled at him. He seemed to forget about Casey for the moment. I missed my parents but I hadn't realized how much until now. It was good to be back in my own life again.

But I’d just left my identical twin on the curb. In my panic, I hadn't even said goodbye to her. Once I got settled at home, I'd have to call her and apologize. Meanwhile, I had to keep my dad thinking that nothing was out of the ordinary. I certainly wasn't ready to tell him or my mom just yet. Once I was sure she was better, I’d be able to explain everything. But that wouldn't happen today. Even if Mom felt better, there was no guarantee how she’d feel tomorrow.

And I worried that telling her might make her condition worse.

"Who was that girl again?" Dad asked, as if he were reading my mind. "The one in the pink top with long brown hair? You said her name was Brie?"

I sighed, knowing I'd have to explain somehow without giving it all away just yet. "Oh, the one in pink with the long wavy hair? That's Casey, Brie's best friend." I didn't want to expand on Casey as I had done with Brie. I didn't want Dad to think any more of her.

"Casey?" he asked, his eyebrows raised curiously. His frown returned as he continued, "It was really odd, but it was like looking at a double of you."

I forced another laugh. "What? Casey?"

Dad slowed the car at a stoplight. "Ali, I could have sworn I was looking at you twice. Just wearing different clothes."

"Are you sure you don't need glasses, Dad?" I asked, brushing it off.

He rubbed his eyes. "I guess I do look at a computer screen all day."

"That's probably it," I said. I'd never lied to him before, but I couldn't let him find out just yet.

"I could have sworn, though," he added stubbornly.

I could almost hear his thoughts and how he still didn't believe me. I only hoped that I'd be able to explain everything before he saw Casey again.

CHAPTER FOUR
Casey

Brie and I stopped at the doors to my bus. "Just call Ali later," Brie said. "I'm sure there's a good explanation for everything. And let me know if you need to talk." She put a hand on my shoulder. "Everything will be okay, Casey."

I nodded. "Thanks, Brie." Although I wasn't fully reassured, I was still grateful to have her to talk to.

We said goodbye, and Brie headed to the next bus behind mine. Not for the first time did I wish we took the same bus. Maybe then she could come home with me and be by my side when I faced Mom and Grandma Ann. I knew I had to do this alone, though.

I sat in the middle of the bus, in my normal seat. I leaned my head against the cool glass window and closed my eyes. What a day!

My backpack shifted on the seat next to me and I opened my eyes, prepared to ask the person who'd just sat down to move to another spot. I wasn't in the mood to chat with anyone.

Instead, I saw Lucas sitting alongside me. I moved my bag onto my lap and stared back at him. He didn't say a word. I glanced around, looking for his friends. They were a few rows up and weren't aware that my brother was sitting with me. Not since the first day of Lucas going to kindergarten had we sat together on the bus. It was an unspoken rule between us.

"What are you doing?" I asked abruptly. I knew I should be happy to see him, but right then, I had more important things on my mind and didn't need my little brother annoying me. Obviously, nothing had changed in the time I was away. I hoped he wasn't planning a stupid prank, or else I'd be sure to embarrass him for trying.

He continued to stare at me with a strange expression.

Finally, I couldn't take it anymore. "What are you staring at?" I couldn't help the irritation in my voice.

He nodded his head and said. "Just checking to make sure it's you. Yeah, it's definitely you!"

I rolled my eyes. He wanted to make sure I was the real Casey and not Ali pretending to be me. I shook my head at him, even more annoyed that he didn't just ask me. He was always doing weird stuff like that. Some things never changed. How had Ali managed to put up with him for a whole weekend?

"Yes, it's me," I said, "you can leave now!"

He let out a dramatic sigh and mumbled under his breath, then went up front to sit with his friends.

I moved my bag back over onto the seat next to me, so no one else would try to sit there. There were enough seats for everyone and I wanted to be alone.

As the bus started forward, the reality that lay ahead for me took a primary place in my thoughts. As much as I was upset with Ali about Jake, I had much more to worry about right then. In less than a half-hour, I'd have to face my mom and Grandma Ann. I still couldn't believe Ali had told them about the swap. That hadn't been a part of the plan.

Neither was the idea of Jake asking Ali out. All the things that had gone wrong with the swap had involved Ali somehow. It wasn't fair. I had done everything right, yet I wasn't the one who Jake wanted to ask on a date.

I could just imagine the response I'd get from my mother and grandmother. Would they even be happy to see me? Would they welcome me or would they—like Lucas—prefer to have Ali there instead? Ali had made a great impression with everyone at school. I wondered what my family thought of her. Ali had only good things to say about them. But how could that be? All my mom did was work, Lucas was incredibly annoying, and Grandma Ann constantly nagged me about homework and a heap of other things.

Would they be angry when I walked through the door because I'd disappeared for the weekend and deceived them? My head started to feel full with all the questions running through my mind. As well, my stomach heaved with each bump in the road. But I knew it had nothing to do with car sickness. It was the fear of what would happen when I got home that was making me feel ill.

But then I reminded myself of one simple fact. I would never have done any of it if they'd been honest with me. I had every right to be upset and they had so much to answer for. Keeping the truth from me was wrong.

I focused on that thought for the rest of the ride home. If they tried to question me about my actions, I would question them right back. I think I deserved an explanation before they confronted me about why Ali and I had switched.

Though when the bus pulled up to our stop, a weight settled in my stomach.

The second Lucas got off the bus, he sprinted for home. Hopefully, he would lose some of that energy by the time I got there. I said goodbye to the bus driver and got off the bus. As I walked alone down the street, each step added more to the anxious feelings bouncing around in my body.

Walking up to the front door, I hesitated. I could hear Lucas talking to someone inside. Imagining my small, stuffy house compared to the huge and luxurious one that Ali was going home to, I sighed heavily. She was returning to her spacious and tidy home, a bedroom closet overflowing with clothes and shoes, and share two parents who adored her.

I took a huge breath to try and boost my resolve. There was nothing I could do about any of it right now. I reached out and turned the knob, opening the front door to face whatever encounter was ahead of me.

CHAPTER FIVE
Ali

Dad managed to drop the questions about Casey for the rest of the ride home. I didn't know if he sensed I was hesitant to talk about it, or if he'd begun to question what he'd really seen. I just hoped he wouldn't say anything to Mom. Though knowing her delicate state, I doubted he'd want to upset her about something he wasn't one hundred percent certain of.

When we turned towards our driveway and the sight of our large house loomed over us, I took a deep breath and felt a sense of deep-seated relief. It was so good to be home.

Once the car pulled up alongside my mother's red sedan, I didn't even wait until the engine was turned off before I jumped out.

Running inside, I raced upstairs. "Mom?" I went

down the hall to her room. The bed was perfectly made without a wrinkle in the quilt. I checked the bathroom and couldn't find her.

When I heard the front door close, I went to the stairs but Dad wasn't anywhere to be seen. He'd probably gone to his office. I knew his work suffered whenever Mom had another episode, so I imagined a lot of late nights for the next week or so. Although that was fine with me. It would give me more time with my mom to watch movies, paint our nails, and do the other fun things we did when she was feeling well.

Hopefully, she was feeling better. And if that was the case, I knew where she'd be. I raced down the stairs, twisted around the banister and headed for the kitchen. Opening the sliding door, I moved quickly onto the patio and was out of breath when I reached the side gate, leading into the garden. I shoved it open and scanned the bright colorful flower beds to find her. I was forced to walk a few feet further before spotting movement out of the corner of my eye.

Her white straw hat was the first thing I saw. She stood up, took the hat from her head and wiped at her brow. I could hardly contain myself at seeing her face again. "Mom!"

Her expression spilled into a wide grin. Everything that had happened since I left for camp was whisked away and replaced by my utter happiness at seeing her again.

I ran over to her and wrapped her in a huge hug. "It's so good to see you." I squeezed her tighter and found that she felt thinner than I remembered.

Mom laughed. "Ali, it's great to see you too. My, you're so affectionate lately." She wriggled out of my grasp and held my hands in hers. "Are you okay? Is everything okay at school?"

I nodded, even though everything in my life wasn't great, other than my parents. I would think about Casey later. I couldn't help the tears that sprang to my eyes at seeing her again after an entire week. "Yes, everything is fine. I've just been so worried about you lately. I miss you terribly when I'm away."

Mom tilted her head back and laughed again. "Is that all? Ali, I'm fine. Really. Don't worry about me."

"I can't help it," I said. "I think about you all day."

And that was the truth. The past week had been the most exciting and the most terrifying all at the same time. Each night I went to sleep, I wondered if I'd wake up to a phone call about my mom. Being with her in that moment was perfect, and it made me feel whole. I never wanted to do another swap again.

"I'm almost done here," Mom said. "Then we can go inside and have some tea?"

"I would love that," I said. I wished I could sit and have tea with her forever.

As much as Mom was smiling, I knew I only had a limited amount of time with her. The seriousness of the situation crashed down on me. My mom's illness wasn't going to get better, and that fact was confirmed when she had to go to the emergency room over the weekend.

At the time, I'd been away, selfishly wanting to meet my biological family when my real family was in turmoil. I couldn't even think of the situation with Jake right then, as that would only add to my guilt. Betraying my twin sister was not something I had ever intended.

It became hard to breathe as I realized how stressful my life had become, it was so hard to deal with. And being back at home in the care of the family I'd grown up with and loved so dearly, I finally broke with the pressure.

Tears flowed down my cheeks and I couldn't help the wracking sobs that broke inside of me. "Mom..." I reached for her, the woman who took me in when no one else wanted me. She soothed me with soft and gentle sounds while rubbing circles around my back with the palm of her hand, the way she had done when I was little.

"What's wrong, Ali?" Mom said. "You know you can tell me anything."

I clung to her. Just like at Casey's house, I knew I wasn't going to be able to keep lying to my parents. An overwhelming sense of guilt flooded my body. I needed to tell them everything, even if it hurt them. I didn't want them to feel bad, but I wondered if I explained myself properly, then they would know how happy I was to meet Casey. They'd had a stranger in their house over the weekend and it was only fair to them to come clean. But would they ever forgive me?

CHAPTER SIX
Casey

When I walked into the house, I expected my mom and Grandma Ann to be standing there with crossed arms and disappointed expressions on their faces. But they weren't in sight. So I was able to take a minute to collect myself. I dropped my backpack by the door and listened for their location. Lucas wasn't talking, which was a total shock to me. Maybe they were all outside.

As I walked into the house, I heard explosion sounds coming from Lucas's room. He was playing his silly fantasy figurine games again. Whenever he did that while I was around, I ended up with his spit all over me. It was disgusting. Even in the time I was away, he hadn't managed to change at all. I wasn't sure I expected him to, but since my whole life had changed over the weekend, I had a small thought that things around here would have as well. At least a little bit.

Ali had tried to tell me that Mom was going to work less. I doubted that. And I was sure Grandma Ann would still be incredibly nosey. The things I'd become used to over the years, such as Lucas's annoying behavior and Mom not wanting anything to do with us, began to niggle at me. Ali's parents didn't have any annoying habits, and even if they did, Ali was able to go to a completely different wing of the house to get away if she needed to. The walls in my home felt as if they were paper thin, and I wasn't able to ever escape my family when it all became too much.

When I heard voices in the kitchen, I hesitated in the hallway. I could easily sneak into my room and close the door, but then I'd just prolong the conversation with them. So I decided to get it over with.

Peering discreetly around the door, I found Mom and Grandma Ann sitting at the table, each with a cup of tea in front of them. I pulled the door open wide and stood in the doorway, waiting for them to make the first move.

"I honestly don't know..." Mom said to Grandma Ann.

Suddenly noticing me, she lifted her eyes lifted to mine. They widened and she stood from her chair. "Casey?"

I stood there, unsure of what to say. I wanted her to start speaking first but we both stared at each other instead. It was the same look that Lucas gave me on the bus at school. Could Mom really not tell Ali and me apart? I knew we were twins but it sort of hurt me that she couldn't pick out the daughter she'd raised from birth.

Grandma Ann stood up. "It's nice to have you back home, Casey. I hope you're feeling well again?"

I didn't take my eyes off my mom. "I'm fine. Ali's parents took good care of me."

The corners of Mom's eyes tightened, and a little sliver of satisfaction bloomed inside of me.

Grandma Ann licked at the corner of her lips. It was a gesture she used if she was nervous or uncomfortable in some way. "Now, if you two will excuse me, I'm going outside to check on my vegetables."

She filled the watering can that she stored under the sink, then left through the back door. Our garden was nowhere near as nice as the one that Ali looked at every day from her kitchen window. But Grandma Ann had a green thumb and she was a very good gardener. I wasn't a fan of vegetables but the ones she grew were definitely fresher than the microwave freezer ones that Mom stocked up for us.

Mom opened her mouth to say something but Lucas's voice filled the room.

"I'm hungry! What is there to eat?" he whined.

I rolled my eyes. Some things would never change

around here. I could not help the same thought from spinning constantly in my head. I doubted Lucas was this annoying when Ali was around, surely she wouldn't have been able to take it. He was probably on his best behavior, tricking her into thinking he was a great brother.

Lucas had his hand on the refrigerator door handle but didn't open it. When there was no answer from anyone, he whipped around and saw Mom and me stock still, staring at each other.

"In case you're wondering," Lucas said to Mom. "Casey's back. The real Casey, I mean. And yes it's definitely her. I can tell the difference now. Casey gets this little crease in her forehead..." he pointed to the space between his eyebrows, "when I'm around."

Mom almost looked relieved to hear that. "Lucas, you may have two cookies. Dinner will be in about an hour and I don't want you to be full."

He let out a war cry and turned to grab a glass from the cabinet. He filled it with milk.

Then he reached inside the cookie jar and took a handful of cookies and left the room.

Mom sighed. "Casey, I have a lot of explaining to do. And a lot to make up for."

All the anger I'd felt when Grandma Ann initially told me the full story built up again and resurfaced. "How could you have done this to me?" Then I thought about Ali and the way I was forced to live her life over the weekend and keep up the disguise. While at the same time, Ali and my family had revealed the truth and were having fun getting acquainted.

Heat flushed through my body and I stomped my foot, unable to hold it in any longer. "I'll never forgive you for this!"

I didn't bother to wait for Mom's reaction to my outburst. I needed to get away from her. She needed to realize what she had done to her daughter. She hurt me worse than anyone could ever have done.

I rushed out of the room. Lucas was standing in the hallway, staring at me. I pushed him roughly against the wall out of the way, ignoring his protest.

He'd be fine. He was exaggerating as usual. When I reached my room, I slammed the door closed. Throwing myself onto the bed, I burst into tears. A stream of hot, angry tears raced down my cheeks, creating a wet patch on the comforter.

Everything was such a mess. Why did this all have to happen to me?

CHAPTER SEVEN
Ali

Mom led me into the kitchen and sat me down on a chair. "Ali, stay here, I'm going to get your father."

I nodded and wiped at the tears that soaked my cheeks.

She rushed off and I took a deep breath. I couldn't believe I'd caved under the pressure once more. First, it was with my biological mom and grandmother, and now it was with the family who had raised me. This time was different though. The reveal had to be on my own time. And I wasn't willing to spend another day lying to my mom since I didn't know how much time I had left with her.

Both my parents came back into the room. Mom looked frantic and she was clasping her hands in front of her. My stomach sank. This wasn't what I wanted.

Dad strode into the room with an expression I'd only seen when he was with important clients. He was concerned, but wanted to appear cool in front of Mom.

"Ali, are you okay?" he asked, sitting in the chair next to me. "What's going on? Your mother told me you burst into tears in the garden. Is something going on at school?"

I couldn't find the words to explain.

Dad leaned forward. "Just yesterday, you told me everything was fine."

"I know," I said. "Everything is fine. But I do have something to tell you."

"Then tell us," Mom pleaded, placing her hand on my shoulder.

I took a deep breath and started at the beginning. "On the first day of school, I saw a girl in my class who looked similar to me."

My parents shared a look. I waited for them to say

something, but Dad nodded his head for me to continue. I was hesitant at first, but once I started, the whole story tumbled out one word after another.

"The girl's name is Casey. I didn't think too much about our similarities until I went to the sleepover. When Casey and I were alone in the bathroom brushing our teeth, we looked into the mirror side by side. It was so weird because we both had our hair down and we looked exactly the same."

My parents stared at me but did not say a word. I took a deep breath and kept talking.

"The other girls couldn't believe how much we looked alike. Then we found out that we shared the same birthday. It seemed too strange to be just a coincidence, and neither of us could stop thinking about it. Our friends even suggested that we might be twins, separated at birth. But we told them that was a ridiculous idea."

My parents' only reaction was to glance briefly at each other as I spoke. Mom looked at me silently, waiting for me to continue.

"Then at camp, Casey told me she'd had a talk with her grandmother, who told her the whole story. Casey's mom had twin girls when she was a teenager. She gave one of them away to be adopted since they were unable to care for two. That was when we both knew we really were twins."

Mom sighed heavily but still did not say a word. I looked quickly at my dad but he remained silent as well. I paused for a moment and took a deep breath. Next was the hard part, telling them that I'd deceived them for the entire weekend.

"We thought it would be a fun idea to trick the other kids and teachers by swapping places at camp. And when we did, no-one noticed. I happened to complain to Casey about not being able to sleep at night because the girls in my cabin were so noisy and never stopped talking. So Casey offered to pretend to be me for a night, so I could sleep in her cabin instead. But then she got sick and the teacher called you to come and pick her up, thinking she was me. We didn't want to get into trouble with the teachers for the swap so we kept pretending to be each other. And Casey came home with you. I stayed on at camp and then went to her place for the weekend."

The final details had poured out in a rush and when I eventually stopped talking, I waited for my parents to say something. But instead, they just stared at me, both of them in shock. I knew I'd messed up by doing the swap, but like Casey had said, both sets of parents had lied to us for years. We weren't the only ones who needed to explain ourselves.

"Why didn't you ever tell me I was a twin? How could you keep something so important from me? I always had this big hole in my heart that needed to be filled. I love both of you so much, but it was so unfair to hide this secret from me!"

Mom let out a little groan and clutched at her chest. She suddenly looked very unwell.

"Ali, stop talking, please," Dad said in a sharp tone.

I covered my mouth with my hand.

He rushed to her side. "Grace, are you okay?"

Her eyelids fluttered, something I'd seen her do before passing out.

"Mom?"

"Ali, help me," Dad said.

I pushed away from the table and went to her other side. Her breathing was so jagged and raspy.

We helped her out of the chair and she leaned heavily into both of us. Dad helped keep her upright while we slowly shuffled to the stairs. No one said a word about what I'd just revealed. Instead, Dad was giving her encouraging words about making it up the stairs.

"You just need to lay down for a little while. I told you being out in the garden all afternoon would take its toll."

Mom muttered something, but I couldn't tell what it was.

We managed to get to the landing at the top. By then, I was breathing just as hard as she was. Once she was in bed, I stepped back and watched Dad put the covers over her. When she closed her eyes her breathing slowed, and she let out a huge sigh before dozing off to sleep.

Dad grabbed my arm. "Let's leave her to rest."

When we got into the hallway, he released his grip, and I looked guiltily towards him. "Dad, I'm sorry…"

He held up a hand to silence me. "No more talk of this today. Your mother is in a terrible condition right now. I think you should just go to your room. We'll talk later."

And with that, he left me standing in the hallway. Alone.

Heat filled my eyes and I struggled to keep my tears at bay.

I ran to my room and closed the door. Pressing my palms against my eyes, I took a deep breath. The memory of Mom's pale face filled my mind. I couldn't believe I'd been so selfish. As much as telling my side of the story had felt good for me, I didn't even realize what it had been doing to her. Now I'd caused the one thing I'd been so afraid of. I paced back and forth across my room, my stomach clenched with fear. I felt sick inside and overwhelmed with guilt. What was going to happen now that the secret was out?

Would she be okay?

CHAPTER EIGHT
Casey

I laid in bed for over an hour, staring at the clock on my bedside table. My tears were dried up and I wallowed in my anger the entire time.

When someone knocked on the door, I buried my face in my pillows. "Go away!"

The door opened and I turned around to see Mom in the doorway. She didn't enter my room, but instead stood there, hesitant and unsure.

Good. She should feel bad about all of this.

I narrowed my eyes at her.

She sighed. "Casey, I'd like to explain. If you would give me a chance."

I sat up and tucked my legs under me. "Fine, explain!"

She sat on the far corner of the bed. "I'm going to explain the same way I did to Ali. Granted, I thought she was you at the time. I should have known since she was so open to everything. You tend to give me a bigger challenge."

I rolled my eyes. The same old thing…Ali being better than me again.

"When I was a teenager and fell pregnant, I was excited about having a child and being with your father for the rest of our lives. But when I told him, he couldn't cope with the idea of being a father. And his family wanted nothing to do with the situation. They all said that he was too young to have kids. He listened to his family and left.

Grandma Ann was there to help me, but with your grandfather's poor health, the pregnancy couldn't have come at a worse time. And then I found out I was having twins. It was all too much for any of us to cope with. I was so young and my dad was so ill. There was no money to pay his medical expenses and we were struggling financially. I had barely enough to support myself, let alone two babies as well.

Guidance counselors tried to advise me and in the end, I decided to give up both of you once you were born. They assured me you both would be taken care of in the way that we couldn't, and that it was the best thing for both my babies. I finally agreed that it was for the best. I only wanted the best for you both.

But then you were born. When you looked up at me with those beautiful eyes and your little hand wrapped around my finger, I knew I wouldn't be able to let you go. Instead, I decided to keep you. And I gave Ali away. That decision haunted me for years. I've felt guilt over it ever since, and not a day has gone past that I haven't thought about your twin. I always wondered where she was, but I knew she'd have a better life than if I had kept both of you."

"So why didn't you tell me I had a twin somewhere?" I asked.

"I wanted to," she said. "When I thought you were old enough to deal with hearing the truth. Then I just kept putting it off, because it was such a difficult thing to admit to, until now."

"You're only telling me now because I've found out on my own!" I could not help my angry tone and I stared at her defiantly.

She sighed heavily and nodded. "That's true. But you should know that I never wanted this to go on as long as it did. I just never knew when to bring it up."

Even though I had her explanation, I still didn't feel satisfied.

Mom reached for my hand and I slid it away. She sat up straighter and spoke, "I'm so sorry, Casey. For everything. I will spend the rest of my life trying to make it up to you."

I wasn't sure that she ever could make it up to me. I

was certain Ali had already forgiven her, but there were some differences between us. I understood if Ali's parents didn't share where she came from since they obviously had issues having their own kid. But I lived with the woman who had given birth to twins and got rid of one. I should have known about Ali before meeting her myself.

"I don't know what else to say," she said, her voice faltering and tears forming in her eyes. "I'm so sorry, Casey. All I wanted was the best for both of you."

I stared back at her but didn't speak.

"Is there anything else you want to ask me?"

I shook my head.

"You don't want to know about your real father? Ali had questions—"

"I'm not Ali," I interrupted. "And besides what would it matter if I knew who he was? He still abandoned us. I don't ever want to meet him."

Mom nodded. "I understand." Pausing for a moment, she took another deep breath before continuing. "So where does that leave us?"

My eyebrows lifted. "Nothing has changed, Mom. I'm so upset that everyone lied to me. I don't know when I'll be able to think about forgiving you."

"Casey, that isn't fair. You have no idea what we went through."

"Only because it took you years to tell me! How can anyone abandon a child? A twin! And never tell your own daughter about it? If I hadn't met Ali, would you ever have told me? Would there ever be a good time to tell me I had a twin sister somewhere in the world?"

She flinched. "To be honest, I don't know."

"Then why should I forgive you? The only reason you stopped lying is because I found out first."

"You're right," she said.

"I know I am," I said crossing my arms.

Lucas barged into my room. "What's going on? What

are you talking about? Casey, were you crying? Your face is all puffy—"

"Lucas, get out of my room!" I yelled.

He jumped back and his lower lip started to tremble.

"Why did *you* have to come home, Casey? I prefer my other sister to you! She's nice to me and doesn't yell all the time."

And with that, he turned on his heel and ran out of the room.

"Casey I know you're upset but don't take it out on your brother."

"Whatever."

"I hope someday you can find it in your heart to

forgive me. I did what I thought was best for you both." She slowly shook her head and crossed the threshold into the hallway, closing the door behind her.

I flung myself back onto the bed and closed my eyes. I had no more tears to cry, but I had plenty of anger left. I was angry at my mom and grandmother for lying. I was mad at Lucas for liking Ali more than me. And I was mad at Ali for being so forgiving to my mother. Ali and I should have been a united front, but at that moment I'd never felt so alone.

CHAPTER NINE
Ali

I must have paced the room a hundred times before I heard a knock on my door. I sprinted to it and whipped it open. Dad stood there.

"Is everything okay with Mom?" I asked. I was still so anxious and my stomach had not stopped churning.

"She's fine," he said. "May I come in?"

I moved out of the way so he could. He put his hand on my shoulder and led me to the bed. I hopped up onto it and he sat down too.

He wiped his hand over his face and then looked at me. "Ali, I don't want you to feel concerned with what happened. We're not mad, it was just a shock. And in your mother's current condition she wasn't able to handle the shock very well."

"Chris! Ali!" Mom called from her room.

Sucking in a sharp breath, I hopped off the bed. I bolted out of my room and down the hall. What if something was wrong with her and I was the one to have caused it?

"Mom?" I asked, when I reached her open doorway. "Are you okay? Do you need something?"

Dad stood behind me. He took my hand, bringing me over to the bed.

"Ali," Mom said, "everything is just fine. I'm sorry I scared you."

"I should be the one who's sorry," I said. "I caused you so much stress."

Mom took a deep breath. "I admit I was a little taken aback by what you told us. But there's no need for you to feel upset by it. We're the ones who need to apologize."

I looked at her and then glanced at my dad. He gripped firmly to my hand as he spoke. "We want to talk to you about your adoption," he said. "We've been so hesitant in the past, but clearly, we owe you an explanation."

"Okay," I replied quietly. Finally, the time had come and I struggled to breathe as I looked from my mom to my dad.

Mom patted a spot next to her and I sat down, taking in every word as she spoke. "I'm so sorry we've kept this from you, Ali. But you must know that it was my decision, not your father's. I was so upset about not being able to give birth to a child of my own. I'd always wanted a large family, so anytime you asked about your adoption, I'd try and change the subject. I just didn't want to talk about it. But there's more than that!"

She stopped there and looked at my dad. I could see she needed help to continue.

"Let's start at the beginning," Dad suggested.

Mom took a deep breath and nodded. "When we found out that we couldn't have a child on our own, the next step for us was adoption. We figured that this was the path we were meant to follow." Mom stroked the top of my head and moved her fingers down my braid.

"We were actually promised a baby twice, but both times the mothers ended up keeping the babies for themselves."

That sounded a lot like my biological mother. If she didn't have twins, would my parents have ever had the chance to raise a child?

"We knew that you were a twin when we adopted you. But we didn't know where the mother and other twin were located. It was a closed adoption so even if we wanted to give you information, we wouldn't have been able to."

"Can you understand where we were coming from?" Dad asked.

I nodded.

"Each time you asked me about your biological family, it broke my heart," Mom said. "Selfishly, I thought it meant you didn't want to be with us. I needed to hold onto you before I lost you. I thought if you knew about your biological family, you wouldn't want to live with us anymore."

"You'd never lose me, Mom," I said. Tears fell from my eyes and plopped onto my lap.

Mom was crying then too. I leaned over and wrapped my arms around her. She held me tightly as if she never wanted to let go and I could feel the shaking of her thin body. Tears streamed down my own cheeks and when I pulled back slightly, she reached for a tissue from the box by her bed, first of all, passing one to me, then taking one for herself.

"Will you ever forgive us, Ali?" she asked quietly, her face full of hope and despair.

I nodded my head, and then looked to my dad who had reached for my hand once more. "It's okay," I replied quietly. "I understand. The important thing is that you're okay, Mom. That's all that matters!"

Mom smiled at me, her face flooded with relief. I smiled back at her, "I feel so much better now that we've talked. I've felt so guilty all weekend, knowing that I'd deceived you."

Mom stared at me and shook her head, "I can't believe you girls managed to do that, and no one realized!"

I grinned at the memory, "It wasn't easy!"

"Tell me about your twin," Mom prodded. "Casey is her name?"

"That's the girl I saw at school?" Dad asked.

I looked towards him. "Yes, but it wasn't the right time for you to find out. I'm sorry I couldn't tell you the truth. I hope you aren't upset."

He laughed. "I'm not upset, Ali. I really did think I was seeing double, though. It's incredible how alike you are."

"And she was here all this weekend?" Mom asked.

"Yes," I nodded. "You two made a good impression on her. She didn't want to leave here."

Mom and Dad shared a look. "I did notice some differences a few times," Mom said. "I wondered if it was because you weren't quite yourself after being unwell. But I wasn't sure. I just couldn't put my finger on it."

"Tell us about your weekend? Casey's family was good to you?" Dad asked, curiously. "I can't believe you spent the entire weekend there! This whole scenario seems surreal!"

"I know," I agreed, "It's as though I've just woken up from the craziest dream. I still can't believe it myself! But my weekend was amazing!" I rushed on excitedly.

I'd been desperate to tell them everything that happened, and now that I'd been given the chance it all came pouring out.

"My birth mother is very nice. She looks like an older version of Casey and me. And Grandma Ann—my mom's mother—is such a sweet woman. Oh! And I have a little brother, his name is Lucas and he's the cutest! He and Casey don't get along very well, but I think he's adorable. And this weekend we went to a carnival, as well as Lucas's baseball game." I failed to mention Jake since I wasn't sure how to explain him to my parents quite yet.

I noticed Mom's smile didn't quite reach her eyes. I knew that look. "Mom, are you okay? Did I say something to upset you?"

"No, dear," she gave Dad another look, then turned to me. "They sound like wonderful people, but I do wonder if you think you might be better off with them?"

"Oh, no!" I said, grabbing onto her hands and squeezing. "You're my parents. I never, ever, want to leave either of you!" I wrapped an arm around each of them and hugged them both. "I'm just so excited that I have two families. And you're both really special to me."

"Well," Dad said, "I guess the next step would be to meet this family."

Mom nodded slowly, as though it was hard for her to agree. I realized this hurt her, but I thought it would be good for everyone in the long run. Once Mom met my biological family, I was sure they would get along really well.

"Yes," I nodded, eagerly. "I want that too. Casey loved you both so much, I know she wants to see you again. She had such a good time getting to know you. Even though you thought she was me!"

I was giddy with excitement and couldn't wait to tell my twin. "I'll call her right now and arrange it. She'll be just as excited as I am!"

I kissed them both on the cheek and then bounced out of their room. Hurrying down the hallway, I went into my own room and reached for my phone. I turned on the screen but suddenly felt reluctant to make the call.

Was Casey in the middle of a conversation with our mom right then? I wondered how it was all going at their house. I hoped that once everything was explained, Casey would be able to forgive our mother and move on.

For some reason though, I hesitated. As much as I wanted to speak to my sister, I had a feeling that it might not be a good time.

CHAPTER TEN
Casey

For the rest of the evening, I didn't come out of my room. My homework sat in my bag at the front door, but I didn't care.

There was no way I wanted to face anyone. If I did, that would open up the conversation again when I saw Grandma Ann or Mom.

I thought about how much homework I had to get done. Because we'd been at camp for a week, we had spent the day reviewing lessons from the week before, and also writing about our experience at camp. I think I only had some math problems to do. Maybe Brie could help me with them in the morning before class.

Since the walls were so thin, I could hear Grandma Ann and Mom in the kitchen, talking.

I ended up getting under the covers and pulling my pillow over my head, to drown out whatever it was they were saying about me.

"Casey," Grandma Ann said through my bedroom door about an hour later. "It's time to eat."

"I'm not hungry!" I called from under my covers. I had barely moved since the talk with Mom. It was all too much to deal with, and there was no way I wanted to sit with my family at the dinner table. I just wanted everyone to leave me alone!

"Casey," Grandma Ann said.

"I'm not coming out, you can't make me!"

I hesitated, waiting to see what she would do next. I knew I was pushing her boundaries but I couldn't shake how angry I was. How had Ali recovered so quickly? She'd just accepted everything our mom had told her. I was smarter than that though. Mom needed to understand the damage she'd caused in my life.

A text came through on my phone. Brie had texted me a bunch earlier, but I hadn't responded yet. I wasn't ready to get into it again just yet.

This text was from Ali: *Are you okay? How did your afternoon go? I told my parents and they're dying to meet you. Are you free to talk?*

I groaned and tossed the phone back onto the bedside table, ignoring her. She hadn't even waited a day to tell her parents. I hoped they weren't too upset with me for lying to them. I'd had the best time with them over the weekend. Though from the text, they seemed willing to meet me without an issue.

I knew if I started the conversation with Ali, she wouldn't stop asking questions. And just like with Brie, I didn't want to talk to anyone right then. I wanted to wallow in my anger for a little while longer. Mom needed to know that her actions had consequences.

I tried to push my mother out of my head for a while. But then thoughts of the school day and the disastrous ending flooded my mind. I'd had so many missed opportunities to catch up with Ali. She was so preoccupied with Jake and his friends during each of the breaks. It was annoying that she got along so well with everyone, while I was the outcast. And I hated that Jake was interested in her when he should have liked me instead!

Then with her Dad interrupting us, I couldn't ask her about what had happened with Jake. Was it true that he'd asked her out? Did she say yes? Did she tell him that I liked him? I really hoped she turned him down without telling him about my crush. I would never be able to look him in the eye again if he knew! But he wasn't even taking any notice of me anymore. He only had eyes for Ali.

My stomach stirred with a feeling of nausea. Pushing through it. I sat up in bed. I stayed there for a moment before feeling well enough to cross the room and turn off the light. Shuffling back to my bed, I pulled the covers over my head again until I couldn't see a sliver of light in my little cocoon. I squeezed my eyes shut, wanting the day to be over. I tried to make myself fall asleep, but instead, all I could think about was the following day.

And I was not looking forward to it.

CHAPTER ELEVEN
Ali

When I woke the next morning, it was still very early. I pulled my phone out from under my pillow and checked for any response from Casey.

Nothing.

I scrolled through the texts, unsure if I'd said something that would upset her. The questions were all straight-forward, nothing that could cause her not to respond.

I rubbed my eyes and rolled back over. I hadn't been able to fall asleep until after eleven because I was worried about the stress I'd caused my family. I was also wondering what had happened between Casey and our mom. I was surprised I was even awake at that moment. Normally, I needed a full night's sleep to function.

It bothered me that Casey hadn't returned my texts. Even a simple "Okay" would have been good enough for me. I knew she usually had her phone with her. But what if she was in trouble over the swap and had her phone taken away? And worse still, what if there was another reason, the one that I'd pushed to the back of my mind? If she'd found out about Jake, she'd be upset with me for sure. I worried that things were not good between us. The thoughts swirled through my head and made me more anxious than ever.

Deep down, I really wanted to say yes to Jake. But it was a fantasy that could never happen. I couldn't do that to Casey, it would be too cruel. And there was no way I would jeopardize my relationship with my twin over a silly boy crush.

And then Jake's face popped into my mind and I thought about all the attention he'd given me at school. I'd tried not to encourage him but it was so much fun hanging out together. I realized that I must have been too friendly though, and he had the impression that I liked him. While that was definitely true, I hadn't meant to show it.

As much as I worried about Casey's reaction, I also wondered what Jake now thought of me. I'd raced off and left him behind as quickly as I could, and then ignored him when he approached me outside the school. Would he think less of me because of it? I really hoped things would still be okay between us.

As far as Casey was concerned, if she had found out, it had to be from Holly or Ronnie. Ronnie loved gossip but Holly was just as bad.

Why did those girls always have to get involved in everyone else's business? I knew if they'd heard something, they would have spread it around, and since Casey and Brie had been down the hall, they would have been the first to find out.

My stomach filled with dread just thinking how upset Casey would have felt to hear that gossip. I had to contact her. Thinking for a moment how to word my text, I slowly typed a message.

Casey, I hope everything is okay? Can I meet you at the bathroom upstairs again so we can talk before school? Please, Casey? We need to talk.

My alarm went off. I scooted to the side of the bed to turn it off. I could have used a couple more hours of sleep but that was impossible. Hoping that Casey would soon reply, I quickly showered and dressed, then finished braiding my hair on the way down the stairs. Stopping at the bottom, I inhaled. The scent of bacon filled my senses. I knew exactly what Mom was cooking up for breakfast. She only cooked bacon in the morning for one special dish…my favorite one.

When I reached the kitchen, I saw her placing bacon on a paper towel-lined plate.

"Good morning," I said.

Dad looked up from his paper and Mom chewed on her lip.

"What's wrong?" I asked.

Mom turned to me in a rush, her face flushed and her expression fearful. "Will you forgive us, Ali? We only ever wanted the best for you. We never meant to hurt you. All night I couldn't help thinking about how upset you must be!"

I moved quickly over to her and gave her a reassuring hug. "Mom, I'm fine. I'm just happy that everything is out in the open."

She kissed the top of my head and squeezed me tighter. "It's such a relief to hear you say that, Ali. What an amazing girl you are!"

I peered over at the counter. "You're making pancake faces, aren't you?"

She laughed. "You guessed it! Now sit down while I finish them."

I hugged Dad before I sat down. I needed them to know I wasn't upset. Tension was the last thing we needed in this house. I was glad all was okay with my family. But when I checked my phone to see how my other family was doing, I saw there was still no word from Casey.

Would she be at our meeting place that morning or not?

CHAPTER TWELVE
Casey

The sound of a text tone woke me from a very deep sleep. My eyes peered open while I reached for my phone.

Ali's text lit up the screen. *Casey, I hope everything is okay? Can I meet you at the bathroom upstairs again so we can talk before school? Please, Casey? We need to talk.*

Once again, I ignored it. Ali was the last person I wanted to talk to. Putting my phone down, I slowly sat up. My stomach was growling because I'd missed dinner the night before.

I wasn't going to starve myself again. I knew I wouldn't last until lunch without eating. I'd have to risk a confrontation with Mom and Grandma Ann just so I could get food into my stomach.

I had a quick shower and then dressed for school after briefly scanning my cupboard. No longer did I have a vast array of expensive designer brands to choose from. With a sigh, I reached for my favorite sky blue top. It had short sleeves and a stand-up kind of collar. I'd had it forever but everyone commented on how nice it looked on me. If I had to face Ali and Jake that day, I may as well try to look my best. Then I waited in my room until there were only about fifteen minutes before I needed to leave for the bus. At least if Mom or Grandma Ann started an argument, I'd be able to have school as an excuse to leave.

Grandma Ann was the only one in the kitchen. At that moment I would have preferred to see Mom. Grandma Ann had no issue with digging into my business. I grabbed a box of cereal from the cabinet, poured some into a bowl and added milk on top.

I quietly sat down at the table where Grandma Ann was sipping from a cup of tea.

"Good morning, Casey," she said.

"Morning," I mumbled quietly.

"Did you sleep okay?" she asked.

"Yes," I replied flatly. I knew what she was doing. She was trying to distract me from the fight Mom and I were having. But I was too stubborn for that.

"We didn't get a chance to talk much yesterday. How was your week at camp?" she asked, leaning forward against the table.

"Fine," I said. I started shoveling the cereal into my mouth, hoping she'd stop with the small talk. It wasn't going to work.

"What did you do there?"

"Stuff."

Grandma Ann frowned. This was what I was waiting for, she was going to try and force me to forgive my mom. Well, she had another thing coming. I started thinking of responses to the questions she hadn't asked yet, but instead, all she did was glance up at the clock and say, "You don't want to be late for school."

I finished my cereal and rinsed the bowl in the sink. I felt her eyes on me the whole time, but I wasn't going to crack.

Lucas came bounding out of his room with his backpack bouncing off his back. He ignored my presence and ran for the door. "Bye, Mom! Bye, Grandma Ann!"

"Slow down, Lucas," Grandma Ann said, coming out of the kitchen.

He stopped suddenly in his tracks and I almost tripped over him.

I bit my tongue to hold back the snappy remark that I wanted to say. I felt bad about yelling at him the night before. I was mad at Mom, not him. Even though his antics got on my nerves so much.

I grabbed my bag from its spot by the door where I'd dropped it the afternoon before. And without another word to my grandmother, I left the house.

On the bus, I found a seat at the very back. I had less than a half-hour before we got to school, to review the homework for math class. When I pulled the book out, my phone tumbled out of my bag. I grabbed it before it hit the ground and shattered. That would be just my luck. Ali's message appeared on the screen again. I opened the message and read through the other texts she'd sent me. My eyes kept falling to the meeting place. Should I meet with her or wait until another opportunity presented itself? I really wanted to hear what happened with Jake from her, instead of through rumors. And knowing Holly and Ronnie, the news of Jake asking Ali out would be all over our grade by now.

Why did they care so much? I only did because I liked Jake, and Ali was my twin. But Holly and Ronnie should have minded their own business. I had enough to worry about.

Shoving the phone back into my bag, I opened my math book. I focused on the problems for the remainder of the ride and managed to finish most of them by the time the bus pulled up at the front of the school. I wasn't sure I had the correct answers, but it didn't matter too much as Mrs. Tucker allowed us to correct our own work. And as long as we put effort into our homework that was all she was concerned about.

I packed up my things and was the last off the bus. By the time I reached the pavement, the rest of the kids from my bus were already inside the building that led to my classroom.

I stood there, still unsure whether I should meet with Ali or not. I could easily have told her that I didn't see the text. But my life was filled with enough lies, I didn't want to add to them.

I sighed and started for the front entrance. Without even thinking, my legs took me up the stairs to the second-floor bathroom to meet with my twin. I stood in front of the door, willing myself to take a step forward.

I hoped that Ali was still on my side and not going on a date with Jake. I wasn't sure if I could handle that, especially with everything going on with my mom.

With that wish in my head, I pushed open the door.

CHAPTER THIRTEEN
Ali

On the way to school, Dad could tell I was nervous about something.

"You okay?" he asked.

I nodded, even though I had the urge to shake my head instead. I wanted nothing more than to stop lying to my family, but this little thing with Casey needed a resolution before I brought my parents into it.

"If you want to talk, I'm here," he said.

I looked over at him and smiled. "I know." I could have come up with an excuse to ease his mind, like a test or something, but avoiding the truth wouldn't technically be lying.

I turned to the window and leaned my head back against the seat. All that morning, I'd been thinking of responses to any of the questions that Casey might have for me. And the only one I was worried about was the conversation with Jake. While I hoped she hadn't heard any gossip, it was only a matter of time before Ronnie and Holly made the conversation between me and Jake known. As much as I tried to deny that they'd heard what he asked me, I knew there was only a very small chance that they hadn't. If Casey asked me about it, I had two options…tell the truth or lie. Telling the truth would be better but not easier. And if I told her that Jake didn't ask me out, and then Ronnie or Holly got to her before I did, she'd never trust me again.

So I decided I would come clean with her about Jake. But I would not tell her about my crush. That part I could keep to myself, since I had to sort through those feelings on my own. The only thing I was worried about was her asking me what I'd said to him. As a good twin sister, I should have said no, right away. But I didn't. I avoided him which didn't help to make Casey think that I wasn't interested.

When one of the school buildings appeared in the distance, my heart began to pound in my chest. I felt each beat rock through me like the steady beating of a drum.

My mouth went dry, and my insides began to twist as Dad pulled the car up at the front of the school.

You can do this, I thought to myself. *Just tell the truth.*

Telling the truth was my new mantra. It applied to our families, and it had to apply to Casey as well.

"Have a nice day, Ali," Dad said when he stopped the car at the curb.

I nodded slowly, unable to move my hand to the handle and open the door.

"Ali?" he prompted.

I blinked a few times, and then took a breath and opened the door. Once I was out of the car I turned to Dad. "Love you."

His eyes narrowed with concern, but he didn't ask me if I was okay again. I was sure he knew I'd tell him when I was ready. "Love you too, Ali."

I closed the door and turned to the school. The car idled behind me, and I knew that Dad wouldn't leave until I was safely in the building.

There weren't many kids there yet so I hoped I would have a few moments to myself before talking to Casey. The buses weren't due for another ten minutes or so.

I took a breath and walked across the grassy area of the school entrance and into the building. When I glanced behind me, I saw that Dad was already down the road.

With a sigh, I made my way up to the second-floor bathroom. My chest fluttered with nerves. For the first time, I felt anxious about talking to Casey. What had I done? This was supposed to be easy. We were twins. And we had a sort of psychic connection. I shouldn't be afraid to see her.

I took a deep breath and pushed open the door to the bathroom. As I expected, it was empty. I checked the stalls to make sure no one was in there. The conversation between Casey and me had to be done in secret.

I dropped my backpack by the door and waited, staring at myself in the mirror until the lines of my face began to blur.

I waited for fifteen minutes before the bathroom door opened.

Turning, I saw Casey in the doorway, looking just as nervous as I felt. All the anxiety burst from me in a rush. I raced over to her just as the door closed.

"Casey, I've been so worried about you." And with that, all thoughts of Jake flew from my mind. She looked upset. And I wasn't sure if it was because of me or our mom. My stomach churned with worry. I hoped by the time we left, everything would be okay between us.

I couldn't stand it if she was mad at me. So at that moment, I decided to avoid the topic of Jake altogether. If she brought it up, I was prepared to talk about it, but I wasn't going to start that on my own. I wasn't sure I would be able to lie to her face about how I felt about Jake. Jake couldn't come between us. I'd only just met my twin sister, and I would hate to ruin everything.

"My parents are so excited to see you again. When I told them that you were with them the whole weekend, they were so surprised. But they said how much they loved you. Now they want to meet our mother, Grandma Ann, and Lucas too! Isn't that exciting?"

Casey smiled. "They liked me?"

I knew how important this was for Casey. She hadn't grown up with two parents. I wanted her to feel the love I felt each day when I was with mine.

"Of course they did. How could they not love you? And once everyone meets each other, you can come over whenever you want. We can have two families. It'll be amazing!"

Casey's smiled widened.

I reached out to her and hugged her. Through our connection, I could feel her excitement. This was all going to work out just the way I'd hoped.

CHAPTER FOURTEEN
Casey

I imagined Ali and me both being in her room together; trying on clothes and doing other things that sisters did. And I'd be able to be honest with her parents about who I was. There would be no more pretending, and that made me feel much happier than I had been over the last day.

"I'm sorry I made you worry," I said, now regretting not answering her texts. "When I saw our mom, things didn't go so well."

"Oh no!" she frowned, "I hope you're okay?"

Ali's concern for me deepened my regret. It wasn't right that I was so upset with her and she didn't know why. There was already enough going on in her life, she didn't need me to hold a grudge against her for anything. And I wanted to talk to someone about my family, hoping that Ali, above anyone else, would understand.

I shrugged. "I can't forgive our mother for what she did. I understand that she had to give you up after birth, but I hate that she kept it from me for so long. When we talked about it, all those feelings from before camp got the best of me. I was so angry with her. I didn't even have dinner last night, I couldn't face Mom or Grandma Ann."

Then I remembered being annoyed with Lucas. Mom had been right about one thing, there was no reason for me to have yelled at him. I made a mental note to apologize to him later.

Ali took my hands. A little electric pulse moved between our fingers. "I'm sure it will all sort itself out in time, Casey. If you can try to understand how things must have been for her, I'm sure it'll help you to forgive her."

I dropped my hands to my sides. "The problem is…we've never been that close. Not like you the way you are with your parents. She's always working, and we just do our own thing. Now, this is something else that's come between us. I don't think it will ever be right."

"Don't you think you should give her a chance though? She was so young when all of this happened."

Admittedly, a part of me did understand, and that's what I told my twin. "I get that part of it, Ali. But she could have said something over the years. If you and I hadn't met, we might never know about each other."

I didn't want to give into our mother that easily. She needed to know how hurtful it was for me to discover all of this on my own. She deserved to suffer a little for such a huge deception.

Ali nodded. "I understand how you feel, Casey. I get it, I really do. And I know it's harder for you than it is for me. Because you're the one who has lived with her your whole life. Anytime you want to talk, I'm here."

"Thank you," I said.

I opened my arms for her and we hugged. It was so nice to have someone who understood me and was able to still be on my side. Brie understood to a certain point, but Ali was my sister and she was directly involved. Having her on my side while the rest of my family wasn't, helped to ease my mind.

And with that part settled, I knew it was time to talk about Jake. I wanted to discuss everything that was bothering me so I could focus on getting things back to normal in my life.

I ended the hug and took a few steps back from Ali. "Ali, there's one other thing."

Ali blinked a few times. "What's that?"

I opened my mouth to speak but just then, the door to the bathroom opened.

I turned around to see Holly and Brie in the doorway.

Holly's eyebrows shot up in surprise.

Brie's gaze darted between Ali and me. "I was

looking for you, Casey."

I took Ali's hand and pushed past Holly. Brie backpedaled into the hallway. Holly was such a gossip; I didn't want her to hear anything we were talking about.

We walked further down the hallway, close to the stairwell where there weren't any other kids or teachers. I needed a chance to talk to Ali and Brie before Holly finished in the bathroom and suddenly appeared at our side again.

"I didn't want her to hear anything," I explained.

"Good idea," Brie said.

I could see Brie looking from Ali to me, wondering if I'd confronted my twin. I didn't want her to bring up the Jake issue. At least not until I was able to.

"Should we come out and tell everyone we're twins?" Ali suggested. "Both our parents know, so it's only a matter of time."

"I guess if we don't do it soon, Lucas might open his big mouth before we get a chance to tell everyone ourselves," I said.

"How are you going to do it?" Brie asked.

Ali and I looked at each other questioningly. Then the warning bell rang.

"How about we think about it while we're in class and work something out during morning break?" I suggested.

"That's a good idea," Ali agreed as she followed Brie and me down the stairs.

While morning classes usually passed by very slowly, that morning the clock seemed to be on double time. It felt like minutes instead of two hours when Ali, Brie, and I sat together for morning recess. We had fifteen minutes between classes to figure everything out.

"Did you think of anything?" I asked Ali. I hadn't come up with any ideas besides simply blurting it out to our friends, the same way Ali had with our mom and her parents.

"What about telling just our group of friends during lunch? And then that will be that?" Ali said.

"Holly and Ronnie do sit near us," Brie said. "If they hear it then it'll be all over our grade by the end of lunch. How about we just tell them and they can spread the news for us!"

As annoying as Holly and Ronnie were with their gossip, this was a good opportunity to use them to our advantage. "That's a good plan."

"So you're telling everyone today?" Brie asked. I could tell she was excited to be included in the secret.

"At lunch," I said to her, silently warning her to keep the secret until then. We only had one class to go, so hopefully, she could.

"Oh, I can't wait!" she said. "This is the most incredible secret to share. It's been so hard to keep it quiet!"

Ali and I smiled. I couldn't wait either.

At lunch, I was too excited to care about what we were eating, but it would have been strange if we didn't get a tray of food. So Brie, Ali, and I went to the hot lunch line and chose a plate of roasted turkey and mashed potatoes. It wasn't my favorite but I wasn't sure I'd be able to eat anything at that point, I was nervous to tell our secret, and to see the others' reactions.

We made sure to sit close to Holly and Ronnie.

"When are you going to announce it?" Brie whispered.

I looked at Ali. "How about now?"

Ali called over Holly and Ronnie.

"Casey and I have something we're dying to share."

Holly and Ronnie's eyes opened into wide saucers. "A secret?" They both said at the same time.

"Sort of," I said. I couldn't help but grin at their curious reactions. They stared silently as they waited for me to continue.

"Ali and I found out this weekend that we're twins." The words left my mouth and it felt so strange to hear them spoken aloud in front of everyone.

Ronnie and Holly stared back at me, their mouths open in shock. I smiled as I watched their reaction. It felt good to be the one sharing such unbelievable news. Usually, Ali was the center of attention, but for a change, it was my turn.

"What?" Holly screeched, finally finding her voice.

"Oh my gosh, you've got to be kidding me!" Ronnie squealed just as loudly. I could feel several pairs of eyes staring in our direction.

Without missing a beat, Ali and I went back and forth explaining our story. And the entire time, Ronnie kept repeating the words, "Oh, my gosh!"

Holly, however, barely made a sound. I didn't think I'd ever seen her stuck for words before.

We didn't mention the swap at all. That would just confuse everyone, and it might ruin my chances with Jake if he realized Ali had been playing me all weekend.

While I tended to know where Jake was at all times, I was surprised to find he'd joined our table, and was sitting amongst the small crowd that formed around both Ali and me.

Then the questions came from everywhere.

"How does it feel to be a twin?"

"Can you read each other's minds?"

"Can your parents tell you apart?"

"Is there any part of you that's different?"

We took turns answering all the questions we could, without revealing the swap.

Until Holly decided to ruin that for us.

"OMG," Holly said. "You two could even swap places. All you'd have to do is change your hair and trade clothing styles. It would be that easy!"

She looked so pleased with herself; as if she'd just thought of the most wonderful idea and was so clever for thinking it.

"That would be fun," Brie said trying to cover up the fact that we'd already done it several times.

I sent her a silent thank you.

"How do we know you already haven't done that?" Ronnie suggested. "You two were a little strange at camp. Did you do it there?"

My mouth dried up like a cotton ball.

And when my eyes flicked towards Jake, I could see that he seemed very interested to hear that answer.

CHAPTER FIFTEEN
Ali

I looked at Casey. Why had Ronnie asked about camp? Did she know we'd swapped already and was messing with us?

Casey let out an uncomfortable laugh, but I think I was the only one to notice her unease.

The bell rang, and Casey and I jumped. Everyone's attention was distracted and I let out a deep breath I hadn't realized I'd been holding. I just hoped that Ronnie would let the idea drop and not bring it up again.

The kids around us hesitated before picking up their trays and heading for the garbage cans to discard their rubbish.

Casey nudged my arm, and we both quickly cleared our trays and moved to the door. Brie was one step behind us.

"Do you think she knows?" I asked Casey in a low whisper.

"She can't," Casey said. "Our parents didn't even know."

"Guys!" Ronnie said, scurrying over to us with her tray. "You didn't answer my question."

"Oh," I said, my stomach fluttering anxiously. "Which question was that?"

"Did you two swap with each other at camp?" Ronnie looked at us expectantly. Her eyebrows were raised curiously and it appeared that she really had no idea if we had or not. I had to think quickly as Casey's lower lip began to tremble slightly and I could see that she was struggling with what to say.

"Of course not!" I said with a laugh. "That hadn't even occurred to us. But it might be fun for Halloween or something."

Casey laughed again, this time less uncomfortable and more like herself. "That's a great idea!" she added quickly.

Ronnie eyed us suspiciously.

"Well, we'd better get to class," Brie said, saving us from more questions.

"Yeah, let's go," I said, pulling Casey away from Ronnie. "You know how annoyed Miss Tucker gets if we're late!"

Ronnie didn't push the issue, but I had a feeling she didn't completely believe our answer. Right then, however, I just wanted to get as far away from her as possible.

After school, I headed out towards the bus stop with Casey and Brie. Throughout the day we'd been bombarded with questions by other kids. None like Ronnie's swap question but everyone was curious about us being twins. I didn't mind the attention, being the new girl, I was used to it. But I could see that Casey was definitely enjoying it. I wished more of the kids talked to her, she was so special and so great to have as a friend. I hoped she'd eventually build her confidence a little more.

"Ali!" Lucas called from behind us.

I turned around just as his little body attached itself to me. I hugged him back, laughing. "Lucas."

"My friend, Jackson told me that he heard you guys are twins! His sister is Lucy, she's in your class." Lucas said. "And I actually kept the secret! I didn't tell anyone!" He grinned proudly at me, clearly very pleased with himself that he'd managed to keep the secret quiet.

"You're the best, Lucas," I said, ruffling his hair.

"I miss you so much. When are you coming back to our house?"

I glanced up at Casey who was sharing a look with Brie. She shook her head and rolled her eyes.

I could tell she was a little jealous. At least I had that feeling. It was strong, just like the other instances with our psychic connection. But I pretended not to notice. As much as I loved his attention, I felt a little awkward about him being so affectionate towards me in front of Casey. I didn't want anything else to come between us.

But I also knew that if she could be just a bit nicer to him, they'd get on so much better. I'd always wanted a brother, and I didn't want to mess things up with him just because he and Casey didn't get along. It was all so complicated.

Wanting to avoid the stares from Casey and Brie, I eased out of his arms and put my hand on his shoulder. "Lucas, since everyone knows we're twins, you can tell people now that you have another sister."

"I can?"

"Sure," I said.

"Cool! I was waiting to tell Matt since I wasn't sure if I was supposed to." He bounded off toward a different school bus where Matt was standing.

Seeing Matt again, reminded me of how alike he and Jake looked.

"Alright," I said to Casey and Brie. "We did it."

Casey let out a relieved sigh and Brie couldn't stop smiling.

"We did do it," Casey said. "Now all we have to do is have our families meet."

I couldn't wait for that. I wanted to show our mom the amazing people who had raised me. I hoped she wouldn't feel bad about it anymore. Even though Casey was still upset with her, I wanted her to know that things had turned out for the best.

"I have to get going," I said. I could see my dad's car behind the line of buses. And I didn't want him approaching me with Casey there, not until we'd had a chance to arrange a proper meeting.

Casey gave me a quick hug. "See you tomorrow, Ali."

"Bye, Casey. Bye Brie." I smiled happily at both of them as I turned away.

Smiling all the way to the car, I felt excited to tell my parents about the great day I'd had. It had started so badly but had ended so well. I felt the smile on my face grow. I'd managed to avoid Jake for most of the day, and Casey's questions about him as well.

Added to that, Ronnie and Brie hadn't mentioned anything about Jake and me. I guessed I was mistaken and they hadn't overheard our conversation after all.

Feeling the happiest I'd felt in days, I made my way to the car.

CHAPTER SIXTEEN
Casey

"I have to get going too," Brie said.

"See you tomorrow," I said and watched her get on her bus.

I started toward my bus but realized Lucas was still talking to Matt.

"Lucas!" I called over to him.

He was so focused on what he was saying to Matt that he didn't hear me. I wanted to get on the bus so I could get a good seat, but if it left without him, I'd never hear the end of it from Grandma Ann.

I quickly marched over there while calling for him. "Lucas! Come on, we have to go"

Was my brother deaf? Even Matt looked at me briefly while I was calling for Lucas. But he had a huge grin on his face and quickly returned his attention to Lucas. He was totally absorbed in the story he was hearing.

I was soon within earshot and heard the words coming from my brother's mouth. He was intent on telling Matt his story and it was as though nothing else existed right then.

"My new sister, Ali, she's so nice!" Lucas was saying to Matt. "She spent the entire weekend at my house and the whole time, we thought it was Casey. Ali even came to our little league game. Casey never comes to those, she says they're boring."

I quickly reached for Lucas' arm to alert him that I was there. I could not believe the words that were coming from his mouth. He was going to ruin everything and I had to stop him, even though I knew I was too late. I could feel my head spinning and a pit of nausea made its way to the bottom of my stomach. I'd completely forgotten to tell him to keep that part a secret!

Looking frantically around to see if any of the kids in my grade had heard him, I did not see any familiar faces. And just as I tried to drag him away, I found myself face to face with Jake. Had he been standing there the whole time? No, he couldn't have been. I would have noticed him on the way over.

Lucas' voice was annoyingly loud. I desperately hoped that Jake hadn't heard what Lucas had just been saying. But I was sick with fear and worry.

"Hi," I said to him, gulping down a small breath of air.

"Hi," he replied.

I stood there for an awkward moment that seemed to freeze time and hold me captive. I was unable to move from my spot. Abruptly snapping out of it, I grabbed Lucas by the shoulder, "Lucas, we have to go."

Lucas gave Matt a high-five and bolted toward our bus.

I turned around and followed him. There was nothing I could say to fix the situation. Jake was near enough that if I told Matt not to say anything about the baseball game, Jake would definitely hear. The best I could do was hope that Matt didn't care enough to share that detail with his brother.

Why did Lucas have to always interfere with my life? One little comment could ruin any chances of Jake and me being together.

I could barely look at my brother when I got onto the bus. My cheeks were flushed, and my whole body was hot. At the same time though, he was oblivious to the drama he'd just caused.

Sitting down, I pulled out my phone and created a group text with Brie and Ali. I had to tell them what had just happened. I needed to tell someone and I needed to be told that it would all be okay. I just couldn't believe my brother! I hoped Ali would finally see how annoying he was after all of this.

Brie texted back with a big angry face emoji.

There was no reply from Ali, and by the time the bus pulled up at my stop, there was still no reply. I guessed that she was probably catching up with her parents.

Lucky her.

It was a good thing Lucas ran all the way home from the bus stop. He wasn't going to like what I was about to tell him.

I prayed that Jake hadn't heard any of the conversation. Hopefully, I was nervous for no reason.

As much as I tried to think about other things instead, the fact that Jake *might* know about the swap this weekend made my head fill with worry. I was close to tears by the time I got home.

When I entered the house, I expected Mom to be locked in her room doing work, but instead, she was sitting on the couch in the living room.

"Hello, Casey," she said, looking tentatively towards me.

I dropped my bag by the door. "Hello, Mom."

"How about we go to Aromas this afternoon?"

Aromas was my favorite cafe in town. What was she up to?

I crossed my arms. "Don't you have work to do?"

She stood up from the couch. "I've finished everything I need to do. Grandma Ann will watch Lucas so we can go. Just the two of us." she added.

"I went the other day with Ali, thinking she was you. I'd like to try that again but with the real Casey this time!" She chuckled slightly at that comment.

I wasn't sure if she wanted me to laugh along, but since I didn't think it was funny, I didn't laugh at all.

"You can get whatever you like," she offered.

"Fine," I said.

If I stayed home, I would wonder about Jake and

drive myself crazy. At least if I went to Amora's, then I could get their amazing hot chocolate. I couldn't remember the last time I went there, it had been so long ago. This was an opportunity that rarely came up, and I knew I'd be the one missing out if I said no.

At the cafe, I ordered hot chocolate and Mom ordered coffee. I eyed the pastries lined up in the cabinet beside our table and had trouble deciding what I wanted.

"I know you're still mad at me," Mom said, after we'd given our final order. "And I get it. But I don't know how many times I can apologize to you."

After being faced with Lucas spilling the beans to Matt, I realized suddenly that my argument with Mom was old news. Neither of us could change the past.

"It's been so hard to hear all of this," I said. "I just wish you'd told me a long time ago. I hate the fact that you kept it a secret. That's what hurts the most."

She reached across the table and took my hands in hers. "I'm so sorry, Casey. I won't keep anything from you ever again."

I stared at her for a moment and locked my eyes on hers.

"Is that a promise?" I asked.

"Yes," she replied solemnly. Her expression was more serious that I'd ever seen on her face before, and I could tell she was being genuine.

Although deep down I was still upset, I could feel the barrier between us beginning to crumble. She was my mom after all. And I knew that I couldn't stay mad at her forever. All I wanted was to have her attention, and finally, she was giving it to me. It was something I wasn't used to, but I had to admit that it felt good.

The waiter brought our drinks, and I blew into the hot liquid, attempting to cool it down before taking a sip.

"Do you want to hear what I did this weekend?" I

asked.

Mom nodded eagerly. "More than anything."

Her eyes were full of hope, and the final shreds of defiance that up until then, would not allow me to forgive her, finally fell away. The release of all the pent up anger and tension that I'd been clinging so tightly to, seemed to disappear into thin air. And smiling at her for the first time in what seemed like forever, I began to speak. Once I started, I could not stop.

The best part about sharing every detail of my wonderful weekend with Ali's parents, was that my mother actually sat and listened. She took a genuine interest in what I had to say, and she really seemed to care. That meant more to me than anything. And when she said she was jealous that I went to see Wicked, and then promised to take me again so I could see the ending, I smiled happily back at her.

That was a big promise for her since those tickets cost a lot of money. But even if I saw the show from the worst seats in the building, I would be overjoyed.

"Ali said that her parents want to meet us," I said. "Officially."

"That sounds like a great idea. Ali's parents seem very nice from the way you've described them." She smiled at me, encouraging me to continue.

"They are! And their house is huge, Mom. Our house could fit inside of it."

"That's impressive," she said. "I'm looking forward to seeing Ali again. She's a lovely girl."

I didn't know why I felt a stab of jealousy in my chest. Ali was her daughter too. But it seemed like everyone in my life preferred her over me.

I tried to push those thoughts away. Ali was my sister after all. I had to stop being jealous of her. Maybe I could try to be more like her so that others would feel the same way about me, as they did her.

I'd pretended to be Ali for most of camp, and over the weekend as well, so it should be easy enough. It was better than being jealous all the time. With a deep sigh, I realized that perhaps behaving more like Ali, was what I needed to do.

CHAPTER SEVENTEEN
Casey

The conversation with Mom eased my mind a little bit about the situation. Even though I continued to feel a dull ache in my body each time I thought of the betrayal, it was nice that we were on the mend. Holding a grudge wouldn't change that, so I had to learn to let go, no matter how long that took.

At school the following day, Brie and I met on the front steps after our buses arrived.

"Are you doing okay?" Brie asked.

I'd texted her the day before about going to Aromas with Mom. "Actually, yes. And we plan on meeting up with Ali and her family soon."

Brie's eyebrows lifted. "Wow, that's going to be interesting!"

I nodded. I already knew and loved Ali's parents. But it would be awkward for the parents the first time around. Maybe they'd make my mom feel a little bit worse about the situation she'd created, as a final act of payback for her lies.

I shoved away the thought. *Be nice,* I warned myself. We were on a path of everyone getting along, and I didn't want to go backward instead of forward.

"Did you ever ask Ali about Jake?" Brie asked, knowing that I hadn't. She'd texted me that I should clear the air with Ali about it, before anything else happened.

"No," I said. "But I will." *Eventually.*

When we got to our homeroom class, Ali was already there. She was sitting in her chair in the back of the room, and I was surprised to see Jake there too, chatting with her. Since when did his bus arrive before mine?

Ali's smile fell when we walked through the doorway. And immediately, that uncomfortable feeling returned deep in my chest.

I tried to channel the Ali-energy I'd had during camp, and walked up to the two of them.

"Morning!" I said cheerfully.

"Hi, Casey," Ali said, and then glanced at Jake.

Jake smiled at me. "Hey."

"We were just talking about us," Ali said.

I jolted.

"You and me, us," Ali corrected. "Jake was wondering how we were separated."

"Oh," I said.

"It's a really interesting story," Jake said. "Like a movie or something."

I stood there awkwardly, unsure of where to take the conversation from there.

The warning bell rang, saving me from myself.

I gave them a small wave and headed to my desk.

I wanted to sink into the chair and never come out. Why did I turn into a puddle of mush around Jake? Even though I tried to be like Ali, it was so hard around him. Why was the swap at camp any different? Maybe it was the excitement of the swap, and now that we were back in real life, that energy was no longer there?

I glanced over my shoulder at Jake and Ali. She was writing something in her notebook, while Jake leaned over the back of his chair to watch her.

Ali had seemed uncomfortable when we walked in. If the rumors had been true about Jake asking her out, maybe she was trying to turn him down gently by being polite, instead of her outgoing and cheerful self. If so, I was sure she was doing this for me. I'd probably imagined her crush on him. I felt sure she'd never do such a thing.

I continued to closely watch the interactions between Ali and Jake throughout the day. He somehow always found a place by her side. And at recess, Ali, Brie, and I were hanging out together when he came up to us.

"Ali, want to come sit with us over there?" Jake asked.

My stomach plummeted. Once again I could not help the jealous pangs.

"No, thanks," she said, politely. "Casey and I need to catch up."

Jake shoved his hands into his pockets. "You two probably have a lot to catch up on."

He gave me and Brie a small wave then walked away.

Ali turning him down made my heart soar.

And I began to feel a little more confident that Jake hadn't heard Lucas and Matt talking about the swap. If he had, surely he would have questioned Ali about it. At least that was something to feel grateful for.

CHAPTER EIGHTEEN
Ali

I tried so hard not to watch Jake walk away from us. He looked so disappointed that I turned him down again. Since Casey and I shared all of our classes, I was aware of her each time Jake approached me. Jake hadn't mentioned going out again and I was hoping he realized I wasn't keen. I'd been trying to ignore him for most of the time, but I didn't want to be mean. Regardless though, he kept trying to get my attention and didn't seem to get the hint.

I had to take my mind off him. And I could do that by planning a huge event in my life. "Casey, do you want to get our families together this weekend?"

Casey clapped her hands together. "Oh, yes, that would be great!"

"How about Sunday?" My dad never worked on Sundays and I knew that day would be perfect for my family.

"I think that should be okay. I'll talk to Mom about it."

"This is all so exciting!" Brie said.

"I know!" Casey agreed.

"Once we confirm the date, where do you think we should meet?" I asked.

"How about your house?" Casey suggested.

I smiled back at her. "I'm sure my parents will be happy with that idea."

"And I could borrow some clothes from you again," Casey said with a smile.

"Yes, of course, you can. Anytime, you want."

Casey then turned to Brie to tell her about the size of my closet. While they were distracted, I threw a glance over my shoulder to see what Jake was up to. He was leaning against the thick trunk of a tall tree, talking to his friends.

And as if sensing me looking at him, he turned directly towards me.

I whipped back around and tried to distract myself by talking about clothes with Brie and Casey.

The date was set with our parents. Since Lucas had his games on Sundays, Grandma Ann would be taking him. Casey and I agreed that the first meeting should just be with our parents. They had a lot to discuss without being distracted by Lucas. He and Grandma Ann could be included the next time we all met.

I got off the phone with Casey and flopped onto my bed, feeling a huge weight lift off my shoulders. This was finally happening! After years of thinking about my biological family, in a few days, they were going to meet face to face!

A text sounded from my phone, and I checked it. It was from Ronnie. My heart sank a little. Was she going to accuse Casey and me of swapping again?

Cheerleader tryouts tomorrow. You better be there ☺

I let out a breath. I sent a text to Casey to see if she was planning to go.

I waited, and she sent back a quick, *Yes if you are.*

I smiled at my phone. I'd always wanted to do cheerleading, but at my old school, the team wasn't great. I hoped doing this together with Casey would bring us closer than ever.

After school the next day, all the girls trying out for the squad met in the locker room to change into more suitable clothes for the tryouts. Everyone was so excited. I noticed a lot of girls had turned up for the practice, and I heard there weren't a lot of spots to be filled. I crossed my fingers that Casey, Brie, and I were able to make the team.

The coach for the squad, Mrs. Caldwell, instructed us to go out to the football field. It was a beautiful day outside and I had a good feeling about my chances.

"I'm so nervous," Brie said.

Casey told me that Brie hadn't been enthusiastic about trying out, but she only did it because Casey and I were. I hoped to change her mind because I thought it would be fun if all of us were involved together.

"You'll do great," Casey said to her best friend. "We all will."

Holly and Ronnie ran past us to get to the front of the group, and we jogged ahead to keep up.

The boys were practicing football on the other side of the field. Some of the girls giggled and waved at the boys while I tried to hide behind Casey. I was nervous enough for the tryouts, I didn't want to be distracted by Jake. I saw some of the boys across the field, staring at our group.

They looked so buff and muscular in their football uniforms. And when I spotted Jake amongst them, he took his helmet off and glanced in my direction, his hair flopping messily over his eyes.

Was it possible to ever stop liking him?

"Wait here, ladies," Mrs. Caldwell said. "I'll be right back."

The boys were taking a water break, and a few of them—Jake included—started to walk over to us.

Casey grabbed my hand, and a big smile appeared on her face. "He's coming over here."

"Yeah, he is," I gulped nervously.

Jake locked eyes with me and came straight toward us.

Shoot!

I tried to act normal and not bounce up and down like my insides were doing.

"Hi, Ali," Jake said, branching off from his group. The rest of the guys spread out to talk with the other girls.

"Hey Jake," Casey said.

Jake glanced at her and smiled, "Oh, hey Casey." He then returned his attention to me.

"Hi, Jake," I said, noticing he hadn't even acknowledged that Casey was there at first. It was the second time he had done that to her today, and I could tell she was crushed each time it happened.

"You're trying out for cheerleading?" he asked.

"Yeah," I said, and moved closer to Casey, so he'd give her some attention as well. "Casey and Brie are too."

He nodded at the two of them and then turned back to me. "There are a few away games that we travel to with the cheerleaders. If you made the team it would be fun."

"All of us girls would have so much fun," I said, trying to include Casey as much as I could. I could feel her becoming a little uncomfortable, probably not as much as me, but close. Why was he giving me so much attention in front of her?

Jake looked at Casey then back to me, and let out a small laugh. "From all the way over there, I couldn't figure out who was who. I know you're twins but it's still strange to see how alike you look. Especially without your braids."

I'd put my hair up in a ponytail like the rest of the girls. I supposed it made sense that he would mix us up. I was sure that didn't help Casey feel any better about the situation though.

"The braids are one way to tell them apart," Brie added, with a small laugh. "And their clothes. But being a boy, you wouldn't have a clue about that!"

Jake smiled. "No, not really."

Mrs. Caldwell came back to the group and clapped her hands together to rally us.

"I'll see you later," Jake said to me. "Good luck."

"Thanks," I said, and bumped Casey's arm.

She said a muffled thanks, and we watched him jog back toward their practice.

Casey walked toward Mrs. Caldwell without another word. My stomach ached, thinking how bad she must feel. I had to figure out a way to make her feel better about the situation with Jake.

But I wasn't sure how.

CHAPTER NINETEEN
Casey

After cheerleading tryouts were over, we all went back to the locker room to change. I felt confident in my chances of getting on the squad. Although I messed up a few times on the cheers that we were taught, because we had done them as a group I hoped Mrs. Caldwell hadn't noticed. Besides, that's what practices were for.

The girls were all excited about their chances of winning a spot. I crossed my fingers that at the very least, Brie and Ali would make it on the team along with me. With Jake on the football team, I'd be closer to him than ever.

I went to bed that night, imagining walking down the halls of school on game days wearing the cheerleading uniform with my sister and best friend. One of the girls from last year's squad was at the try-outs to demonstrate some moves.

She'd been dressed in the new uniform and all the girls had agreed that it was such a cool design

I really loved the matching orange and black pom poms and could hardly wait to have my own set.

But that great feeling disappeared the morning that

the team was announced. On the bus, my stomach knotted with anxiety. What if Brie didn't make it? Would she feel bad? I knew she didn't want to do it, to begin with, but I didn't want her to be upset with Ali and me.

I headed to the locker room the second I got to school. I was sure Ali had already been there that morning since her dad always dropped her off early. And I didn't want to wait at the bus stop for Brie to arrive. At least if I didn't see her name on the list then I'd be able to comfort her.

The white piece of paper taped on the wall was like a beacon. I practically ran over to the list. Thank goodness no one else was in the hallway to see.

I was out of breath when I reached it and took a second to collect myself before checking it.

I started at the top and moved my finger down the list so I wouldn't miss my name.

Ali's name was at the top of the list. Then I saw Brie after that. It appeared the names were in alphabetical order. But I didn't see my name after Brie's. Instead, the next one was Holly's, then I found Ronnie's. There had to be some mistake.

My throat thickened as I looked through each name on the list again, and still didn't see mine. But when I finally did find it, my stomach sank.

Mine and two other names were listed on the reserves team at the very bottom. Which meant that if someone dropped out, only then did I have a chance of being on the team.

The corners of my mouth twitched and heat pricked behind my eyes.

Loud voices from down the hall, snapped me back to reality. It was Holly and Ronnie. I swiped at my eyes and quickly headed towards the other end of the hallway.

It was hard to control my disappointment about not making the team. I went into the second-floor bathroom and grabbed a paper towel to blot my face. I didn't want the other girls to know I'd been crying. That feeling of jealousy over Ali overwhelmed me again. I felt like I had on the first day she arrived at our school. And the same way I did every time Jake talked to her instead of me.

Why did everything always work out for Ali? And not for me?

It wasn't fair!

CHAPTER TWENTY
Ali

I asked Dad to take me to school extra early on Friday morning because I was so excited to see if I'd made the team. Casey and I had texted all night about how cool it would be when we both made the squad.

When I arrived, Mrs. Caldwell was in the process of posting the list on the noticeboard.

She smiled when she saw me. "You're here early."

"I couldn't wait to check the list," I grinned.

"Well, here it is," Mrs. Caldwell said, crossing her arms in front of her and taking a few steps back from the board.

I didn't have to look too hard because my name was

listed at the very top.

I let out a little squeal, and Mrs. Caldwell laughed.

"I guess you're happy," she said.

"Thank you so much!" I said, my body buzzing with excitement.

"You deserved it. I'll see you at practice."

She walked down the hall, and I turned back to the list to see who else had made the team. Brie was on there, then Holly, Jacey, Ronnie, …

I scanned the list another time, still not seeing Casey's name.

"Oh, no," I said to myself. Casey was first on the reserves list which meant she hadn't made the official team.

I wondered if I should warn her ahead of time. But then I decided not to. She was going to be so upset, and I wasn't sure if she'd want me around when she realized what had happened.

I went to my locker and pulled out some books that I'd need for morning classes. All I could think about was Casey. I felt so bad. I hated the thought of her not being on the team. It was so disappointing, and knowing how upset she would be, made it worse.

But what could I do? I checked my phone. The buses weren't due to arrive for at least fifteen minutes. What if I talked to Mrs. Caldwell about Casey? Would she change her mind and add Casey's name to the official list before Casey got to school?

It was worth a shot.

I stuffed my backpack into my locker and closed the door, spinning the combination lock.

Hurrying down the hallway, I pushed through the double doors to the stairs. Mrs. Caldwell was also a math teacher for one of the lower grades. Her office wasn't too far away from my homeroom class. If this was going to happen for Casey, I needed to do it quickly!

I knocked on the door to her office. It was open a

crack, so I barged in after knocking.

"Ali?" Mrs. Caldwell said, putting down her glasses. She had a stack of papers on her desk, and she held a red pen in her hand. "Come in."

I sat down on the chair in front of her desk. "Mrs. Caldwell, I saw that Casey didn't make the squad."

She put down her pen and folded her arms on her desk. "Ali, we only have a certain amount of spots. I'm sorry she didn't make the team this time around."

"But she really wants this," I insisted.

"All of the girls really want this, Ali. I'm sorry, but my decision is final."

"Is there anything I can do?"

"Well, since Casey is on the reserve list, you can give up your spot for her if you'd like."

I frowned. I guessed it was something I could do. But I knew it wouldn't really solve the problem. I was sure Casey would feel bad if I had to give up my spot for her. Besides, we wanted to do this together.

"I don't think that would work," I murmured quietly. "But if someone else couldn't make the team for some reason, then Casey would be added?"

"Yes, that's right. She's on the top of the reserve list, so if anyone couldn't commit, she'd be the first one for that spot."

"Okay, thanks," I said, feeling defeated.

Mrs. Caldwell gave me a pitying look and then I left the room.

I stood outside her office and leaned up against the wall. Casey was going to be devastated.

And as much as I knew she'd want to be alone, as she always did when she was upset, I was her sister and I had to help.

I went to the first floor, passing Holly and Ronnie on the way.

"Did you see the list?" Ronnie asked.

"Yeah, I did," I said. "Congrats."

"You too!" they said in unison, and then skipped down the hallway reciting one of the cheers we'd learned the day before.

Jacey stood in front of the list digging in her bag. I wished she'd leave so that when Casey got there, she wouldn't have to see the list in front of someone else who'd made the team over her.

Jacey pulled out her phone and dialed. I stayed in my spot further down the hallway so she wouldn't think I was eavesdropping.

"Yeah, Mom," Jacey said into her phone. "I made the team. But I'm going to see Mrs. Caldwell now and tell her that I won't be able to do it."

My heart leaped into my throat. *Oh, my gosh, I can't believe this!* My head was spinning with the words I was hearing from Jacey.

"I know, I know," she said. "I just wanted to see if I could make it. I wanted another option in case Mrs. Johnson couldn't fit me in for cello lessons."

Jacey's voice faded as she walked down the hallway.

I could have jumped up and down at that moment. Casey would be on the team after all! It was a good thing I'd made it there in time. Even if she saw her name on the reserve list, then I'd be able to tell her that Mrs. Caldwell had made a mistake.

I thought about taking down the list, but I wasn't sure who'd seen it yet. It was better not to get involved in that.

Brie came around the corner and scurried toward me. "Is that the list?"

"Yes," I said, trying to hold back a smile. I wanted her to be happy about making it, without me ruining the surprise.

Brie saw her name and clapped her hands over her mouth. "Casey was right! I didn't believe her when she texted me."

My smile fell. "She saw the list?"

"Yeah," Brie said. "She's not happy about being on the reserve list. To be honest, I didn't believe her when she said I'd made it. I think I'm going to drop out so she can have my spot. She's the one who asked me! She deserves to be on the team!"

I touched her arm. "You don't have to do that, Brie. I just heard Jacey talking to her mom. She said that she's not going to be able to do cheerleading after all, because of cello practice or something."

"We need to tell Casey right away!"

"Yes, we do!" I said.

There was no reason for her to be upset.

Everything had worked out for all of us and I couldn't wait to tell her.

Cheerleading was going to be so much fun!

CHAPTER TWENTY-ONE
Casey

I woke Sunday morning with a big smile on my face. Today was the day that I was going to see Ali's parents again. But this time I would be myself instead of pretending to play their adopted daughter. I didn't hear anyone else in the house moving yet, so I took the opportunity to get ready early. I showered and spent a considerable amount of time choosing an outfit. Even though my style was more casual, today was special for all of us and I wanted to look good. First impressions and all that.

I decided on a pretty pink top that had a swirly sequined pattern on the front and a white skirt. It was an outfit that I saved only for special occasions. I went through my jewelry box and pulled out a long necklace that I hadn't worn in ages. It was a gift from Grandma Ann. She bought it after seeing me admire it in one of the stores in the mall.

When I was finally ready, I left my room and headed for the kitchen. I felt anxious about the meeting ahead but hoped some breakfast would help to calm me down.

Lucas was already in the living room watching cartoons. He held a bowl of cereal in his lap and slurped sloppily from a spoon.

I rolled my eyes.

Grandma Ann and my mom were in the kitchen.

"Good morning!" I said.

"Good morning, Casey," Grandma Ann said.

Mom sat at the table, staring at her coffee mug.

"Mom?" I asked.

Grandma Ann and I both looked at her.

She glanced up with wide eyes. Her face looked a little pale, and her eyes were bleary. Had she managed to get any sleep the night before?

"Morning," she said.

"What's wrong?" I asked.

Grandma Ann patted Mom's shoulder. "Someone is a bit nervous about today."

It was Mom's turn to roll her eyes. And I thought it funny that relationships between mother and daughter didn't change as they became older.

"I'm worried about meeting Ali's parents," Mom said. "I tried to pick out something to wear this morning, but nothing seems appropriate. And I feel I should take something along with us – it would be rude to go empty-handed. But you know I'm hopeless at baking, Casey. Perhaps I should pick something up from the bakery?" Her words tumbled out in a rush as she stared at me, an expression of overwhelm filling her features.

For any other occasion, I would have agreed with her. But last night, Ali was texting me about helping her mom make a batch of intricate cupcakes and two gourmet home-baked pies. If Mom showed up with something in a bag, no matter how good it was, it would be an embarrassing addition to the homemade ones that Ali's mom had worked all night on.

"How about you get flowers instead?" Grandma Ann suggested.

I looked at her, and she winked at me. Mom didn't notice. For once, I was happy for Grandma Ann's advice.

"I think flowers would be great, Mom," I said. And to change the subject, I added, "I'll help you pick an outfit, as well."

Mom's shoulders relaxed a little and she looked at me with relief. "Thanks, Casey. That would be fabulous!"

Grandma Ann cooked pancakes and eggs, while I helped Mom choose an outfit from her cupboard. I pulled out my favorite, it was one that made her look even younger than she already was, and when she put it on, I remembered for the first time in a long time, how pretty she was.

Normally when she wore her hair back and her usual professional clothes, she looked more like a business-woman. But with the change in outfit, it changed her style completely. For a second, I wondered if Ali and I would look as young as her when we were her age.

After breakfast when Mom and I were heading for the door, my phone rang.

"Oh, it's Ali," I said, and stopped there in the doorway to answer it. "Hey!"

"Casey!" Ali said in a frantic tone.

I looked at Mom, who raised her eyebrows curiously. "What's wrong, Ali?" I asked.

"We're in the car right now."

"I thought we were meeting at your house?"

"We're on the way to the hospital," she said.

"Oh no! Is it your mom?"

"Yes," Ali replied, her voice cracking with emotion. "She passed out and we need to get her to the hospital as quickly as possible."

"Oh no!" I repeated the words, as my own memories of racing to the hospital came flooding vividly back. I didn't think I would ever forget that terrible journey with Ali's mom so sick in the front seat, while her dad sped along the highway. "Is there anything I can do?"

"No, not really," she said, "but I'm sorry, we have to

cancel."

"Don't worry about that," I said. "Text me as soon as you find out anything."

"I will." Her reply came through the speaker and then she was gone.

"What happened?" Mom asked.

Before I could answer, a text appeared from Ali. *I'm really scared*

I guessed she hadn't wanted to say that in front of her parents. I quickly texted her back. *I'm sure your mom will be okay, Ali. I'm thinking of you. Text me as soon as you hear anything!*

Okay

"Casey?" Mom prompted.

"They're taking Ali's mom to the hospital. She's not doing well."

"Should we go there?" Mom asked.

"I don't think so," I said. "We'd probably just be in the way."

Mom started to chew on her fingernails, something I hadn't seen her do in years.

"Mom," I said. "You should go to the little league game with Lucas and Grandma Ann. I'm going to stay home and wait to hear from Ali. She needs me right now."

"Are you sure?"

"Yes," I said. "I have some homework to finish up before tomorrow."

Mom bobbed her head then went into her room to change.

I'd already finished my homework but I didn't want to go to the game, and my homework was a good excuse to stay at home. In the back of my mind, I knew Jake was probably going to be there, but I wasn't ready to face him. If he asked me something about the game from the weekend before, I wouldn't know what to say.

Mom checked in with me one more time before

leaving. Once they were all gone, I was happy for the silence.

I texted Ali again to see if there were any updates.

Her reply came back straight away. *They admitted her – We still don't know what's wrong*

I put down my phone, uncertain of what to say to comfort her.

All I could do as I tried to think of a suitable reply, was to hope that Ali's mom was okay.

We'd planned such a wonderful day together, and I worried that it might never take place. If the worst happened, I was so worried about how Ali would ever cope.

CHAPTER TWENTY-TWO
Casey

On Monday, I figured out soon enough that Ali wasn't coming to school. When I arrived at the classroom, I saw that her seat was empty, when normally she got there before everyone else.

Before class started, I texted her for an update. I hadn't wanted to bother her earlier since I thought I was going to see her at school. She'd been at the hospital all day, the day before, and had indicated that she hoped to be at school that day. But obviously, she didn't want to leave her mom.

After a few moments, I received her reply. *No school today. We're at the hospital again. Can you get some work for me?*

Of course, I replied back. *Let me know if you need anything.*

Ali didn't respond.

I thought of her all day during school and everyone was asking where she was. I told whoever asked that she was sick. It wasn't my place to explain about her mom's illness.

At our first cheerleading practice that afternoon, I had to tell Mrs. Caldwell that Ali wasn't feeling well. I hoped by missing practice that Ali wouldn't get into trouble. But Mrs. Caldwell said it couldn't be helped.

"Alright, ladies," Mrs. Caldwell said. "Today we're going to determine the positions for the formations of the cheers. There will be one lead spot, and that person will be in charge of starting the cheers for the other girls. Initially, I was going to choose Ali for the spot since she showed clear leadership, but since she's not here today, then I'm forced to make another choice."

I felt bad that Ali was missing out on the leader spot,

but I was sure she'd rather be with her mom at that moment.

Mrs. Caldwell moved us into different places to determine the best spots, then each of us had a turn at being the leader in the front and center position.

Holly was the most vocal, but she kept messing up the cheers. Ronnie wasn't loud enough. And Brie requested not to be the leader. Some of the other girls were good, which made me a little nervous.

I never liked being in the spotlight, but I wanted to try my hardest and prove that I belonged on the squad, even though I'd almost missed the opportunity.

After our practice was over, Mrs. Caldwell sent us for a drink of water and said she'd tell us her decision when we returned.

All of the girls were excited and tried to figure out who had done the best. Brie and I went off to the side on our own.

"You did really well," Brie said.

"Thanks, but I'm not sure I have a good shot. I mean, on Friday morning I wasn't even on the team."

I looked across the field to see the boys at their football practice.

"It would be nice if I were the leader," I said. "Jake would definitely notice me then."

"How good do the boys look in their practice uniforms?" Ronnie said, from a little further away.

"Totally," Melissa said.

"Don't bother with Jake," Holly added. "Everyone knows he has a huge crush on Ali."

I felt like I'd been punched in the stomach.

Ronnie dug her elbow into Holly's ribs, and Holly let out a squeal. Then she looked at me. Her face fell, and her cheeks flushed tomato red.

"I mean, I think so. I'm not really sure," Holly said.

Brie leaned in and whispered to me. "Don't worry about it."

Holly turned back to Ronnie, and they spoke to each other in a low voice. I didn't care what they were saying, even though I had an idea it had to do with Jake and Ali.

"Besides," Brie said, putting her arm around my shoulder, "some of Jake's friends are far better looking than him."

I laughed at her attempt to make me feel better. Even though Ali was my sister, we'd yet to have a bond as close as Brie and I had. Brie understood me.

"What about his friend, Josh?" Brie asked.

I rolled my eyes at her attempt to make me feel better.

"Come back over," Mrs. Caldwell said.

I squeezed Brie's hand, excited for the announcement.

We all crowded around Mrs. Caldwell in anticipation of her decision. "Based on your efforts today, I've chosen Casey as the leader of the squad."

My jaw dropped, and Brie gasped.

"Me?" I asked, unsure if I'd heard her correctly.

Mrs. Caldwell smiled, and the other girls clapped.

Brie took my arm and raised it in the air, then grabbed both my shoulders and gave me an excited shake. "Way to go, Casey. You did it!"

I couldn't believe I was going to be the leader of the squad! Everything was looking up for me. Being compared to Ali in such a good way was such a welcome change.

But thinking of Ali brought down my mood considerably. Here I was celebrating when she and her mom were in the hospital. My stomach twisted, and I hoped that Ali wouldn't feel too bad that she'd lost her spot.

I was thankful that the practice was over after the announcement. My head felt light with a mixture of emotions. And I wasn't sure I'd be able to focus on anything else. I waited by the curb for Grandma Ann to pick me up. But I was surprised to see Mom's car driving down the road.

"Hi," I said when I got into the car.

"How was your first practice?" she asked.

"It was great!" I said, unable to hold back a smile. "I

made leader of the squad."

Mom squeezed my arm affectionately. "Honey, that's fantastic! Congratulations."

I grinned back at her. I was so pleased, and was still trying to believe it was true. But then I thought of Ali and her missed opportunity. Pulling out my phone, I quickly texted her to see what was going on with her mom.

I'm in the waiting room, she texted back. *I couldn't watch them put another needle in her.*

My heart broke for Ali. "Mom? Can you drop me off at the hospital?"

"I don't know if you should go," she said. "This is their time to be together as a family." It was as if she knew exactly how serious it all was.

"I am her family," I said firmly.

Mom sighed. "Okay, I'll take you. But you should probably only make it a quick visit."

When we arrived at the hospital, I asked Mom if I could go in alone. It wasn't the time for a family meeting right then.

I found Ali in the Emergency Room waiting area. Wouldn't they have brought Ali's mom into another wing by now?

I spotted the unfriendly nurse from my previous visit at the hospital. She did a double-take when she saw me. And then glanced towards Ali who was sitting in a nearby chair. Being back there reminded me of the last time Ali's mom was in the hospital, which was only the weekend before. So much had happened since, it seemed such a long time ago!

"Casey!" Ali called, a surprised expression on her face as soon as she spotted me.

I rushed over to her and hugged her tightly. "I wanted to see how you were. How come your mom's still in the emergency room?"

"We were able to take her home last night, but then she relapsed again this morning."

"Ali, I'm so sorry."

She slumped down in her seat and closed her eyes. "This is really bad, Casey. She's never been in the ER this much before. Dad won't tell me much, but I know we're close to the end."

Streaks of tears flowed down her cheeks, and she began to sob.

"Shh," I said into her ear.

I felt so bad for her, it was horrible to see my sister so upset. I held tightly to her hand and tried to comfort her by pulling her towards me in a gentle hug. Soon her sobs became light sniffles. "Sorry."

"Don't be sorry," I whispered back.

"Dad said he'd be back soon to get me, but it's been over an hour." She glanced towards the double doors that remained firmly closed in front of us.

"Have you tried talking to the nurses?"

She scoffed. "They're no help. They won't tell me anything."

I smirked, remembering that they were the same way when I was there last.

We sat together in silence while we waited for her dad to return. Ali didn't ask about cheerleading. She'd probably forgotten all about the scheduled practice that afternoon. And I didn't bother to mention it. It wasn't the time to be talking about cheerleading.

About fifteen minutes later, Ali's dad finally appeared through the double doors.

Ali jumped from her chair and went to him. I stood close behind her. I couldn't help feeling a little nervous seeing him again, after he knew the truth about the swap.

His eyes darted between us as we approached. "Hi, Casey," he said in a quiet voice.

"Hello," I replied with a small smile.

"I'm sorry to do this but, Ali, you need to come with me."

"I want Casey to come too," Ali said.

"I'm afraid that's not the best idea," he said. "Mom's not doing well, and it's better that only you and I go in to see her."

"It's fine," I offered. "I'll wait here for you."

Ali hesitated, but I smiled at her, silently encouraging her to go without me.

They disappeared through the doors and I was left in the waiting room, once again, worrying about Ali's mom.

I sat back down in a chair and watched the news on the television. It had distracted me last time, but this time I couldn't focus. Unable to sit still, I got to my feet and paced around the room, my mind a whirlwind of worry for Ali and her parents.

After waiting half an hour, I texted my twin. I didn't want to bother them, but I was anxious to know what was going on. When ten minutes had passed and there was no response, I texted again. But still there was no answer and I wondered if Ali had turned her phone off.

Deciding to approach the familiar nurse, I took in her unfriendly expression as I waited for her to acknowledge me. When she finally looked up at me, I asked her as politely as possible, "Are you able to check on my friend's mom for me?"

"Not in the emergency room, no," she said with a grimace.

It wasn't worth my effort to push her. I already knew what she was going to say. So with no other alternative, I returned to my seat in the corner.

Soon afterward, I saw my mom enter the waiting room.

"Mom?" I called over to her.

"What's happening?" she asked, coming to my side. "How's Ali's mom?"

I sighed heavily as I looked up at her.

She dropped down into the chair alongside me. "Oh,

Casey, did something happen?"

I could feel tears forming at the corners of my eyes. But I didn't try to stop them. "I don't know. I haven't heard from Ali in over an hour. What if something happened? What if her mother died?" I didn't want to utter the words, but I couldn't prevent them.

Mom wrapped her arms around me and made soothing sounds in my ear.

I let go and sobbed into her shoulder. I didn't remember the last time I hugged my mom. We hadn't been that close in a very long time. I sensed that everything, including our relationship, was about to change.

CHAPTER TWENTY-THREE
Ali

It had been almost two hours since I left Casey in the waiting room. "Dad, I should probably go out there and tell Casey to head home."

Mom had just fallen asleep. Before that, she was woozy from all the drugs the doctors were giving her. We'd watched reruns of her favorite sitcom while we waited for the medicine to kick in. It was a relief once her eyes closed and she breathed steadily. The nurse turned down the volume of the heart monitor so it wouldn't wake her.

It was the perfect time to go out and see Casey. I hoped she wasn't upset with me for leaving her for so long.

"I'll come with you," Dad said.

When I pushed through the double doors that led to the waiting room, I was shocked to find our mom sitting alongside Ali.

It wasn't the introduction to my family that I'd hoped for, but neither was coming to the hospital.

I glanced up at Dad who had his serious business face on. I wondered if he was hiding his nerves under that look.

"Ali!" Casey got up from her chair and came over to us. "What's going on?"

I gave our mom a little wave. "She's stable for now."

Our mom stood next to Casey, and she held her hand out to my dad. "I'm Jackie."

Dad shook her hand a little too long before he let go. "I'm Chris."

"It's nice to finally meet you, even though this isn't the best situation. I'm deeply sorry for your wife."

Dad nodded, not saying anything.

"I wanted to make sure you were okay," I said, breaking the awkwardness. "We should probably head back inside. I think we're going to be here the whole night."

"Why don't you stay at our house?" our mom suggested suddenly.

Casey looked as surprised as I felt.

She shrugged. "If it's alright with your dad?"

"That's actually a good idea," Dad said. "You shouldn't have to stay here all night, Ali."

"I want to be here," I said to him. "It's a nice offer but what if Mom wants to see me?"

Dad gently took hold of my shoulder. "We're hoping she sleeps the whole night. How about you keep your phone handy, and I'll contact you the minute there is any news or if anything happens."

I wasn't sure. I wanted to be there, but I knew I'd get no sleep if I was in the hospital all night. At least if Dad promised to contact me, then I guessed it would be okay.

I took a moment more to think about it before nodding my head, "Alright," I said, "as long as you remember to call me if there are any problems with Mom!"

Casey took my hand and squeezed it.

"Thank you," Dad said to our mom.

"It's not a problem. Ali is a lovely girl. You and your wife raised her well."

Dad gave her a quick smile before reaching down to hug me. "I love you, Ali. I'll text you in a little while." Without another word, he turned back to the double doors and disappeared through them.

"Okay," Mom said. "How about we pick up some dinner on the way home?"

"Sounds good," Casey said, and we walked side-by-side following our mom out of the hospital.

We grabbed some take-out food and ended up with much more than we needed. When we arrived at the house, Lucas barely let me in the door before he bounced over and hugged me.

"Ali! Are you staying over tonight?" he asked.

"Yes," I said.

"Oh, that's so cool!" He beamed happily back at me.

Grandma Ann came over and hugged me as well. "It's good to see you again so soon Ali, even though the circumstances aren't ideal. How is your mother?"

We talked about Mom while we ate, but then Lucas started talking about his baseball game the day before, recounting each play. It was a good distraction for me.

It was getting late by the time we finished dinner, and I was exhausted.

Casey took me to her room and pulled out the trundle bed from underneath her bed for me to sleep on. "It's not as comfortable as your bed," she apologized.

"It's fine," I said. I was so tired I could have slept on the floor.

She loaned me a pair of pajamas, and we quickly changed, brushed our teeth and climbed into bed.

When Casey turned the lights off, I closed my eyes. I was so happy to be with her. Staying with my biological family was something I needed at that moment. They truly cared enough to take me into their home. And having a sleepover with Casey was the best thing I could have done. But I couldn't help the deep sense of dread that filled me when I thought about my mother laying in the hospital emergency room. I just prayed that she would be okay.

The next day, I woke up early and immediately checked my phone. I'd set the alarm for six but had it on vibrate so I wouldn't disturb Casey. I texted my Dad asking about Mom.

He replied straight away. *She was steady all night.*

I'll ask for a ride to the hospital this morning, I typed back.

You should go to school. You already missed a day.

I want to be with Mom, I replied.

She's going to be in and out of consciousness all day. I

think you should go to school. Keep your phone on you and text me between classes.

Okay, I typed, even though I didn't feel okay about not being with my mom. How did Dad expect me to concentrate when she was lying in a hospital bed?

I laid back down and tried to fall back asleep, but I couldn't. I stared at the ceiling until Casey's alarm clock went off. She rolled over and looked down at me.

"Did you sleep okay?" she asked.

"Not really."

"If you want to stay here today, I'm sure Mom wouldn't mind."

"No," I said sitting up, "I think I should go to school today. It'll take my mind off everything."

It was the first time I'd ever taken a bus to school, and I had to admit it was a little fun. Casey didn't seem as excited as me, in fact, she seemed a little nervous. I wasn't sure why. Thinking back, I realized I had never asked her about the first cheerleading practice.

But as much as I wanted to know what happened, I didn't want to feel as if I was missing out on anything. I'd ask her about it when Mom was better.

When we got to school, we arrived much later than I normally did, and the front of the school was packed with kids and teachers, almost like it was at the end of each day.

Right when we got off the bus, we came face to face with Jake and his little brother, Matt.

Matt stared at Casey and me, wearing a funny expression on his face. "Wow, Lucas was right, you two really look alike."

"That's because we're twins," Casey explained.

Matt looked from Casey to me. "Are you going to come to our little league game again this weekend? Maybe if you come then Jake will come too! He really liked it when you were there last weekend!"

I stared at Matt, not knowing what to say. At the

same time, I could feel Casey's eyes on mine and I felt the nudge of her arm.

I took a big breath as I watched Jake's eyes widen with comprehension. Then his mouth fell open.

The problem was, I had no idea what was going on in his head.

Had Matt told Jake about the swap the weekend before, and all about me going to the little league game in Casey's place? Was that why Jake was looking at us so strangely?

Or was he embarrassed that Matt had revealed his crush on me?

My mind went blank, and I could tell Casey's had as well.

What was Jake thinking?

And how were Casey and I going to get out of this one?

***

Book 5

Turmoil

CHAPTER ONE
Casey

Hopping off the bus at school with Ali was different and exciting. With our twin-status out in the open, I didn't have to be nervous about walking into school with her, and someone spilling the beans. That morning while we were getting ready, I was excited to share clothes with her. I had a smaller collection of clothes, and they weren't nearly as nice as hers, but she was just as excited as me. It was something sisters did, and with us being twins, it was even cooler.

She'd decided on a turquoise colored skirt that buttoned down the front and a white top with little flared sleeves. I hadn't worn either of those things for ages, but Ali really liked them. I was so glad to see her happy with what she was wearing.

And the headband that she found in my cupboard was a perfect match for the turquoise skirt.

While I missed the quality and selection of her beautiful designer clothes, I felt happier wearing my own things. I guess I just felt more comfortable being me in my usual shorts, jeans, and t-shirts.

That morning I was dressed in my favorite black jeans and a striped pink and white top, and I was hoping for a glimpse of Jake getting off his bus. Whether I was being Casey or Ali, I had a special radar for him. When I did spot him, he was with his little brother, Matt. He had his hand on Matt's shoulder and they were heading towards us.

Jake smiled broadly, and my whole body broke into tingles. Then an explosion of butterflies fluttered around in my stomach, making it a struggle to appear calm and as though nothing was out of the ordinary.

As they approached, Matt wrinkled his nose at us. "Wow, Lucas was right, you two really do look alike."

"That's because we're twins," I explained, catching Jake's eyes.

If he had a crush on Ali, I was hoping he realized that she and I looked exactly alike; but we were just different in personality. From what Brie said, Ali had played me well during the swap. And he had got along so well with her that nothing should be different now.

Matt turned from me to Ali. "It was so cool having you at our little league game, Ali. Are you going to watch us again this weekend? Maybe if you come then Jake will as well!"

I grabbed Ali's arm, and we both let out a small gasp of surprise.

Jake's eyes widened, and his mouth fell open.

I stared at him, unable to move. A whooshing sound filled my ears, and the dancing butterflies in my stomach turned into a pit of jittery nausea.

Jake shifted on his feet, his eyes darting between Ali and me. His lips turned down into a frown, and he shoved his hands into his pockets.

My skin prickled with embarrassment. My mind went blank, and there was no way that I could explain away what Matt had said. We'd been careful in all of this, and of course, it was Lucas' big mouth that had ruined everything.

Jake pulled his fingers through his hair. "I, um, I have to meet my friend. S-See you," he mumbled and hurried off toward the school buildings.

Butterflies erupted in my stomach once more. But these weren't the right kind. I watched Jake walk away from us. And when he entered the school grounds, I turned back to Ali.

"What's wrong with him?" Matt asked. "Did I say something wrong?"

I glared at Matt. Of course, he'd said something wrong! He had ruined all of this for me by opening his big mouth about the swap. I couldn't believe he had no idea about what he'd done!

I began to say something, but Ali beat me to the punch.

"Everything is fine," she said, giving me a wide-eyed look. The look said, "Don't worry about it."

I clenched my jaw. Of course I was going to worry about it! Jake's silly brother had just revealed to Jake that Ali had been at the game and not me. Now Jake knew that she'd been pretending to be me. How was she so calm? Ali had no idea how annoying little brothers could be. This was a prime example, but regardless, she was more concerned about Matt being upset than anything else.

However, Matt seemed to have no idea of the effect of his big mouth. Shrugging as if it were no big deal, he headed in the direction of the school gate. I watched him skip away, probably heading off to find Lucas so they could plot together how to destroy their older siblings' lives…mine in particular.

I turned to Ali and grabbed her by the shoulders. "Now Jake knows it was you at the little league game last week!"

Ali opened her mouth, but nothing came out.

I groaned. "This is such a mess. What chance do I have now? Jake will think I've been messing with him and he'll never talk to me again!" My head felt light, almost as though I was going to pass out.

Ali sighed. "I think it'll be okay."

"How are you so calm about this?" I asked.

Ali shrugged one shoulder. "He might have thought that Matt just mixed us up."

I wished I would have thought of that. If I'd been quick on my feet, I could have corrected all of this with a few words. I could simply have said that it was me at the little league game and not Ali. But I was terrible when put on the spot and I could never think quickly enough.

Sighing heavily, I shook my head. "You saw the

expression on Jake's face. He definitely had a problem with something!"

Ali chewed on her lip. "Well, maybe he was embarrassed because Matt made it sound as though Jake had a crush going on."

I dropped my hands to my sides and thought about that. Did Ali mean that Jake had a crush on her? Clearly, that was the question that kept popping up between us. I wasn't willing to explore that mess quite yet. I had to fix this whole mix-up before getting into that with Ali.

"We should get to class," Ali said quickly.

I could sense she didn't want to talk about it either. Once again, our twin psychic connection was taking over and we each knew what the other was thinking.

We headed in the direction of our lockers to get the books we'd need for our morning classes. Brie was there waiting and when Ali joined us, I stood uncomfortably alongside her.

"What's going on with you two?" Brie asked, shouldering her bag.

She had obviously sensed that something was wrong, and I decided there was no use hiding what had happened.

"This morning, Jake's brother basically told Jake about the swap," I said.

"We don't know that for sure," Ali said quickly.

Brie's mouth opened in surprise.

"Exactly," I said, watching Brie's reaction. "That's how I feel."

"Do you want me to say something to him?" Ali asked. "He sits in front of me in class. I can probably make him think that Matt mixed everything up."

"No, it's probably best not to," I said. "Let's just leave it and pretend everything is fine."

Although Ali still looked doubtful, she nodded in agreement. "Okay, if that's what you want. I won't say anything."

I nodded. I didn't know what was best in this situation. If Jake did have a crush on Ali, maybe he would just come out and say something. And I wasn't sure I was ready to know that just yet.

The bell rang and the three of us walked into class together. Ali was first inside, and she went straight to her desk. I couldn't help watching her. My stomach churned as Jake looked up at me. Then his eyes flicked to Ali and back to me again. I had to stop looking at him. It was hard for me to hide my guilty expression. But I didn't want him thinking anything was wrong.

Slumping down into my seat, I dropped my bag to the ground. I had trouble drawing air into my lungs and I felt as though I were suffocating.

Turning around discreetly, I peered back at Ali without Jake noticing. She was sitting at her desk. Usually, when she arrived each morning, Jake turned around and talked to her, but today he ignored her and continued to face the front of the room.

I made eye contact with Ali, and she looked upset. Jake was normally so friendly to her, but it was quite obvious that he wasn't interested in talking to her at all.

I sent her a silent message, *I think he knows!*

Ali quirked her lips and nodded, clearly understanding what I'd said.

I squeezed my eyes shut and turned back to the front of the room.

"Alright, class," Mrs. Halliday said, "We're going to look at last night's homework and check your comprehension of the reading passage."

She handed stacks of blank paper to the front row of students. As they passed the papers back to the kids behind them, someone tapped my shoulder.

I turned to the boy who sat behind me, whose name was Everett. His green eyes looked hopeful. "Want to work on this together?" he asked with a shy smile.

Everett and I had a lot in common. Like me, he loved to read. And we'd worked together on a few assignments in the past. He was a little nerdy, but not in a weird way. He was incredibly smart and funny. But why couldn't Jake look at me the way Everett did?

I tried to push Jake out of my mind while working on the activity. But I found myself glancing behind me for most of the morning, trying to figure out what was going on in Jake's head. While he would normally pair up with Ali in class, he'd quickly picked Ben who sat in the seat beside him. Had I wrecked everything between Jake and me? If he wasn't talking to Ali, then I was sure that he wouldn't want anything to do with me either.

I hoped that this would work itself out, but I knew that either Ali or myself would have to explain ourselves soon enough.

CHAPTER TWO
Ali

Our day had started off so well. It had been fun to share clothes with Casey and then catching the bus to school together. But from the moment when Matt revealed the swap to Jake, everything changed.

In the hallway before class, I tried really hard to stop Casey from worrying. I felt responsible because I was the one to tell Casey's family about our swap in the first place. But I didn't expect Lucas to tell Matt all about it. I guess I should have thought of that, but I'd rushed in without thinking of all the consequences.

I pretended to Casey that I was okay, but inside my stomach was twisted into knots, and my palms were sweaty. I tried to keep myself together but I felt sick inside. It was my fault that everything was ruined and I felt so bad about it. I thought about the odd look on Jake's face after Matt had spoken up about little league. I could almost see Jake's mind ticking over. It had been hard to look away from him when his gaze bounced between Casey and me.

I was sure that I knew what he was thinking, and I could have easily said that Matt was mistaken. But for some reason, the lie didn't come. And we couldn't blame poor Matt as it wasn't his fault. With everything going on, I wasn't thinking straight. If only I'd spoken up, everything would be fine now.

But I desperately wanted to know what was going on in Jake's head. As much as I knew he was Casey's crush and I had no right to feel the same way, I was worried that now he wouldn't want to be friends with either of us.

As well as worrying about my own feelings for Jake, I wasn't sure if Casey would forgive me for the mess we'd found ourselves in. The swap was my idea in the first place and I was to blame. She hadn't said anything, but I knew the thought was on her mind.

When I entered the classroom my nerves slowed down a little, so I was able to clear my head and think of what to say to Jake. Even though Casey didn't want me to, I had to make things right again. I made sure to walk slowly down the aisle to give Jake a chance to greet me as he did every morning. That would give me the opportunity to jump in with the lie.

When I reached his desk, he continued to stare down at his book. I stood there for a second, waiting for him to look up. But he didn't. Instead, he ignored me completely.

I swallowed the painful lump in my throat and sat down in my chair. Staring at the back of his head for a moment, I waited but he still didn't turn around. Something was definitely wrong. Should I tap his shoulder? Or was he making it clear that he didn't want to speak to me?

We were in bigger trouble than I originally thought.

While I was trying to decide what to do, Casey caught my attention. It was obvious to her what was going on, and that made me feel even worse. As if I didn't have enough to worry about already, with Mom in the hospital. Things just weren't working out at all.

Thinking of Mom, I decided to check for any messages from my dad. I also needed to turn my phone to silent mode. The school had a strict policy about cell phones, and I didn't want to get into trouble if he called me in the middle of class.

Reaching down, I plucked my phone from my bag and hid it under my desk, so I could check without Mrs. Halliday noticing. Shifting my body slightly, I made sure that I was hidden behind Jake, and out of the teacher's view.

"Okay guys," Mrs. Halliday said. "Can you please open your homework books to the reading passage?"

Ignoring her request, I focused on my phone instead.

But there were no messages. So I quickly typed a short text to let Dad know my phone would be in silent mode during class.

"Hey, Ben," Jake said to the boy alongside him. "Want to work together?"

While I was mid-text, I glanced up at Jake. Ever since my first day, Jake had asked me to work on class assignments with him. There had not been a single time where he hadn't turned to me with his usual beaming smile. But now he wanted to work with Ben. Something was definitely wrong.

Jake shifted his seat closer to Ben's.

"Ali Jackson!" Mrs. Halliday said, her voice sounding sharply above the scrape of chairs around the room.

I jolted upright and my eyes snapped towards hers.

With her arms crossed over her chest and her eyes directed at the phone in my hands, I knew I had been caught. Because Jake had moved his chair, he'd given her a clear view of my desk and the phone hidden underneath.

The entire class, except for Jake, turned in their seats to look at me. With everyone's attention directed my way, I felt my face heat up so intensely that I was sure I'd burst into flames at any moment. My mouth had dropped open and I couldn't take my eyes away from the phone that I'd placed in her hands.

"You can have this back at the end of the day," she said. She clicked her tongue disapprovingly. "I never expected this from you, Ali."

My fingers tingled, and my head spun. My phone was my lifeline. Right then, it was my only connection to my parents and what was going on with my mom at the hospital.

Mrs. Halliday started down the aisle toward her desk.

"Um…Mrs. Halliday, um…can I please have it back," I stammered.

She turned around, her lips pursed. Then her

eyebrows drew together, "Excuse me?"

"I really need my phone," I said, looking her fearfully in the eye.

My heart pounded against my chest. I had to have that phone by my desk. Even if it was on vibrate, at least I'd know that Dad was trying to contact me.

"You know the rules, Ali—"

With my pulse racing frantically, I lost all control, "Please give it back!" I shouted the words, and then realized the mistake I'd made.

Wringing my hands together in my lap, I wished that

Mrs. Halliday could somehow understand my desperation. But I had no way of letting her know how important that phone was to me; unless I confessed right then to everything going on in my life. And that was something I could not do. Not in front of the entire class.

Mrs. Halliday's eyes narrowed. "I will not accept that rude tone, Ali Jackson!"

"I'm not being rude, I— "

She barely let me speak before she cut me off. "Ali, you will be staying behind this afternoon for an after school detention. I will not tolerate this type of behavior in my classroom. Let this be a lesson to everyone!"

She scanned the room and then her eyes fell back on me. "And your parents will be getting a phone call from me about your behavior."

Tears began to well in my eyes. "If you would just listen— "

"No, you listen to me," Mrs. Halliday continued, her face turning red. "This is *my* classroom, and my word is *final.*"

Mrs. Halliday stared me down, and I realized I'd completely overstepped the mark. She wasn't willing to listen to anything I had to say. After speaking to her the way I had, she refused to hear another word.

I knew I should have just told her that my mother was in the hospital and I needed my phone in case something happened. Surely she would have understood. But it was too late now and she probably wouldn't believe me anyway. At least not until she attempted to call my parents and they weren't home. But that could be hours from now. And anything could happen in that span of time.

Even though I'd been right for demanding my phone back, my parents would be so disappointed in me for yelling at my teacher. I wasn't sure what had come over me. If I was calm about it, she might have returned it. Or at the very least I wouldn't have detention.

I should have never left the hospital. Now I wouldn't know anything until the end of the day. What if something happened and I wasn't there? I would never forgive myself.

CHAPTER THREE
Casey

I cringed while watching the entire scene unfold between Mrs. Halliday and Ali. Initially, when Mrs. Halliday noticed Ali's phone, I thought she was going to either lightly scold Ali or take it away. But Ali made it so much worse by talking back. I'd never seen her get worked up like that before. I understood that she wanted to stay connected with her parents at the hospital, but Mrs. Halliday didn't know the real reason.

Why hadn't Ali said anything? If it were me, I wouldn't care what the other kids thought, as long as I got my phone back. Mrs. Halliday would have understood her need to have it. And I bet Ali only had her phone out for that reason. She wasn't the type to distract herself during class.

I had a strong urge to stand up for Ali, and I had almost raised my hand to try and explain the situation. But I had a bad feeling that it would only add to the problem. Mrs. Halliday was a stickler for the rules and could be very short-tempered when it came to kids who broke them. Today she seemed in an unusually bad mood, which made all of this so much worse.

So instead I sat there in silence while Mrs. Halliday gave Ali a detention, in addition to taking away her phone.

I could feel Ali's embarrassment and anger. Even though she kept a straight face, I was sure she was dying inside.

I tried to catch her attention to let her know I was there and that I understood. But when I leaned over in my seat so she could notice me, she remained stone-faced, her eyes fixed on Mrs. Halliday. Even though by that point, the entire class was looking in her direction.

It was a different side to Ali that I had not seen before, and I was surprised by her defiant manner. It was something that I knew I was guilty of when someone made me upset. But I had never thought that sort of behavior could exist inside of my twin, who so far, had seemed perfect in every way. Up until now, she never seemed to do anything wrong.

I wished she'd just explain herself! But whatever the stubborn trait was that existed in my personality, was obviously also present inside of Ali. And I knew she wouldn't budge. At least not until she calmed down.

The edge in Mrs. Halliday's face was unmistakable. I'd only seen my teacher get this angry a few times before. I wished Ali would look at me so I could tell her not to make the situation any worse. Mrs. Halliday was renowned for holding grudges, and if any kids got on her bad side, then it was a hard situation to reverse.

I recalled Leon Peters from last year's class. He was often outspoken and caused a lot of trouble in class. He thought he was the class clown and was always trying to get everyone's attention.

He was often in trouble with his teachers, especially Mrs. Halliday. Early in the year she'd yelled at him, and then seemed to pick on him regularly after that. Since everyone was aware of what she was like, no one dared to get on her bad side. But Leon persisted.

Then a couple of months later, he managed to be switched to another class. I thought that because the situation had become so bad, perhaps his parents had probably requested it. But I didn't want the same thing to happen to my twin sister over a cell phone. Especially as she had such a good reason to keep it on her during class.

After Mrs. Halliday had ended the conversation with Ali, she put the phone into her desk drawer and continued with the lesson. I partnered with Everett, but I couldn't pay much attention to anything he or Mrs. Halliday said.

Ali sat with her partner, a girl called Jessie who sat alongside her. But every time I checked, she didn't seem to look up once from the book in front of her; at least until Mrs. Halliday called on her to answer a question. She answered correctly but only half-heartedly, and had an edge to her voice when she spoke. This seemed to spur on Mrs. Halliday, and she asked her three more questions before the end of class. It was a good thing Ali was smart. I think Mrs. Halliday was searching for another reason to get Ali into trouble.

Each time the teacher said her name, I cringed. I knew I had to do something, even if Ali didn't want me to. At least she'd be able to know her mom was okay during the school day instead of after it.

As I usually did, I stared at the clock, counting down the minutes until the bell rang.

When it finally sounded at the end of class, I jumped up and headed straight towards Mrs. Halliday's desk. I was sure that Ali wouldn't ask for her phone back again, for fear of getting into more trouble. So I knew I had to make an effort.

"Mrs. Halliday?" I said when I got to her desk.

She glanced up at me over her reading glasses.

I took a breath. "Ali's mom is very unwell. She's been in the hospital overnight and Ali was using her phone to check up on her."

Mrs. Halliday blinked. Then she tilted her head to the side, glancing over my shoulder at Ali who was coming down the aisle toward the front of the room.

Ali was on the verge of tears, and I wanted to give her a hug and tell her everything was going to be okay.

"Ali?" Mrs. Halliday asked, as my twin approached.

"Yes, Mrs. Halliday?" Ali asked.

"Is it true that your mother is in the hospital?" Mrs. Halliday looked at Ali, her eyebrows raised in concern.

Ali frowned and glanced at me. I hoped she didn't feel that I'd betrayed her. Most of the kids were out of the classroom by then, so I knew none of them had heard. And even if they did, it was worth it to get her phone back.

Ali's lower lip trembled, and she nodded silently.

Mrs. Halliday touched her fingers to her mouth. "I'm sorry, dear. I didn't know. But you do realize that if you need to be contacted, phone calls can go through to the school office. If there was an emergency of any kind, you'd be told immediately."

"I know," Ali replied, trying to blink away her tears. "But I wanted to keep my phone with me so I could check up on my mom. I just wanted to be sure she's okay."

Mrs. Halliday took in Ali's words. Then, reaching into her desk drawer, she retrieved the phone and handed it to Ali. "The rules are no cell phones in class. But we'll make an exception this time."

Ali's eyes lit up as she nodded. "Thank you, Mrs. Halliday."

Without hesitating, she quickly swiped her fingers over the screen to check for messages.

When I glanced down at her phone and didn't see

anything, I breathed a relieved sigh.

"My dad said he'll message me if anything happens," Ali explained to Mrs. Halliday. I could hear the relief in her voice and I knew I'd done the right thing for her.

"Well, I hope that your mom is okay and everything turns out fine," Mrs. Halliday said, giving Ali a genuine smile.

I patted Ali's shoulder while she studied her phone.

"You know, girls," Mrs. Halliday remarked, "I've heard you two are actually related. Is it true that you're twins?"

"Yes, we are," I replied, a wide smile spreading across my face.

Ali smiled too, and I knew she'd forgiven me for talking to Mrs. Halliday about her mom's condition.

"That's remarkable," Mrs. Halliday shook her head, the disbelief at our situation showing clearly in her expression.

It appeared that her bad mood had lifted as well. "I always thought you two looked so similar. I think twins are fascinating. How did you find each other?"

"By accident," Ali and I said at the same time.

I glanced at Ali and smiled.

Mrs. Halliday sat there with her hands clasped together, apparently wanting to know more. But I knew that Ali wouldn't want to spend the break sharing our story. I was sure that she was desperate to leave the classroom so she could call her dad.

"Thanks for giving my phone back," Ali said, nudging my arm.

I could tell she wanted to leave. "See you after the break," I said to Mrs. Halliday, and I turned towards the door.

"If any other teacher asks about the phone, have them come speak to me," Mrs. Halliday said, as we made our way towards the door.

"Thanks, Mrs. Halliday," Ali replied.

I couldn't believe how easy that had been. Once we reached the hallway, I noticed the tears on Ali's face.

"Oh, Ali!" I said. "What's wrong? Did your dad just text you?"

She shook her head. "I didn't want Mrs. Halliday to know—"

"I know it wasn't my place," I said quickly.

"No," Ali said. "It's fine. It was just me being stubborn. She made me so angry and nothing made sense. I've never yelled at a teacher like that before."

I slung my arm over her shoulder. "I've done it plenty of times. But I never knew you had it in you!" Grinning at her I added, "It's good to see we have something else in common!"

Ali smiled back at me as she put her phone to her ear. From my spot alongside her, I could hear the dial tone and I waited anxiously for her dad to answer.

I just hoped that he would have good news.

CHAPTER FOUR
Ali

I couldn't wait to get outside to call Dad. I practically ran out of the building with Casey by my side. The whole situation from class had been mortifying for me. I still couldn't believe I'd shouted at Mrs. Halliday like that. I wanted to do something nice for her to make up for my attitude. But that would have to wait until after I got an update about Mom.

"Thank you, again, Casey," I said, pushing through the door. I didn't know how long the conversation would go with Dad, and I wanted to make sure that Casey knew how much her speaking with Mrs. Halliday meant to me.

"No problem, you would have done it for me, right?" she asked.

"Yeah of course I would have," I smiled gratefully.

After I got everything with my mom sorted, I hoped I could come up with a plan to get her and Jake together. My crush had to be pushed aside for my sister. She'd done so much for me and was so supportive when I needed her. That outweighed any crush. At least I hoped it could.

Brie came up to us the moment we got outside. She saw my phone. "How did you get it back?"

"I'll tell you about it," Casey said, leading Brie away.

I silently thanked her for giving me privacy. I was unsure what to expect, so I wanted to be alone. Pressing the green telephone button, I dialed Dad's cell number.

"Dad?" I asked the moment he picked up the phone. "Is Mom okay? The teacher took away my phone in class. I didn't see any messages from you, so I wanted to make sure nothing had happened."

"Ali," Dad said. "Slow down. Everything is fine right

now."

"What do you mean, now?" I asked frantically. "What happened that she wasn't fine?"

There was a long pause on the other end, in which a million possibilities of something going wrong filled my mind. Had she passed out again? Was the medication not helping her? What?

"She had a rough night," Dad said.

"Why didn't you text me?" I asked.

"She's stable now," he replied.

I glanced around me to make sure no one was listening to my conversation. Everyone seemed preoccupied with whatever they were doing right then. "You said you were going to contact me if something happened."

"And I will, Ali. Last night wasn't out of the ordinary. It wasn't worth you worrying. School is important. Get on with your day, and I will call you if something happens."

I heard voices and equipment moving around in the background. Was he in Mom's room, or outside? I wondered what was going on there that he wasn't telling me.

"Should I come to the hospital?" I could call my biological mom to take me. I was sure she wouldn't mind. She often worked from home and could be at the school quickly.

"No, you should stay in school," Dad said. "There's no need for you to be here. I'll text you every hour if you want, and give you an update."

"That'd be good," I said. "But if you want me to come, I can ask Jackie."

"Okay, but I have to go now," he said. "I can see the doctor on his way."

I opened my mouth to speak, but he cut me off.

"I'll send you a text about what he says."

I breathed a sigh of relief. "Thank you."

"Love you," he said.

"Love you too, Dad."

He hung up first. I pulled the phone away from my ear and flipped on the vibrate switch. I didn't want a repeat incident of the issue with Mrs. Halliday. Even though this time I was sure she wouldn't pose a problem, I didn't want to create another fuss. Once Mom was better, I knew I wouldn't be given a free pass with my phone again.

I took a moment to allow the conversation with Dad to settle over me, while I took in the rest of my classmates hanging out in different areas together. It was a beautiful day with a warm breeze. The movement of my hair reminded me of how my mom raked her fingers through it every once in a while. A wave of tingles rippled over my head, thinking of the sensation. I took another breath. Mom was okay for the time being. I could concentrate on school, at least until I heard something different.

Casey came over to me, her face filled with concern, "How is she?"

Brie twisted her hands together. Casey had told her. It was a reaction I knew very well from people who found out about Mom. I recognized the pity in her eyes.

There was no reason to be upset with Casey though. She'd helped me get my phone back. And Brie had become a close friend. It would be easier for everyone if we kept secrets to a minimum; at least between those people who mattered.

"I'm sorry about your mom," Brie said.

"Thank you," I said absently.

I was distracted by the sight of Jake as I spotted him from the corner of my eye, heading our way.

I held my breath as he and his friends walked in our direction. Casey and Brie quickly caught on, and the three of us watched them approach.

They were only a few feet away when they turned towards the small field in the back.

I let out the breath through my teeth as Jake looked at us. Instead of his usual friendly smile, his frown had returned. And as quickly as he acknowledged us, he continued on his way without a second glance.

He said something to one of his friends, but I didn't hear his words. I hoped it wasn't something about us. It was bad enough that he was upset with Casey and me, I didn't want him to start rumors of the swap. That would complicate things even more.

"I think he knows," I sighed heavily. "He must know, or why would he be acting like this?"

Casey groaned into her hands. "Everything is ruined now. I'll be lucky if Jake ever speaks to me again."

"He didn't speak with you much before," Brie commented.

Casey gave her a look. "I know that. But he spoke with Ali pretending to be me. We'd made progress, and now we're back to the start."

It wasn't the start for me though. Jake had been friendly with me since my first day at this school. But I didn't want to show Casey how upset Jake's attitude made me. She was the one with the obvious crush. I had to keep my feelings to myself or else risk hurting her. Even so, I worried that he wouldn't speak to me again either.

And then I wondered if all of this had happened for the best. If Jake continued to ignore us, then Casey wouldn't suspect he had feelings for me. And I wouldn't be on her bad side about Jake's crush issue.

But would it all come out regardless? Once Jake got over the initial shock would he or someone else confront us? If Ronnie or Holly suspected that we'd swapped places for so long, we'd never hear the end of it. And then the teachers might even find out.

A sour taste filled my mouth, and I doubted that anything would make it go away. Why did we think we'd get away with this? All I'd wanted to do was meet my mom, and now everything was a mess.

Brie talked to Casey about the situation, giving me a

moment to steal a quick glance in Jake's direction. His laughter filled my ears, even from that distance.

It appeared he was only in a bad mood when Casey and I were around. A sharp pang hit me as it always did when I saw him. Even with everything that had happened today, I still couldn't help my crush on him. And I had no idea what to do about it.

CHAPTER FIVE
Casey

While Ali was on the phone with her dad, my attention split between her and Jake. Concentrating on anything else was difficult. When he walked by us earlier, I was sure he was going to confront Ali and me about what Matt had said this morning. Again, my mind went blank looking for an excuse. I'd thought of plenty, but transferring thoughts to my mouth was too difficult, and instead, I stood there like a statue.

Would we need an excuse though? I bet Ali was sick of lying as much as I was. Although I wasn't sure what could we say to him that would still keep us on his good side? If we said it was a joke, then he might feel embarrassed for being tricked about who he was spending time with; or he might feel angry that we'd purposefully lied to him. Either way, there was no chance that we could tell the truth. I'd just have to talk to Ali about it once her mom was stable again. In the meantime, we'd have to deal with whatever happened.

"What's up with Ali today?" Brie asked.

While I told Brie about Ali's mom, I found it hard to stop looking at Jake. He had made a point to frown at Ali and me, and now he was joking and laughing with his friends.

All of this would have been easier to handle if he was simply in a bad mood. At least that would explain his attitude. But clearly, he was only acting that way around Ali and me. And that thought made my stomach hurt.

The swap had obviously had more of an effect on our lives than we realized. Each day something new popped up to remind us of that. For some reason, I dwelled on the fact that it was going to get worse from here. If Jake had told any of his friends about the swap, then I was sure Ronnie and Holly would also hear soon enough. If that happened, I'd glue myself to Ali's body so we'd be able to answer all of the questions together, to keep our answers straight.

When Ali finished speaking with her dad, she came over to join us. Brie told Ali how sorry she was to hear about her mom. But thankfully, according to Ali's dad, her mom seemed to be okay. I just hoped that really was the case.

Brie then pulled a notebook out from her bag and waved it in front of me. "I'm so nervous about our history test. I can't even remember anything from what I studied, my brain is too full of names and dates."

"When's the test?" I asked her, as I glanced towards Jake once more.

I wished I was a lip-reader, then I'd be able to know for sure what he and his friends were talking about.

"Um, after the break," Brie said.

I whipped around to look at her. "What?" I exclaimed. "Are you serious?" Thinking about it, I briefly remembered today's date as an important one. But with Ali's mom going back into the hospital and all the drama surrounding Jake, I'd completely forgotten to study! History was my least favorite subject, and I rarely listened in class. Without preparing for the test, there was no way I could hope to pass. Then I remembered that our test result would make up a huge part of our grade for the semester. I couldn't believe I'd forgotten!

"Casey?" Brie asked. "You did study, right?"

I shook my head slowly. "I didn't." My entire body vibrated, and I thought I was going to be sick.

"Well, um, you have like ten minutes before class to check the notes from the review class last week," Brie said, offering her notebook.

"Ten minutes isn't going to help," I said, tears forming in my eyes.

Even in the review class, I'd barely paid any attention. Since Ali had come into my life, school work wasn't as important to me. But it should have been since Ali was the smartest girl in our class. I should have tried harder to prove myself as an equal twin to her, not just in our appearance but with school work as well. Now I was going to bomb out on this test, and my mom and grandma would freak out at me!

My breathing came faster, and I had to sit down on the concrete. My stomach was a bundle of nerves and I found it difficult to breathe. I focused on the grooves in the pavement and wondered how I was going to get through this.

Ali and Brie sat down next to me, so I wouldn't look strange on the ground by myself. If I could speak, I would have thanked them.

"It's okay," Ali said, as she touched my shoulder, trying to reassure me.

"Don't worry about it, Casey," Brie said. "It's all multiple choice. I'm sure it will come back to you."

"I don't think so. I guess I'll just have to try harder on the next test." One stray tear slipped from the corner of my eye. I stared at the droplet on the leg of my jeans where it had landed. Even if I aced the other tests—which was going to be hard enough—Mom wouldn't forgive me if I bombed this one.

I rested my head against my knees and closed my eyes. I wished I could disappear right then and there. Or possibly some virus could attack me at that moment, and I'd have to go home sick. Why didn't anything ever happen in my favor?

"Here," Ali said. "Let's take a look at the notes. If we can at least help you get a passing grade—"

"Why don't you two swap places again?" Brie suddenly interrupted.

I lifted my head and looked at her. "How would that help?"

"Ali, haven't you been excused from the test since you've already done the whole unit of work, plus the final assessment at your other school?" Brie asked.

"Yeah, Mrs. Halliday said I don't have to do this test," Ali replied. "Because all my results were transferred to this school," her words trailed off as if she were starting to understand where Brie was going with this.

I remembered Mrs. Halliday telling Ali there was no need for her to take the test again. Ali had brought all of her paperwork into school, and I recalled seeing a big red A-plus on the paper. Our teacher even held it up in front of the class to show everyone, as she was so impressed. At the time, I remembered wondering if there was anything Ali wasn't good at.

"No, we can't do this," I shook my head at the silly idea from Brie, even though a small part of me was hopeful that Ali would agree.

It would be the answer to my problem...if only Ali would do it. But I could never ask her to swap again. It wouldn't be fair with everything going on with her mom, and now Jake. Besides, we were still struggling with the consequences from the previous swap.

Though if we hadn't swapped, I might not have been so distracted with those consequences and might have had more time to study. I wasn't blaming Ali exactly, but she did technically owe me for the first swap.

A small part of me was hopeful that Ali would say yes. I held my breath, waiting for her reaction.

CHAPTER SIX
Ali

I'd just started to calm down after the conversation with Dad. But then my heart began to race again; first of all when I spotted Jake and realized he might be talking about us, and then when Casey told us she'd forgotten to study. If I was taking the test myself, I would have remembered about it and we could have studied together. But since I'd already completed the entire unit, Mrs. Halliday said I could work on my class project, instead of doing the exam a second time. So I'd totally forgotten that today was exam day.

I hated seeing Casey so stressed. There were only ten minutes remaining until the bell went, so it was pointless her even bothering with the notes. My heart went out to her.

On the other hand, though, I knew she'd done this to herself. I never received a good grade without hard work. That was something my parents had forced me to learn. But I guessed they paid a lot of attention to me and what was going on in my life, so they always encouraged me to make time for study and homework.

Casey however, kept insisting that our mom was so preoccupied with work that she barely had time for her. Although I knew I shouldn't judge, I wondered if Casey exaggerated about that. She didn't seem to appreciate any advice that our mom or Grandma Ann gave her, and I had the impression that she preferred to do the opposite of whatever they asked. I never understood that part of her. But she was my sister, and I'd grown up in a different house so I had no right to compare.

And then, out of the blue, Brie came up with a totally unexpected suggestion. "Why don't you two swap places again?" She looked at us, her eyes wide with excitement.

I could see she thought her idea a genius one, but the moment she suggested another swap, my stomach sank. Even though I enjoyed History and knew I could probably do really well in the test, I thought it a bad idea. I'd already experienced Mrs. Halliday's anger and certainly didn't want to risk upsetting her again. If she caught us cheating, that would be far worse than using a cell phone in class. I could only imagine the consequences.

Casey's expression was hopeful, and I stared back at her, silent and unsure. This really was not something I wanted to be a part of. And besides that, I wasn't sure if we'd be able to pull it off.

"Ali," Brie pressed. "I think you should help Casey out. You weren't caught for the last swap. It was so easy. No one had any idea!"

"I know, but it was close," I said, avoiding any eye contact with Casey.

I didn't like how Brie was pushing me to make this choice. My stomach churned uneasily. We needed to think this through, not like the last time when it all happened without us being properly prepared.

"Casey's mom threatened to ground Casey for the entire summer if her grades don't improve," Brie added, a persuasive tone in her voice.

"What?" I asked Casey. "Did she really?

Casey nodded solemnly.

Sighing heavily, I looked at her. While I knew Casey had more potential than she showed in class, I was also aware how distracted she'd been lately. There was so much going on and school work was the last thing on her mind.

I kind of felt that I was to blame for that. Suddenly appearing in her life, asking her to swap places with me so I could meet my biological family, and then creating all the problems with Jake, had all been my doing. An invisible weight rested on my shoulders, and I had no idea what to do.

With the risk of Casey missing out on her entire summer, I began to convince myself that I couldn't let that happen. I would feel so guilty if I didn't help her and she was stuck inside for three months. She was my sister, and weren't sisters supposed to help each other out?

We'd done this before with no one realizing, except for Grandma Ann. But Grandma Ann wasn't here right now. And the swap would only be for a short amount of time. If we went straight to class after changing clothes, we could avoid any chance of being caught. And if we changed back right after the exam, what harm would there be?

But then Casey spoke. Shaking her head adamantly, I could see she'd thought about the idea and had made up her mind. "No, we can't do this. It's a great idea, Brie, but I don't think we should."

I could have easily agreed with her. It was wrong. The consequences if we were caught would be horrendous. But my mind continued to tick over. I didn't see many risks with a short swap, and in a way, I felt obligated.

I was the one to insist on the last swap and Casey had agreed willingly. I felt that I owed it to her. As well, it would be a way to make up for everything that had happened.

The more I thought about it, the more convinced I became. Mr. Edwards, my old history teacher, had spent so much time on that unit of work. I could still remember everything like the back of my hand. I also realized that after everything Casey and I had managed so far, this was really no big deal.

"Okay," I said abruptly, nodding my head in agreement.

I stared at Casey's surprised reaction as I jumped up from the ground, a wave of nervous energy moving through my body.

"How much time do we have?" I asked, quickly turning to Brie.

"Not much," she said, looking at her watch. "If you're

going to do this, you'd better hurry!"

"Are you sure?" Casey asked, frowning worriedly at me as she got to her feet. "This is huge, Ali. You don't have to. It's my fault for not studying."

Brie looked at Casey encouragingly, "Seriously, Casey…I would not be saying no to someone as smart as Ali doing the test for me. You're so lucky! And besides, I want to be able to hang out with you during the summer. If you're grounded, it'll be the worst summer ever!"

I could see Casey processing Brie's words. But not wanting to waste another second, I grabbed her hand and tugged her along with me. "Come on, we only have a few minutes before the bell rings. We're going to have to be quick!"

"Oh my gosh!" Brie exclaimed, the grin on her face stretching from one ear to the other. "This is so exciting!"

CHAPTER SEVEN
Casey

Waiting for Ali to make the decision had my stomach in knots. I would have been okay with her refusing to do the swap. There was a chance we'd be caught. And with Mrs. Halliday's attitude that morning, we ran a greater risk of getting into more trouble than ever. But I didn't want to lose all hope of getting a passing grade on the History exam. I still couldn't believe I'd forgotten all about it.

When Mom had given me the ultimatum after my last report card, I made sure to keep that in the back of my mind when any exam came up. But this time, I had completely forgotten.

I decided that from now on, I was going to mark the calendar in my room so I'd remember, no matter what else was going on in my life. And I would ask Ali to study with me for future tests. She was the smartest person in the class, and I was sure she wouldn't refuse. In fact, it might bring us closer than we already were.

When Ali agreed to help me, I could have hugged her right there on the spot. But there was no time for that. I just wished Brie had mentioned the test earlier. With us rushing to the bathroom, I hoped none of the other kids would think anything of it.

Ali and I raced towards the school building and the stairs that led to the upstairs bathroom. I couldn't believe my luck! For once, I'd get a passing grade in History. My mom would be thrilled, and Grandma Ann might actually stop hounding me about homework for a change. That would be the best thing ever.

Grandma Ann had such high expectations for me. It wasn't fair! I knew she only did that because she had never pushed my mom to try harder when she was at school. And I guessed she didn't want me to follow in my mom's footsteps and bomb out of school at a young age.

In the past, I'd tried to block out my grandmother's nagging. But now that Ali was in our lives, I felt as though I had something to prove. And getting a good grade in the subject I often did badly in, would be a good start.

Also, knowing my mother so well, I knew she'd probably follow through on the threat of being grounded if I failed the test. That was something I wanted to avoid at all costs.

"When we entered the building, Brie went in a different direction. "I'll meet you in class," she said. "It might look suspicious if we all head to the upstairs bathroom together."

Brie had a big grin on her face. She loved being a part of our secret. I nodded and waved to her, as I took the stairs two at a time.

By the time we made it to the bathroom door, I was out of breath. Ali was too. Pushing the door open, I crossed my fingers that no one else was in there. Luckily, however, during lunch breaks the school buildings were pretty much deserted. And today was no different. I closed myself inside of a stall then Ali and I swapped our clothes quicker than we'd ever done before.

My body buzzed with nervous energy.

"I can't believe we're doing this again," I gasped.

"Me neither," Ali said with a small laugh.

We met outside the stall and giggled to ourselves. I still found it so crazy how alike we looked!

With barely a moment to check ourselves in the mirror before the bell rang for class, we glanced quickly at each other and headed out the door.

"Thank you so much for doing this," I said to Ali, as we raced down the stairs.

"No problem," she grinned back.

My heart was racing and I guessed that she was probably feeling the same way. Taking a deep breath, I pushed open the classroom door.

We were the last ones back to class. I entered the room first, and Ali was right behind me. I exchanged a glance with Brie, who gave me a small thumbs up. I didn't respond because I was playing Ali now. Though Ali was friends with Brie too, they weren't that close. And I didn't want to bring any unnecessary attention to myself or my twin.

I could feel all eyes on me, and I hoped that no one suspected anything. Is this what it felt like to be the new girl? At camp, the rest of the kids were so excited to be away from home that they never paid this much attention to either Ali or me. Though I wondered if this morning's issue with Mrs. Halliday was the reason for all the extra attention.

Mrs. Halliday was already standing at the front of the room with the test papers in her hands. She gave us an annoyed look but didn't say anything. After the chat we'd had earlier, maybe she thought Ali had been on the phone with her Dad during the break. I had a feeling our teacher was more supportive toward us now, and especially toward Ali.

And now with Ali in my place, I was prepared to get an A!

As I navigated my way around the desks, I imagined Mrs. Halliday holding up my test like she always did with Ali's work. Even though it wouldn't be my earned grade, at the very least, it would make me feel included in the smart group. And I vowed to work much harder in future to genuinely get that attention for myself from my teacher.

As I headed towards Ali's desk at the back of the room, for some reason, my eyes fell on Holly, who was eyeing me curiously. I tugged on the hem of the top that Ali had been wearing, self-conscious and full of guilt. Did Holly somehow know what we had done? But how could she? Ali and I looked so alike, surely no one could tell the difference?

Brushing away my fears as I passed Jake's desk, I glanced at him, but he was too busy staring at his paper and trying to ignore me. I felt sure he was still upset with us. If we didn't have an exam, I might have tried to talk to him. Being Ali always made my confidence soar. But the reason for the swap was for the exam so I'd have to find another way to get to him.

I sighed and sat down. While Mrs. Halliday passed out the exams and offered instructions, I watched Ali sitting in my seat near the front of the room. It was so strange to see her from this angle. If I didn't know any better, I would have thought she was me. And I knew instantly that our plan was going to work out.

Pulling Ali's project book out of her bag, I glanced around at the other kids whose attention was on the test paper in front of them. It felt a little strange looking through Ali's things, but I was a little excited at the same time. Shuffling through the pages of her book, I investigated the work that Ali had already done at her previous school. Everything was so beautifully presented; neat writing, perfectly illustrated sections that were neatly colored, and every page had wonderful comments written by her previous teacher:

Awesome work, Ali!
Excellent!
Fabulous effort! A+
Love your illustrations, Ali. Very impressive!

I couldn't help rolling my eyes as I turned to the current project page and suddenly felt the pressure of maintaining such a high standard. I would have to try to look busy, so I could pass the time without making too much of a mess of Ali's book.

Glancing toward the front of the room, I could see Ali

busily writing on the test paper in front of her. As if she could feel my eyes on her, she turned back and smiled. With a quick nod and a smile in return, I felt reassured that everything would be fine. Then she returned to the test.

I imagined once more, Mrs. Halliday adding the first "A" I'd ever received for History to the paper in front of Ali.

Except this time, the paper would have my name on it!

CHAPTER EIGHT
Ali

Casey entered the classroom first, and I watched her walk ahead of me toward my seat at the back of the room. I took a breath and walked in behind her. No one even looked at me. I let out the breath I'd been holding and made an effort to concentrate on going to the right desk.

Brie smiled at me, and I smiled back, my confidence building again. I could do this. Right?

Entering the room as Casey seemed very strange; even though I'd swapped places with her numerous times since we had met.

I watched everyone glance up when Casey walked down the aisle to my seat. I never noticed how others looked at me. To be honest, I normally had eyes for Jake when I entered the classroom.

Jake didn't budge when Casey slid into my seat. His head was down, and his frown had returned. I plopped into Casey's chair and sat there with my shoulders slumped. I hoped Jake would get over this soon. Each time I saw him, I felt worse for lying to him.

Maybe I should have told him everything over the weekend of the swap. Especially after the baseball game. Mom and Grandma Ann knew at that point, so letting Jake in on the secret wouldn't have been a big deal. Casey wouldn't have been happy, though. The only reason she'd agreed to the swap was for me to get Jake to notice her. And right now, he didn't notice either of us.

"Are you ready for the test?" the boy next to me asked. I remembered that Everett was his name.

I nodded, not wanting to talk to anyone. This swap was for the exam only.

Facing forward, I hoped he wouldn't keep talking to me. If he and Casey were friendly with each other, I didn't want to ruin things. Perhaps he liked Casey. Although she had never mentioned anything much about him, even though he was kind of good looking in a nerdy sort of way, a bit shy though.

"Alright class," Mrs. Halliday said, gathering our attention. "Clear your desks of everything except for a number two pencil. This test is multiple choice using the scan sheet. Each packet with the test questions has a number at the top, place that number in the upper part of your scan sheet. Keep your eyes on your own work, and if you studied the review questions we went over in class, you'll do fine."

I swallowed the lump in my throat, and as much as I wanted to turn around and give Casey a reassuring look, I needed to avoid drawing attention to myself. I felt her eyes on me and closed my eyes, telling her I would ace the test for her.

When I got the test packet and scan sheet, I realized my hands were shaking.

Although I wanted to help Casey out—I owed her that—I found myself struggling with the task. The idea of cheating, even for my sister, made my stomach flip-flop. I tried to concentrate on the test, while at the same time worrying about my mom. I thought the test would be a distraction, but it had been the other way around.

I tried to assure myself by knowing that Dad would call if there were an issue.

Even though I'd swapped clothes with Casey, I kept my phone in the pocket of her jeans. I did not want it leaving my side again.

Over the course of the exam, I developed a nervous habit of constantly checking the phone in my pocket. Even though it was on vibrate, I wanted to check for messages. But each time, I'd make sure Mrs. Halliday was busy looking at something else.

There had been no word from Dad as of yet. Dressed in Casey's jeans, I could feel the phone at my side. I loved the idea of having a sister and swapping clothes. What I never imagined was the idea of swapping lives too. Thankfully, we'd both chosen tops with sleeves that morning, so the birthmark on my shoulder wasn't in view. That would have been a huge problem.

When I was mid-way through the exam, I felt an urge to turn towards the back of the room. When I did, I saw Casey looking my way. I gave her a discreet thumbs up sign to let her know that all was going well with the test.

She gave me a smile and returned to my project binder. A part of me hoped that she wouldn't move things around too much. But if she did, I wouldn't mind. If I were sitting there, I would have done the same to appear busy.

I turned back to my test and reread the question. This exam was set up differently to the one I'd already done in my previous school. There were a few questions that I struggled to remember the answers to, but they eventually came to me after enough concentration.

I knew I was doing well enough for Casey to pass. Luckily for Casey, I had a good memory. I didn't have to answer all the questions correctly, just enough for her to get a passing grade. Besides, Casey didn't usually do well on this subject. If she got all of the questions right, Mrs. Halliday might think that was strange. One or two questions wrong would stop her from being suspicious.

I was working on a particularly confusing question when I adjusted my headband. It had slipped forward and pushed hair into my eyes. I tugged it down over my chin so it sat loosely around my neck. Then I smoothed the strands of hair back off my face.

Just as I slid the headband back into place, a sudden thought registered in my head.

Oh, my gosh…I'm still wearing this headband!

I'd borrowed it from Casey's room that morning, and

we'd both completely forgotten about it!

For the first time since being myself again, I hadn't bothered to braid my hair. Instead, Casey and I had decided to go to school with our hair loose, the way that Casey always wore it. We'd already revealed the secret at school the day before and decided we may as well flaunt the fact that we are identical. Mrs. Halliday had heard the rumor, so I knew it had probably spread all over the school. This definitely seemed to be the case because we were constantly being approached by kids asking about our incredible story.

After breakfast that morning, though, I'd asked Casey for a headband to help keep my hair back from my face. I was used to having it tied back and never liked it hanging in my eyes. This was one reason I always wore it in a braid. I much preferred that to a ponytail or a bun, and I loved the different styles of braids that I could experiment with.

That morning I'd chosen a pretty turquoise headband to match the skirt I had borrowed from Casey. This created the only difference in our hairstyles.

But how could we have forgotten about that? With every other swap, we'd always been sure to swap everything, including shoes, jewelry, hairstyles, absolutely anything we could think of.

Today we'd been in such a rush to get changed that we'd literally shoved our clothing under the walls of the bathroom stalls and got dressed as quickly as we could. We hadn't had a chance to check ourselves in the mirror. Instead, we rushed out the bathroom door and down the stairs to the classroom, as we—me in particular— were so worried about being late and getting into trouble from Mrs. Halliday again.

I pulled the headband off my head entirely and shoved it into my lap. Then I looked around discreetly to make sure no one had noticed. Surely none of my classmates would have picked up on something like that. It was such a tiny detail.

I glanced around the room again and happened to lock eyes on Holly. She was staring directly towards me, watching my every move.

CHAPTER NINE
Casey

It had only been fifteen minutes into the test, and I was dead bored. I tried to look busy while everyone else worked on the paper on their desks, but I found my eyes wandering around the room instead. When Mrs. Halliday wasn't looking, I glanced discreetly at Jake.

Everyone had to separate their desks further before the test began, and he had shuffled his over to the left. From my spot at an angle behind him, I could see that his hair had flopped down over his forehead. And each time he tilted his head, I could see the frown of concentration as he chewed on his pencil.

Maybe after the test, I could pretend to be Ali and set the record straight about the little league game. I would tell him that it was Casey at the game and that Matt had been mistaken. Then I'd tell Ali about the lie and make sure we both stuck to that. I also decided to warn Lucas to keep his big mouth closed, or else. If he ruined this for me, I was going to be so mad at him.

I hoped that wasn't too much to hope for. I wanted to move on to more important things; like becoming better friends with Jake and maybe more.

My gaze wandered around the room again. The clock had barely moved an inch. Perhaps I should have taken the test! At least class would have moved faster. Right now it was too slow for me and the waiting was endless.

Many of the other kids wore the same anxious or blank expressions as Jake while working on their test papers. Several of them were clearly in the same situation as me. They hadn't prepared well enough for the test and were struggling badly. Once again, I was so grateful for my twin who had her head down and was busy filling in those little bubbles for each question.

I watched her for a moment. Her shoulders lifted and she rubbed her chin on her arm, glancing back at me. I looked away and then did it again. And so did Ali! It was as though she could feel me watching. She smiled at me, and I checked to make sure Mrs. Halliday was busy before smiling back.

My eyes wandered around the room again until they fell on Mrs. Halliday once more. She stared back at me, a slight frown creasing her brow. I flinched and put my head down, pretending to be busy with the project.

I didn't dare look around the room again for fear of Mrs. Halliday catching me. I would be mortified if she thought "Ali" was somehow sending answers across the room to "Casey" since she'd already completed the test at her previous school.

Looking down, I tried to put Ali's paperwork in some order. Pretending to be Ali in school was a lot harder than it had been at camp.

Staring at Ali's work, I wasn't sure what do to. I worried about messing up the perfect work in front of me. Maybe I could get started on reading ahead for class. I pulled out the novel we were reading in English and read one sentence about ten times before I gave up.

I couldn't concentrate! Especially with Jake sitting so close to me! How did Ali manage to finish anything with him right there? Well, she didn't have a crush on him. That was the difference between us.

Looking back at the clock, I could see that only ten minutes had passed.

I knew I wouldn't be able to get any work done, so I stared at the project book and pretended to read what I'd written. The words blurred in front of my eyes and my mind wandered back to earlier that morning when Matt spilled the beans. Little kids are so annoying. Why couldn't he have kept his comments to himself? He was just as bad as Lucas! No wonder they were best friends. They were exactly the same.

Jake's confused expression after listening to Matt babble on lingered in my mind. Jake had never looked at me for that amount of time before, and his expression was stamped in the front of my mind. Then he'd just left us standing there without another word! My cheeks heated while remembering how awkward it had been.

It was then I decided to make a list of pros and cons. Grandma Ann loved a pro's and con's list. It was how she made any big decision.

I flipped over the sheet of scrap paper I'd copied Ali's notes onto, and drew a line down the middle of it. On the left side was the Pro column and on the right was the Con.

Thinking about telling Jake the truth was the main question I had. And by the time I listed everything I could think of, I saw the Con list had grown much bigger than the Pro-side.

I stared at the list and took in everything that I'd written. We had to keep this a secret or else there was a strong possibility that Jake wouldn't want to have anything to do with us, or perhaps it'd just be me who he'd want nothing to do with. It might even push him to like Ali more than I suspected he already did. It just wasn't fair.

I folded the list and shoved it under Ali's books. I wished I had some idea of what to do. Instead, I made myself more anxious by wondering what was going to happen now.

CHAPTER TEN
Ali

Holly's eyes locked on mine for a moment and then she glanced down to the top I was wearing. As quickly as she had turned in her seat, she was back facing forward. I waited for her to turn around again, but she didn't.

When Mrs. Halliday looked up from her desk to make sure everyone was working, I returned my gaze to the test. I didn't want her to think Casey was cheating.

Sighing heavily, I scrunched the headband hidden beneath my desk, into a ball in my fist. There was nothing I could do except hope that Holly wasn't smart enough to realize what was going on. Ever since finding out about our swap, she had constantly been asking questions. It was as though she knew something but was unwilling to say it. Why was she so interested in Casey and me? Holly needed to mind her own business.

Checking to make sure that Mrs. Halliday was busy again, I glanced at Holly's test paper and could see there were very few questions answered. There were also a lot of eraser marks. She was obviously having trouble with the test. Maybe she was trying to distract herself by looking around the room. Without being inside of her head, I had no idea what she was thinking. And did she pay that much attention to Casey and me that she would notice one little fashion accessory such as a headband?

I hoped not.

Again, focusing on the paper in front of me, I looked at Casey's name at the top of the page. I'd added it when I sat down. At the time, I'd grabbed one of Casey's books from her school bag, in an attempt to copy her writing. Her books were labeled with her messy scrawl, and I tried to copy her style the best I could before shoving the book back into the bag. There were so many other bits of paper and notebooks crammed inside, that it was a struggle to return the book I'd pulled out. Casey was clearly messier than me, and it made me cringe to see all of the papers crinkled at the edges. This wasn't my book bag, though. I had to act the part of Casey, at least until class was over. Me cleaning up her papers would have been a sign that neither of us was who we pretended to be.

I squeezed the bottom part of the pencil, letting out a little of my anxiety.

After this, no more swaps. I was done pretending. We were even now. I couldn't keep doing this to myself. It wasn't fun anymore and I wanted to be me again.

All of a sudden I felt my pocket vibrate and knew instantly that my dad must be calling. The vibrating stopped. It had been a text. Dad said he'd contact me after the doctor came in. I wanted to check it, but I knew that wasn't possible. If it were something important, he would call –

But then the vibrating started again, and I knew straight away that it wasn't just a text, but a phone call.

When the vibrating stopped, I let out a sigh.

Then it started again, and my palms broke out into a sweat.

He said he'd only call if it were an emergency. And he said to keep my phone on me at all times, not in my bag, but in my pocket. I'd done what he asked but now I was in the middle of Casey's test.

I couldn't answer the phone. Mrs. Halliday and everyone else thought I was Casey. Why would I be answering my phone during a test? Mrs. Halliday had made it quite clear to all of us that cell phones were banned in class. She had given me, Ali, permission to answer my phone if I needed to, but certainly not Casey, nor anyone else.

Why hadn't I thought of that before? I could have given my phone to Casey so she could answer it, pretending to be me. I was sure she could have somehow found a way to get me out of class if my phone rang, but now I was stuck.

I hadn't had time to think of anything other than swapping clothes. This was a disaster! Not thinking of the headband was bad enough, now my phone!

My heart raced with fear. I looked to the front of the room where Mrs. Halliday was continuously scanning the class. Hopefully, she'd be distracted by something on her desk, even just for a short time so I could pull out my phone and message my dad. If I didn't contact him soon, he'd wonder why I wasn't answering. And I wanted to know why he was calling in the first place.

As I reached into the pocket, I quickly pulled my hand out. I couldn't risk it. I wouldn't dare. Not after this morning's episode. And being labeled a cheater would get Casey and me into so much trouble.

Unable to concentrate on the test, my hands moved of their own accord, twisting into my hair, tugging at the ends. I was frantic with worry and seriously panicking about the whole situation. Mom's condition and health were at stake, and if Dad was calling me numerous times, it couldn't be good news. The hairs on the back of my neck prickled and I had the sudden need to burst into tears.

Why did I do this? Why hadn't I thought it through before agreeing? If this were any other day, it would have been fine. But between Mom in the hospital and my guilt for having a crush on Jake, especially when my sister clearly liked him first, my brain was a jumbled mess.

Then the familiar tingling in the back of my mind made me turn my head toward Casey. I tried to make it look like I was thinking really hard in case Mrs. Halliday glanced my way. I couldn't wait the ten minutes to find out what Dad wanted. My only hope was to use the mental connection that Casey and I shared so we could come up with a plan.

Pressing my lips together, I stared at her, hoping she'd be able to figure out what I was thinking.

Her eyebrows furrowed.

I patted my pocket that concealed the cell phone.

Then her eyes widened. She'd received my message.

I turned around to face the front of the room. Now Casey knew about Dad's call. But what were we going to do about it?

I tried to think of another excuse to leave the room, or even just to look at my phone. Maybe Dad had called to make sure I got his text? Though wouldn't he know I was in class if I hadn't picked up? There had to be something wrong with Mom. He'd only called twice, though. I hoped he realized I was in class now and was unable to answer.

The sound of the ticking wall clock was louder with each *click*. I couldn't sit there for a minute longer when something could be wrong with my mom.

I weighed the options in my head and furiously chewed on my lip.

I shoved my hand into my pocket and held it there, unsure of what to do. If I pulled out my phone now, Mrs. Halliday was sure to see it. But why would Casey be on her phone in class? Especially after Mrs. Halliday made it clear to the class that this wasn't acceptable, especially during a test. That would give her a reason to think Casey was cheating.

I raked my hands through my hair once more. I wanted to put the headband back on to give me some relief from the tresses sticking to my heated face. I wished I had never agreed to the swap, and then I could explain to Mrs. Halliday that I needed to take my dad's call. This wasn't going to work. This whole situation was forcing me to admit to the swap.

I imagined the never-ending detentions and possible suspension as the consequences of our actions.

If I was going to get into trouble, I wished it was for a fun swap. A swap for a test wasn't fun at all. I could imagine Mrs. Halliday's reaction to the news.

I chewed on the eraser part of my pencil, trying to ignore the gross taste in my mouth. Should I risk getting caught? Or not?

I took a breath and made a decision. It was the best I could think of. Raising my hand, I got Mrs. Halliday's attention. Her eyes narrowed, and she nodded.

"Can I please use the bathroom?" I asked.

Everyone looked in my direction. The same feeling of embarrassment moved over me as it had earlier that day.

Mrs. Halliday glanced at the clock. "Casey, you will have to wait until the test time is over. There are only ten minutes left." Raising her eyebrows she added with a sigh, "Surely you can wait until then?"

I nodded. Casey could wait, but I certainly couldn't. My stomach churned anxiously. This was a disaster!

CHAPTER ELEVEN
Casey

Ali's voice caught my attention. "Can I please use the bathroom?"

I glanced up and noticed that the entire class had also looked up from their papers to stare at her. Everyone knew not to talk during a test, especially to ask for the bathroom pass. I knew that rule, everyone in our class knew that rule. But apparently, Ali didn't. I cringed and waited to hear Mrs. Halliday's response. If Ali had been the one to ask for the bathroom pass, I was sure Mrs. Halliday would have granted it, since it could have been an excuse to talk to her dad. But with her pretending to be me, there was no reason for the request.

Mrs. Halliday glanced at the clock.

"Casey, you will have to wait until the test time is over. There are only ten minutes left. Surely you can wait until then?"

I watched Ali nod in agreement. What was wrong with her? Asking to use the bathroom in the middle of a test seemed really strange. Ali never asked in class to go to the bathroom, for fear of missing any part of a lesson. Why was she doing this when she was me?

I tried to send her a silent message, hoping that our strange connection would help bring the words to her. "Ali, are you okay? Is everything okay?"

Ali slowly turned around, and I saw the expression of fear on her face.

I gave her a look that said, "What?" Did she forget some of the questions on the test? I wanted to reassure her that I only needed a passing grade.

Ali patted her pocket, and I realized she must be

referring to her phone. And that could only mean one thing.

Oh no! Of all times for this to happen. It must be her dad calling her. He'd only call if there were a problem at the hospital.

Shivers of fear raced up and down my spine. What were we going to do? She was clearly distraught by the situation. She couldn't possibly convince Mrs. Halliday to let her go to the bathroom if she was supposed to be taking the test for me. Why would I have Ali's phone and need to make a phone call?

This was very, very bad.

I was so selfish to expect Ali to do this swap. As if Ali hadn't had enough going on right now. And then I put her in this terrible situation. I should have never listened to Brie. I would rather fail the test than something happen to Ali's mom with Ali unable to reach her dad.

This is all your fault, my mind screamed at me. *You have to do something NOW!*

I thought of all the consequences but knew I had to do the right thing for Ali. I would have to accept whatever happened as long as I never had to see that look on Ali's face again. I would tell Mrs. Halliday I'd forced Ali to swap with me for the test because I didn't study. I would take full responsibility for everything.

Jake would probably never talk to me again, but that wouldn't be any different than the way he was acting now. Ali needed to talk to her parents, and I knew she was too good of a person to purposefully get caught and get me into trouble.

I was already doomed from the start with this test. I shouldn't have dragged her down with me. This was the only way to make up for the terrible choice I'd forced her into.

I pushed my chair back, scraping the legs noisily against the floor, and stood in my spot.

A few kids jolted in their chairs, and I heard Ronnie

let out a girlish squeak. The rest of the class turned to face me.

Mrs. Halliday looked at me, and I took in her concerned expression. She didn't seem as annoyed with me as she had been with Ali that morning. But she also knew what Ali was going through and as I was her twin, perhaps she had sympathy for me as well. "What is it, Ali?"

I glanced around the room and took a deep breath before opening my mouth to speak.

CHAPTER TWELVE
Ali

I was attempting to finish the exam but the words jumbled together before my eyes. I nervously tapped the eraser of my pencil against the desk. Was there anything I could do without telling Mrs. Halliday about the swap?

Then a loud scraping sound pierced my ears. Mrs. Halliday glanced up, and so did most of the class. Someone let out a tiny squeal of surprise. My heart leaped. Was that enough of a distraction to check my phone?

But when I turned around, I realized it was Casey standing. I had to do a double-take since I was once again struck by how similar we looked.

And for the first time since the conversation that morning, Jake turned around to look at her too.

Casey's eyes met mine for a brief moment before turning back to Mrs. Halliday.

She looked nervous. And I knew deep down that Casey was going to give up our swap. She somehow knew about the phone call and had swooped in to rescue me. My stomach clenched and my pounding heart filled my ears like a booming bass drum, loud and relentless.

Casey opened her mouth to speak and then closed it. She did that a few times, but no words came out.

We were going to get into serious trouble at any moment. My hand rested on the phone in my pocket. I was desperate to move it just enough to see the screen. Maybe if it was a false alarm from Dad, I could tell Casey to sit down, and I could finish the test before we got into trouble.

Then my entire world slowed down as if I were watching a moving play out in slow motion…the scrape of Casey's chair…turning to stare at my unfinished exam in front of me, and then glancing at our teacher…Mrs. Halliday's words questioning Casey about her interruption during a test...then the look of utter fear on my twin's face.

I felt as if I were an observer, floating above the entire room. As if I weren't really there. It was surreal, and my head began to feel fuzzy from it. I watched the events unfold in front of me, rather than being a part of what was happening.

The moment stretched on for what seemed like minutes, but in reality, it was only a few seconds. What was she going to say? How was she going to say it? Why did she want to do it in front of the entire class? Had she intended to do that before her chair scraped? Had that noise been an accident? Now there was no turning back for her. "Ali" had to say something.

Casey's voice filled my ears. "Mrs. Halliday? I have um, I have something, um, I need to—"

Then right in the middle of her sentence, the intercom came alive with the sound of an abrupt voice. We all looked at the box behind Mrs. Halliday's desk as we tuned into the voice sounding through the speaker.

CHAPTER THIRTEEN
Casey

I stared at Mrs. Halliday. My mouth opened but nothing came out of it. Was I really doing this? I couldn't believe this was happening. Both Ali and I were going to get into serious trouble because of me. If I'd studied when I was supposed to, instead of obsessing over Jake, neither of us would be in this situation right now.

I hoped that Mrs. Halliday would be lenient on Ali if I told her this was my idea. I would take all responsibility. I would tell her that I was the one to blame. I tried to think of a good excuse but right then my mind was blank with fear.

All I could think about was getting Ali out of the classroom so she could contact her dad. I would tell Mrs. Halliday that Ali was sitting in my seat and had to check her phone right away. This was too important to ignore. This wasn't a game anymore, and I had to speak up.

I'd intended to walk up to Mrs. Halliday's desk and tell her everything, but the movement of my chair had been much louder than I anticipated, and the entire class looked up from their tests to see what was going on. Their eyes pinned me in place and my legs remained fixed, refusing to move.

I felt the eyes of every other person in the room. An embarrassed flush crept over my skin. The words to explain my guilt were on the tip of my tongue waiting to come out. But they seemed stuck, and I struggled to say them. It was as though I had an uncontrollable stutter.

I wished I could make myself move toward the teacher's desk. Then Ali would have been excused from class, and I would be left suffering the consequences. Now, with everyone looking at me, they would all know about the swap.

I really hadn't thought this through. It was a habit that continued to follow me around each time a swap was suggested.

I licked my lips and forced the words out of my mouth. "Mrs. Halliday? I have um, I have something, um, I need to—"

Then the sound of the classroom intercom came to life. I sucked in the words hanging off the tip of my tongue. Before I could say anything else, I was silenced by the voice on the intercom. "Can Ali Jackson please report to the office with her bag immediately? I repeat…Ali Jackson to the office immediately. Thank you."

A crackling sound came from the intercom and then it went silent.

I clamped my hands over my mouth. No! This couldn't be happening again!

From that announcement I already knew what the message was about. Ali's dad must have been trying to get in touch with her. And since she was taking my exam, she wasn't able to answer her phone.

For Ali's Dad to call the school, it had to be bad.

I gulped with despair and looked to Ali for advice. I sent her a silent message. *What are we going to do?*

*Just go….*was the message she seemed to be sending me. She flicked her hand and nodded toward the door, urging me to leave.

This had gone on too far. I debated on revealing the swap anyway, but it seemed that this announcement had saved us from that. What was I going to do when I got to the office though? If Ali's dad was on the phone would I be able to talk to him as though I were Ali? I'd done it before, but what would Ali think?

"Ali," Mrs. Halliday said.

My head snapped in her direction.

"You may go," she said.

Without taking another moment to think any more about the situation, I grabbed Ali's bag from the floor, shoved her project book and pencils inside, and raced for the classroom door. I'd figure everything out when I got to the office.

Mrs. Halliday's eyes were filled with pity, but she didn't say anything to me. She knew the call must be related to Ali's mom's illness and was most likely serious. Poor Ali! I felt the same way as I had when Ali's parents picked me up from camp. I was in the wrong place at the wrong time, and yet I still didn't do anything to prevent it from happening again.

I paused for a moment in the doorway, glancing helplessly at Ali who remained seated at my desk. My heart pinched seeing her face in a mask of shock and despair.

She did tell me to go though. Maybe she'd find a way to get out of class before I made it to the office. I thought about walking slowly, but I didn't want to risk another announcement sounding through the intercom. Then Mrs. Halliday would be suspicious of something going on between Ali and me. And while we were in the clear for this swap, I didn't want to chance anything at this point.

I couldn't believe what I'd been about to do. And as Ali had taken an important test for me, this was a test I had to pass for her.

When I arrived at the office, one of the secretaries, Mrs. Johnson, walked over to me. "Ali, you need to call your father immediately. He said you have your cell phone with you."

Mrs. Johnson wanted me to call Ali's dad? I thought he'd be on the phone!

She stood there watching me as I pulled my cell from my pocket. I turned the phone on, and I moved the screen out of her view so she wouldn't see that I didn't have his number. What was I going to do?

There was no reason why Ali wouldn't have her own father's number on her cell phone. Another roadblock. Maybe he would call back in a few minutes?

"Is there a problem?" Mrs. Johnson asked.

I had to think fast. I pretended to struggle to turn the phone on, even though it was on and fully charged. "I think my phone is dead."

"Come over here, then," Mrs. Johnson said, leading me to her desk.

She sat down and lifted the phone from her desk. Her

fingers hovered over the keypad. "What's your father's number?"

I sighed and licked my lips. Of course she'd ask that. Just when I thought I'd avoided the problem of not knowing his number. Didn't she have caller ID?

"Do you know his number?" she asked.

I chewed on my lip. "His number was stored in my contacts. I don't remember it exactly. But he's at the emergency room with Al—my mom."

"You kids these days," she said with a shake of her head. "I had to remember everyone's number when I was your age, or else I could never to talk to anyone! I still recall my best friend's number from high school." She smiled at me and then clicked on her computer. "I'll just do a search for his number. We'll have it stored in our records." Within seconds of her search, she was on the phone and speaking with Ali's dad.

I stared at her, my mind racing. What was I going to say to him? I still had to pretend I was Ali. I decided to make the conversation short so that neither Mrs. Johnson nor Ali's dad would think something strange was going on.

Mrs. Johnson handed me the phone then sat back in her chair and glanced at her computer screen as if she were trying to give me some privacy. She wasn't even five feet away from me, she'd hear every word. I had to be sneaky.

"Ali?" Ali's dad's voice filled my ear.

"Yeah, D-Dad?" I said shakily. I cleared my throat and tried again. "How's Mom?"

"You need to come down here right away." His voice was abrupt. "Ali, I've explained to Mrs. Johnson that I ordered a cab, and it should be there within five minutes. The company has my credit card, so you don't need any money. The driver will bring you to the hospital. Don't panic, things are...okay, but I want you here with me. I have to go now but come straight through to the emergency room when you get here. The nurses will be expecting you and will let you through. I'll see you soon."

"O-okay," I said.

"I love you," he hung up, and I pulled the phone away from my ear, dropping it to my side.

My mind raced. This was a disaster. The situation from camp was happening all over again. I'd already been forced to go the emergency room in Ali's place. There was no way I could let that happen again. This time, I had a feeling something bad was going to happen. Ali had to go to the hospital, not me!

I placed the phone onto the desk and hurried over to the office door. I didn't want Mrs. Johnson to ask me what was wrong. Everything was so complicated, I wasn't sure if I'd be able to find the words to explain. What a mess!

There was nothing I could do right then. Outside, a bright yellow cab pulled up to the school and beeped the horn twice. If I didn't go out there, Mrs. Johnson would definitely ask questions.

Instead, I pushed through the door and decided to go to the car, hoping that I'd be able to figure out something on the way to the hospital. Maybe I could have Grandma Ann or Mom call the school for "Casey" and pick her up too. It might look suspicious, but I didn't care. Besides, we were sisters. I doubted anyone would think it strange that we'd leave to go somewhere at the same time, especially if there was an emergency.

As the door to the office closed behind me, I heard the sound of rapid footfalls on the tiled floor. I turned to see Ali rushing down the hallway in my direction.

I could not have been happier to see her face!

CHAPTER FOURTEEN
Ali

Along with every other pair of eyes in the room, I stared at Casey. I sensed that she was going to reveal our swap and my heart pounded in my chest at the thought of Mrs. Halliday and the entire class finding out that we were cheating on the test.

But just as she began to speak, the intercom buzzed loudly and interrupted her. I sat with my mouth open in disbelief at how close she had come to telling everyone that she was me.

While the message from the office had saved her from spilling the beans, it was difficult to watch her leave the room in my place. Dad had been calling me about Mom, yet I was the one still sitting at my desk.

Now Casey was going to know more about Mom than I did. And who knew when she was going to come back? I needed to speak to my dad. I had to know what was going on with Mom.

How could this be happening to me?

"Alright everyone, back to work," Mrs. Halliday said, breaking through the turmoil in my head.

Everyone returned to their papers except for me. I stared at the clock on the wall above the door, willing the hands to move faster. The seconds seemed to tick past at a snail's pace. A minute felt like an hour.

I didn't care if Mrs. Halliday looked over and saw me not paying attention to my paper. Each second that went by was agony, and I needed to know what Casey had found out.

When ten minutes had passed, my hand flew up into the air. After frantically waving my arm to catch her attention, Mrs. Halliday finally noticed me.

"Yes, Casey?" she asked, even though I was sure she remembered what I needed.

"May I use the bathroom, now?" I asked quickly.

"You may," she said and waved her hand for me to go.

I bolted from the room, leaving the unfinished exam on the desk. I only had one question remaining, but that was the least of my concerns. I knew most of my answers were correct. Casey would get the grade she needed to prevent her from being grounded. And hopefully, I'd make it to the office in time to find out what was going on with Mom.

In the hallway, I bumped into another student carrying a hall pass.

"Watch it!" he said, giving me a small shove.

"S-sorry," I said, rubbing my arm.

I grabbed my phone from my pocket as I ran toward the office.

Dad's text and two missed calls filled the screen. His text read, *Call me* And there was no voicemail. When I didn't return his call, he probably thought that calling the school would get me out of class. And his plan worked, but it had been the wrong twin to answer his phone call.

My mind was a blur as I quickly made my way to the office foyer where I saw Casey standing by the door immobile, her face filled with dread. She pushed open the door and started to head toward the foyer exit.

I rounded the corner to meet her on the other side. I didn't want anyone asking questions.

"Ali!" I shouted, trying to catch her attention. At least if anyone saw me, they would think I was Casey. But not for long. I wasn't letting my twin out of my sight until we'd changed back.

Casey turned around, her mouth dropping open in relief as soon as she saw me.

"I'm so glad you're here!" she gasped, her face white

with worry. "What happened in class?"

"Mrs. Halliday gave me permission to use the bathroom," I whispered. My breath came quickly as I tried to catch it. I had sped along the corridors, desperate to reach Casey as fast as possible.

Pulling her aside, I glanced behind her toward the office area where Mrs. Johnson was watching us curiously.

Casey turned to see what had caught my attention. "Hold on a sec," she said. And I waited while she opened the office door to speak to Mrs. Johnson. "Mrs. Johnson, I just have to use the restroom. I'll be back in a minute."

"Okay, hon, just make it quick," Mrs. Johnson replied. "I'll make sure the cab driver doesn't leave."

Following Casey into the nearby bathroom, I closed the door behind us and Casey checked under the stalls. It seemed to be our normal procedure for entering bathrooms lately.

"Was that my dad calling me to go to the hospital?" I asked. My throat thickened and I had to force the words out. "I haven't called him yet. Did you talk to him? What's going on, Casey? What did he say?"

"He said your mom isn't doing well," she explained in a rush. "But he said not to panic. He called a cab to take you to the hospital. It's outside now. So we have to hurry! The nurses will be expecting you and you have to go straight through to the emergency ward. Oh my gosh, Ali, I was so afraid that I was going to be the one who had to go to the hospital. This is all my fault!"

It was the quickest I'd ever heard Casey speak. Her face had paled, and she seemed really affected by this whole situation.

"Don't worry. I'm here now," I said reassuringly. "Let's hurry and change."

Casey nodded, and we rushed into the stalls to swap clothes.

Once we were dressed again, I gave my twin a quick hug.

"I'm so worried, Ali," Casey said. "Text me as soon as you know what's going on. I wish I could go with you!"

"Me too," I said softly.

But both of us knew that wasn't possible. I needed to be with my adopted family. I wasn't sure if it would be the last time I would ever see my mom again.

I blinked and fresh tears warmed my eyes. Before Casey could say another word, I grabbed my bag and raced out of the bathroom, through the double front doors to the cab waiting by the curb.

As I fell into the seat behind the driver, I felt a deep fear settle over me.

The prayer in my head repeated itself over and over, as if on constant rewind.

Please let Mom be okay.

Please let Mom be okay.

Please let Mom be okay.

I asked the driver to hurry. Then I watched the school building disappear behind me as I repeated the words of my silent prayer in my mind.

CHAPTER FIFTEEN
Casey

Ali rushed out of the bathroom so quickly, I was left to stand there on my own, still in shock over what had just happened. Taking a moment to catch my breath, I headed back into the hallway. As I passed the front doors, I looked through the glass into the distance and saw the taxi turning out of the school parking lot onto the main road. I just hoped that Ali would make it in time to see her mother before anything worse happened.

Crossing my fingers as I walked, I wished that Ali's mom would recover and be able to come home soon. Ali's dad said not to panic, so I held onto the tiny glimmer of hope that it wasn't too serious. Even though most of my body responded differently.

My heart went out to Ali. If there were some way for me to be there for her, I would.

I took one last look at the taillights of the cab and continued on my way.

When I reached the classroom, I hesitated outside the doorway. As I peered through the window that was set into the door, I could see everyone chatting to each other. All of the desks were cleared of exam papers. I couldn't believe Casey and I had pulled it off.

Taking a deep breath, I pushed through the door.

Mrs. Halliday glanced at me and then continued to sort the scan sheets and packets on her desk. "Take a seat, Casey. You can chat quietly until the bell rings for lunch."

I nodded at her, then almost went down the aisle toward Ali's seat. But I remembered that I was myself again and at the last minute, changed course and headed to my own desk. Jake hadn't noticed—or was trying not to notice—my entrance into the room. The rest of the kids didn't glance up at me either. Being myself was very different to playing Ali. I sort of missed all the attention she seemed to get.

Once I sat down in my seat, I turned towards Brie.

She was the only one aware of the situation. Shaking my head at her, I tried to convey my disbelief about what had just happened; the exam, the frantic phone call from Ali's dad, and the swap. It had all been so intense.

Brie's eyebrows rose questioningly, but it wasn't the right place to talk about it all.

I leaned closer towards her. "I'll tell you later," I whispered.

My head was swimming with visions of the scenario that had just taken place. I felt as though I were standing on a pond of thin ice. But I did not want to risk cracking the thin layer and falling in, so I turned around in my seat and remained there quietly waiting for the bell.

While I hadn't seen Ali jumping into the waiting cab, I imagined her sitting in the back seat while the taxi made its way through the suburban streets heading towards the hospital. Was this another part of our connection? Was I feeling her anxiety or mine?

Sometimes our connection confused me. I could feel things, or at least I thought I felt things that Ali was feeling. Once everything settled down, I wanted to explore our close-knit link further. But with her mom being sick and the issues with Jake, that would take some time.

The bell rang, and I jumped out of my seat. Grabbing a firm hold of Brie's arm, I pulled her from the room.

"Ow," she said when we got into the hallway.

"Sorry," I said, shaking my head apologetically. "But I had to get out of there. I've got to tell you what just happened. Oh my gosh! It was seriously intense!"

She grinned at me. "Okay, but let's get food first, I'm

starving. Then we can grab a table on our own so you can fill me in on all the details."

It was then Brie's turn to drag me along. We were the first ones in the cafeteria, so we didn't have to queue to get our lunch. My stomach was in knots, so I took the same food that Brie did, but with no intention of eating it. If I didn't have a tray in front of me, it would probably look strange. After the close call I'd had in the classroom, I had to stay under the radar.

Brie and I picked a table at the back of the room, in the corner. I wanted to get everything off my chest before the room filled up and there was a chance of someone overhearing.

"So…" I began, as I watched Brie munching hungrily on her food, "Ali's dad called in the middle of class," I said.

"I know," Brie said, chewing on a French fry. "I heard the announcement."

"No," I said, leaning closer to her. "Before that."

Her eyes widened. "Really?"

"Yeah. Ali and I have this strange connection, and I could just tell that something was wrong. She pointed to her pocket and I knew it must be her phone buzzing, which could only mean that her dad had tried to call. But obviously, she couldn't answer it because she was supposed to be me. So I had to do something."

"Is that why you stood up?" Brie asked. "Were you going to tell the whole class about the swap?"

"Well I didn't really want to tell the whole class, but Ali needed to talk to her dad," I explained, "It was my fault she was in the wrong seat, to begin with, so I had to say something. I just wasn't sure what!"

"And then the announcement came over the intercom?" Brie said, her eyebrows shooting up in surprise.

I let out a massive breath of relief at the memory. "Yes! OMG, it was the best timing!"

"Whoa," she said. "That was so close. Imagine if Mrs.

Halliday found out that Ali was taking your test?"

"I know," I nodded, equally as bothered by the thought. "But what else was I supposed to do?"

"I don't know," she replied, thoughtfully. "But I think someone is watching over you two. The timing of that intercom announcement was crazy. It literally saved you from confessing to everything."

Thinking it over some more, she added, "That was such a close call."

"It really was," I agreed, my stomach still churning anxiously.

The more I recalled what had happened, the more my body buzzed with nervous energy. It was over, but I still felt like I was going to be caught.

"At least you'll get a passing grade on your test," Brie grinned. "Now we can talk about the summer. There are so many cool things coming up, it's going to be the best!"

As Brie went into a list of possible choices, my mind wandered to Ali.

Placing my phone on my lap, I kept checking it for messages from my twin. She should have arrived at the hospital by now. I knew she had a lot on her mind, but I wanted to make sure that everything was okay.

Deciding to send her a quick text, I typed a brief message.

Thinking of you. Hope everything is okay. Message me when you get a chance.

For the rest of break, I tried to unwind from the hectic morning. I even ate a few French fries and finished off my chocolate milk. But when the bell rang for afternoon classes, there was still no reply from Ali.

Throughout the afternoon, I felt the same way Ali must have felt, earlier in the day when she was waiting for messages from her dad. I constantly checked my phone between classes and sometimes when my teachers had their backs turned. Ali hadn't reached out to me at all.

I thought about texting her again, but there was probably a reason she wasn't responding. And I didn't want to intrude on her time with her parents. I'd have Ali for the rest of my life. But I had a strong feeling that she would only have her mom for a short while longer.

CHAPTER SIXTEEN
Casey

After school, I had cheerleading practice. I hoped that would distract me enough to get through the rest of the afternoon. I'd become particularly attached to my phone, and I needed a little break.

We were changing into our practice outfits when Brie asked, "Have you talked to Ali about cheerleading?"

"Not yet," I said.

I knew that I still hadn't told Ali about Mrs. Caldwell choosing me for lead cheerleader, but there had been so much going on, I'd completely forgotten. Ali hadn't had a chance to come to any practice sessions at all since she'd been chosen for the team. I just hoped Mrs. Caldwell would be as lenient as Mrs. Halliday and give Ali a pass because of her mom. Mrs. Caldwell was very strict on her rules though, and if anyone signed up for a team, the condition was that they had to be available for practices.

I decided to approach Mrs. Caldwell in the same way I had done with Mrs. Halliday and tell her about Ali before practice began.

"Ali got an emergency call at school today…her mom's in the hospital and she had to leave straight away, so she won't be at practice this afternoon," I explained.

Mrs. Caldwell looked appropriately distraught. "That's very unfortunate, Casey. I appreciate you telling me. But if Ali misses too many more practices, I'll be forced to find a replacement."

I looked at Mrs. Caldwell hopefully as she spoke. I certainly didn't want it to come to that.

"And since you're the lead now, be sure to tell her to speak with me if any more issues arise. She can come and talk to me anytime."

"Thanks, Mrs. Caldwell," I replied with a nod. "I'll tell her that."

Mrs. Caldwell turned to the rest of the group. "Girls, practice will begin in two minutes!"

I went over to my bag and pulled out my phone.

"Have you heard anything from Ali?" Brie asked.

I looked at the screen and opened the messaging app. "Not yet."

Brie put her hand on my shoulder. "I'm sure she'll message you soon."

"It's so hard waiting," I said. "I'm really worried. I just want to know what's going on."

"Well, maybe cheerleading will take your mind off it."

"Maybe," I said.

"Okay girls," Mrs. Caldwell called to us with a smile, "let's get started."

As part of my leader position, it was my job to rally the girls at the beginning of practice. The girls were a chattering bunch and tended to take a while to get into formation. But I took my job seriously and managed to get everyone in place within a few minutes.

No one noticed how distracted I was during our workout. With each lull, as Mrs. Caldwell worked individually with some girls, my mind wandered to Ali and her mom. I kept looking towards my bag, trying to figure out a way to get to my phone. But I knew it wouldn't be possible until after practice. Like Mrs. Halliday, most of the coaches followed the same rules about cell phones.

Midway through practice, the football coach blew his whistle loud enough to echo across the field. The football players gathered together in one group at the other end of the field and then starting running toward us.

My stomach fluttered as I spotted Jake heading our

way. They'd all removed their helmets and even from that distance, I could see how hot and sweaty they were from practice. Regardless of that though, Jake still looked good.

The other girls began to whisper to each other, and some started giggling.

I clapped my hands together. "Come on girls, let's get back into formation!"

I caught a look of approval from Mrs. Caldwell. Then she counted down for us.

We did the first few steps together at half pace to make sure we were doing them properly. Because there were a few spins, I was able to get a peek at Jake as his team approached us. During each practice session, they did three laps around the field. It was something I looked forward to every time.

"Stay in your positions," Mrs. Caldwell instructed, and then she began directing the girls on the outer edge of the group to their next locations.

Holly was alongside me, practicing one of her moves.

"How do you think you did on the test today, Ali, er, I mean, Casey," she snickered quietly in my ear.

I whipped my head in her direction. What was she talking about? And why had she said that? I could tell from her sarcastic tone that there was something going on. She stared at me with her eyebrows raised questioningly and a smirk attached to her face.

"Um, it was okay, I guess," I murmured in reply.

Holly smirked again but said nothing else.

I turned away, and my heart raced. When I'd entered the classroom as Ali after morning break, Holly had given me an odd look and this seemed to continue throughout the test.

She couldn't think we'd swapped! How would she know? But she obviously suspected something. What if she'd already told Ronnie about it? Would she tell anyone else? The questions raced through my mind.

Mrs. Caldwell called us all to attention and I tried to brush the thoughts away so I could concentrate. Even if Holly thought we'd swapped, Ali and I could just deny it. If she came right out and asked us, we could say it wasn't true. There was no way for her to prove it, anyhow.

Refocusing on the cheerleading routine, I tried to ignore the looks from Holly.

Mrs. Caldwell was demonstrating the next steps in our routine when a football landed right in front of me. Seeing the ball at my feet, I turned to see where it had come from. Nearby, a group of boys from the football team was practicing kicking skills.

I bent down to pick up the ball so I could pass it back to them. But when I stood, I locked eyes with Jake who was running in my direction. I met him halfway and tossed him the ball.

"Here you are," I said, looking shyly towards him.

He smiled at me for the first time in what seemed like

forever. "Thanks."

I watched him walk away before returning to my group. My stomach fluttered, and I couldn't help the smile on my own face. Maybe Jake wasn't as angry as I had thought. He'd avoided us all day, so he didn't need to smile now unless it meant that he'd forgiven us.

Someone snorted nearby, and I peeked over my shoulder.

"She may as well forget about Jake. Everyone knows he likes Ali," Ronnie said loud enough for me to hear.

Holly snorted again and let out a forced laugh.

I fisted my hands by my sides. "You two should mind your own business and keep your comments to yourselves!"

Holly placed her hands on her hips. "And you should do your own tests rather than relying on your brainiac sister to do them for you!"

My face heated up and I felt as though I were inside a piping hot oven. I stared at the girls, with no idea of what to say in return. My gaze slipped to Brie, and I could see that her mouth had dropped open in shock.

Loud clapping brought me back to reality. Mrs. Caldwell blew her whistle. "We need to focus. There isn't much time left, and I want this routine completed by the end of today's session. Casey, please come up here. We'll take it from the top."

I felt Holly and Ronnie's eyes on me as I passed them on my way to the front of the formation. Neither one said anything to me, but I knew that nothing else needed to be said. They knew! The issue was, how did they know? Had they heard our conversation during morning break? I couldn't recall them anywhere near us. And I was sure that Brie and Ali hadn't said anything. When would there have been time? And besides that, there's no way they would have mentioned it to Holly and Ronnie anyway.

During the rest of practice, the two girls glared at me. A few times, I messed up the routine and they laughed aloud, clearly intending to mock me. Even though Mrs. Caldwell scolded them, they still continued to watch my every move.

I'd never been so happy for a practice to end. And I was close to tears when I reached my bag.

"Great job everyone," Mrs. Caldwell said. "See you tomorrow afternoon."

We all said goodbye to her and then started toward the locker rooms. Brie walked alongside me, but neither of us mentioned Holly and Ronnie. It wasn't safe to talk until Brie and I were alone. We'd have to figure out a plan. And this definitely wasn't the time to worry Ali about it.

When I opened the door leading to the girls' locker room, something hard shoved against my shoulder.

"Ow!" I said, turning to see Holly and Ronnie pushing roughly past me.

Holly stuck out her lower lip in a fake pout. "Ooh, sorry Ali, er…I mean Casey, or whoever you are."

She and Ronnie threw back their heads with laughter and then locked arms before continuing into the locker room.

"How did they find out?" Brie whispered.

"I have no idea," I said.

CHAPTER SEVENTEEN
Ali

The cab driver kept glancing at me through the rearview mirror. He had obviously noticed the distressed expression on my face and was probably worried that I might burst into tears at any moment. He was correct to think that I might. I held myself together for the entire ride, though. I needed to be strong for Mom.

During the ride, my mind abruptly wandered back to the events of the day so far. It had been a whirlwind, and just when I thought I could catch my breath, the fate of my mom had crashed over me.

But I couldn't believe how reckless Casey and I had been. It almost had us in serious trouble. How could I have agreed to take a test for her? My guilt about Jake had overwhelmed me, and we were almost caught out for it. But I pushed all those thoughts aside, realizing that I needed to stay focused on my mother. She was my priority now and the silent prayers returned to my lips.

I just hoped Dad would allow me to stay at the hospital until Mom was ready to come home. School and Jake didn't matter anymore. My nerves amplified the closer I got to the hospital. I felt a hot flush flood my body and I was forced to lower the window to get some fresh air.

Today had been a beautiful day, sunny and bright. It was the kind of day where my mom would love to be in her garden. Instead, she was in a hospital bed, only able to see the sunlight from the window. Casey hadn't been given much information from my dad, so I had no idea about my mother's condition. And I couldn't call him to find out because he'd already spoken to Casey.

When the driver pulled into the hospital parking lot, I

felt my anxiety become worse. He dropped me near the entrance to the emergency room and I thanked him as I got out of the car. Staring at the sliding doors that loomed ahead of me, I wondered for a moment if my mother would ever walk through them again.

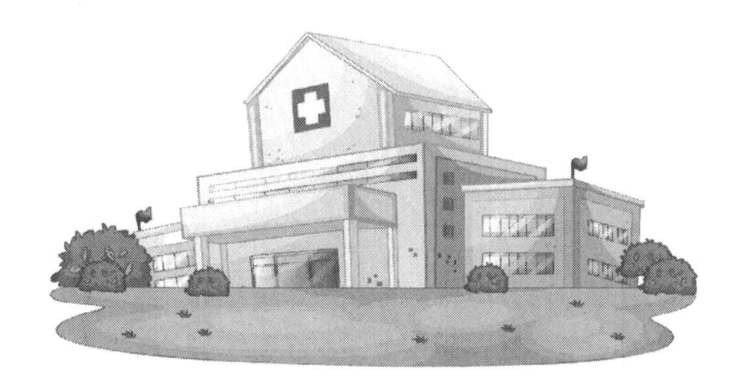

At that thought, I allowed one tear to escape. Wiping it away, I promised myself to be strong. That was what Mom needed and it was the way I intended to be.

The moment I stepped through the doors, the familiar sterile smell assaulted my senses. As I approached the front desk, one of the nurse's glanced up towards me and I could see the recognition in her expression. She picked up the phone handset at her side before I'd even made it to the desk.

Nodding at me, she spoke into the phone. "Your daughter is here."

She then hung up the phone and looked at me. "Your dad will be out in a minute."

"Thank you," I said. I had a sudden urge to ask her about my mom, but I doubted she'd tell me anything. Dad always tried to keep everything positive, but nothing was positive about him taking me out of school to come to the hospital. All I wanted was to know the truth.

Ignoring the sympathetic look from the nurse, I

headed over to the double doors of the emergency room. But Dad pushed his way through them before I arrived.

As soon as he reached me, he scooped me up into a hug. "Ali," he said against my hair.

My lower lip trembled, and I had to bite down on it to keep from crying. The sharp pain brought me back to the reality we were facing.

I leaned away from him. "How is she?"

His face told me everything.

"I should have stayed," I said.

"No," he said. "Everything has happened within the past few hours. Come on, let's go see her."

I took my dad's hand, and we walked together down the hallway. Each step felt as though I were walking in someone else's shoes. But reality began to settle in, and I had to fight to keep myself from breaking down right then and there.

"Mom will be so happy to see you," Dad said.

"She's awake?" That was good news.

Dad sighed. "She wants to see you..."

His words hung in the air and I didn't want to believe in what was unsaid.

We stopped in front of the room. The curtain was drawn around her bed so I couldn't see her from the hallway.

"Dad," I said, and I couldn't help the wobble in my voice.

He took my hand in his. "We're going to be okay."

I didn't need to tell him how I felt. He already knew. Our little family was so close that losing one of us felt as though I were losing a body part. This was so unfair.

We went into the room, and Dad pushed the curtain aside.

Mom sat up against her pillows, and her eyes were half-lidded. I wondered how hard she was working to remain awake, waiting for me. Or maybe she was afraid to close her eyes.

I shook away the terrible thought.

"Mom," I said and went to her side.

Her lips twitched, and I knew she was too weak to smile. Her face was a grayish color, and her hands were freezing. I held onto them anyway. I wanted to be able to feel her and make sure she knew I was with her.

Dad went to the other side of the bed and sat.

"How are you feeling?" I asked.

Mom licked her lips slowly. "Better now. The doctors gave me something to ease the pain."

"You're in pain?"

"Not anymore," she said. "Tell me about your school day."

I pulled up a chair and sat next to her, refusing to let go of her hand. After school, each day, Mom and I would sit down with a cup of tea and talk. Today would be no different. Except for the fact that there would be no tea, and it might be our last opportunity ever.

I began to tell her about taking the bus with Casey. I planned on leaving out all the other details of our swap as well as cheating on the test for my twin because that was something I never wanted to share with her.

My phone buzzed from my pocket, and I knew it was Casey without even looking at the screen. But I didn't want anything to interrupt the time I had left with my mother. I was too overwhelmed to talk to anyone other than her. And I wasn't sure how much more time we had together.

A few moments later, she began drifting to sleep. I stopped talking so she could rest. With a kiss on her forehead, I smoothed her hair away from her face.

It was then that I let all of my emotions go. Tears flowed down my cheeks, and I dropped my head on her pillow and sobbed. I could hear her shallow breathing and I could still smell the familiar perfume scent on her. That unique and beautiful scent would be something that I would always remember about her.

Dad and I sat in silence for a while, watching her sleep as we listened to the steady slow rhythm of the monitors.

A short while later, a nurse popped her head in the doorway and signaled for Dad.

"I'll be right back," he said to me.

Sitting back in my chair, I felt my phone in my pocket. I'd forgotten about Casey's texts from earlier.

I read through them and then typed a few replies, before deleting them and starting over again. When I settled on one message, I read it twice over and then pressed send.

Mom's not doing well. I'm scared…

CHAPTER EIGHTEEN
Casey

In the locker room, Brie and I avoided any further contact with Holly and Ronnie. They didn't come over to us, and I avoided all eye contact. It was easier now that practice was over and we weren't under Mrs. Caldwell's watchful eye.

I could tell that Brie wanted to discuss the situation, but I shook my head each time she tried to say something. This had to stay between Ali, Brie and me. If anyone else found out, then we'd be in serious trouble.

We waited until all the girls were out of the locker room before heading out into the hallway. Everyone was outside either getting into their parent's cars or waiting to be picked up.

"There's no way that they could know about the swap today," I whispered to Brie.

"They certainly made it seem like they know," she said. "You heard Holly. She practically came right out and said it."

Brie had a point.

"Ali and I have to keep denying it," I said.

"Those girls can be pretty persistent," Brie said.

"I know, but we'll get into so much trouble if Mrs. Halliday finds out." I felt sick again thinking about how I had almost told my teacher all the details. Now I never wanted the secret getting out. It couldn't.

"I'll help you guys," Brie said. "I could say I was with you the whole day or something."

"That might help," I said. "Thanks, Brie."

She shrugged. "It was my idea for the swap this time. So I should take some responsibility."

Brie looked out through the window. "My mom's here. Let's text later?"

"Okay," I said and gave her a quick hug.

I waited until I was sure that Holly and Ronnie had gone home before I went outside to wait for Grandma Ann.

I sat on the steps for a few minutes before checking my phone again. While I didn't expect anything from Ali, I was surprised when I saw her text.

When I opened it up, my chest squeezed tightly.

Mom's not doing well. I'm scared…

I looked up worriedly and checked the parking lot. Where was Grandma Ann? I should be there to support Ali, instead of sitting on a curb at school. But would Ali want me there? From her text, it seemed as though she wanted someone to talk to. I was sure her dad had enough to worry about, so maybe I should go to the hospital, even if I had to sit in that horrible waiting room again.

I wasn't sure what to say in reply, so I put my phone away to think it over. I wanted to be supportive, but I'd never been in a situation like this. What could I say to ease her mind and let her know I was there for her?

The scraping sound of cleats over the sidewalk caught my attention. The football players were heading past, after their practice. I stood up and moved aside, out of their way. None of them paid much attention to me and I pretended to search in my bag for something. It gave me an excuse to look busy and avoid looking at them. And then I heard a familiar voice.

"See you tomorrow, Casey," Jake said.

My head snapped up to see a smiling Jake as he headed past me towards the boys' locker room.

I stared at him in surprise. I couldn't believe that he'd not only smiled at me but spoken to me as well! It was the same way he usually talked to Ali. But he'd used my name this time.

My heart soared and filled with hope that things had

turned around and somehow sorted themselves out. Perhaps he was over the idea of both Ali and me swapping and tricking him. Or maybe we'd been mistaken and he was unaware of the swap altogether.

But when I thought about it some more, I realized it was also possible that Jake was simply embarrassed after Matt implied that he was interested in Ali.

While I didn't want to think about Jake liking Ali, whatever the reason, he seemed to be over it. And he'd called me Casey, so he knew exactly who he was speaking to. Finally, I had something to smile about after such a stressful day.

The sound of a sudden car horn caught my attention and I turned to see my mom's car idling by the curb.

My eyebrows drew together. Why was she here instead of Grandma Ann? I jogged down the steps, now with a spring in my step, and hopped into the car.

"How come Grandma Ann didn't come today?" I asked.

"She had an appointment at the hairdresser. She told you that this morning," Mom said.

I didn't remember that at all. I also didn't remember I had a test, so I guessed Grandma Ann could easily have told me anything and I wouldn't have remembered.

"Don't be so upset that I came to pick you up," Mom said, half-joking.

"I'm not upset," I smiled. "I'm surprised, that's all. In a good way."

"Ah, that's alright then," Mom replied, a pleased expression on her face.

As she pulled away from the curb, she spoke again. "How's Ali doing today? Did she head over to the hospital after school?"

The mention of Ali created a surge of guilt to flow through me. How could I have been obsessing over Jake while my twin was sitting by her mom's hospital bed? What sort of sister was I?

"Ali rushed to the hospital earlier this afternoon during our exam," I said.

"Oh, no," Mom frowned. "Have you heard anything?"

I shook my head. As much as I wanted to go to the hospital to be with Ali, I didn't want to intrude on their family time together. So I decided to leave that decision in her hands.

Taking out my phone, I typed a quick text to her, now knowing what to say.

If there's anything we can do, let me know. We'll come right away if you need us. Thinking of you xxx

The rest of the afternoon dragged on. I kept checking my phone to see if Ali had texted back, and I could barely concentrate on my homework. By the time I went to bed, there was still no news from Ali.

It was so hard for me not to text her again. But I had to stay strong for her and not keep bothering her with constant messages. As I turned off the lights, I felt a sudden uncomfortable sensation forming in the pit of my stomach. I didn't know if it was intuition or our psychic connection, but I had a strong feeling that things weren't going well at the hospital at all.

Sighing, I crawled into bed and curled up under my covers, at the same time, thinking of Ali probably sitting in a chair next to her mother's bed. The tears came quickly. I knew in my heart that Ali was suffering. And right then, I was suffering too.

At some point, I drifted off, but I jolted awake when the text tone sounded on my phone. Earlier that evening, I'd turned the volume up all the way so I'd be able to hear it from anywhere in the house.

Quickly grabbing it from my bedside table, I could

see the screen was already lit up and that the message was from Ali; although, I'd already known that would be the case. In the darkness of my room, I blinked my eyes, trying to take in the words that jumped out at me. There on my phone screen were two simple words; words that I had been dreading.

She's gone.

A tightness settled in my chest, and my heart ached. I broke down into choking sobs. Pushing my face into the pillow, I was overwhelmed with a devastating sadness that I could not comprehend. I'd only spent a weekend with Ali's mother but Ali was my identical twin, and right then I was sure that I was feeling the exact same emotions as her.

The loss was so great that a hole seemed to open up inside me, one that I was sure would never be refilled.

This wasn't supposed to happen. Our families were meant to meet, and everything was supposed to be great between all of us. Ali and I would have two mothers. That had been our plan.

But that plan would never take place now.

My door opened, and the light from the hallway spilled into my room. Mom stood there.

"Casey? What's wrong?" She came over to me and sat on my bed.

"She's gone, Mom," I said. "She's gone."

I was unable to say anything else, only repeat Ali's words from her text, over and over again. Each time I said them, the more they became real and the deeper the loss became.

Mom pulled me to her and wrapped her arms around me. She made soothing sounds against my hair. I clung to her, the tears spilling down my cheeks. But then in a flash, a mixture of thoughts raced through my head, all combining into one terrible nightmare.

If Ali's mom had passed away, what was going to happen now? They had only moved so she could get the treatment she needed. But now that she was gone, would Ali and her dad stay or would they return to their old home on the other side of the country? It was where Ali grew up and had friends. And it was the main location for her dad's work.

What if in the process of Ali losing her adopted mom, I also lost my twin. I had never even known that she existed until such a short time ago. But she was my sister, and I'd connected more with her in that time than I ever had with the rest of my family.

If I lost Ali now, after being thrown together by fate, it would be the ultimate act of cruelty. I could not bear the thought. But the possibility was so real. I found it hard to breathe.

I hugged my mom and hoped that Ali wouldn't leave me, but the uneasy feeling deep inside me would not go away. And through my tears and the sensation of loss, was another deep emotion…a choking fear of what might lay ahead.

***

Book 6

MOVING ON

CHAPTER ONE

Casey

The rumbling of the school bus numbed my entire body. I stared out the window at the dreary morning. Dark clouds blocked any sunlight, and the window was streaked with running water trails as the rain tumbled down onto the bus. It sounded like pebbles pecking at the roof, each one of them counting the passing seconds.

Tick.

Tick.

Tick.

My eyelids were heavy from lack of sleep. Keeping with the gloomy mood, I thought of Ali and her family. It was hard to believe that it had only been a week since Ali's mom had died. While I wanted to be there for Ali, there were a lot of arrangements to take care of, and my sister didn't have time for me. She'd barely responded to my texts and the few phone calls we had shared were very short.

I hadn't pushed to see her, but since she was my twin, I had the *need* to see her; more than anything. I wanted to support her and be there for her during this sad time in her life. For me, the loss of Ali's mom, even though I'd known her only a short while, had opened up more emotions in the past week than I'd ever felt before. I had never experienced such overwhelming sadness; although I knew it must be minor in comparison to what Ali was feeling. I just wished she would share her feelings with me. Being around her always made me feel better, though maybe it wasn't the same on her side.

The weather right then was the exact opposite of a few days earlier at the funeral. There, the sun had shone across a cloudless sky. It was bright and sunny, just like Ali's mom. It was as though she were right there with us. The warmth of the sun reminded me of the feeling I'd had whenever she hugged me or gently caressed my face. At the time, she had thought I was Ali, but her love for her adopted daughter came through with a single touch. It was something I rarely felt with my own mother, and even in the brief time I was able to spend with Ali's mom, I discovered that she was the most special person I'd ever met.

Although it had been a sunny day for the funeral, the mood was anything but bright. They'd only lived in the area for a short while but there was a big turn-out for the ceremony. Friends and family had flown in from around the country to support Ali and her dad.

Mom, Grandma Ann, and I sat a few rows behind Ali, yet it didn't seem like she cared if anyone was there, including me. When we arrived at the church, I went up to Ali and hugged her fiercely, trying to show her how much I would also miss her mom. The connection we shared tingled between us, but she either didn't notice, or she pushed it aside. I felt her pain through our bond. It overwhelmed me.

She thanked me for coming, and then someone else pulled her away to be seated at the front of the church.

She didn't even say goodbye to me.

I wasn't upset about the way she acted. I was sure I'd be the same way if I were in her shoes.

It was my first funeral ever, and I had no idea how to act or what to say, so I went along with whatever Grandma Ann and my mother did. We sat quietly through the service and at the cemetery. Ali didn't approach me again, and her tear-soaked face was the last I saw of her.

When the bus took a sharp turn into the school parking lot, the jostling broke through my thoughts. I was transported from that somber day back to the present, a day with somber weather. It was the theme of the week, and I didn't know when it would improve.

A day like today reminded me that Ali's mom was

really gone now. Her suffering was over, but Ali and her dad's suffering had just begun.

I worried that Ali would not return to school. And grabbing my phone from my bag, I re-read her reply to my last message.

The night before, I'd texted her...*When do you think you'll come back to school?*

Her response... *I'm not sure...*was the last message of our text chain.

My fingers hovered over the keyboard, but I didn't know what to say. What did her message mean?

I'm not sure.

Was she taking a break for a few days to grieve over her mother, or was she never coming back, like ever? I couldn't imagine that! I didn't want to push her into returning to school before she was ready, but I wondered if Ali and her dad were considering moving away now that her mom was gone. Even though I was her sister, they had nothing else to keep them here. They originally came for Ali's mom's treatment at the hospital. But now that she had passed, what were they going to do? Would they move away? Would staying in their house constantly remind them of Ali's mom?

My chest hurt just thinking of my sister leaving.

The unknown terrified me. I'd missed her so much in these past few days. I couldn't bear the thought of not having her around at all.

The bus pulled up to the curb and stopped. I stood up, waiting for the kids in front of me to get off before I headed down the aisle. School would be a good distraction, as long as I didn't focus on Ali's empty seat all day. It was lucky she sat at the back of the room, so I wouldn't see her empty chair, though I knew she wouldn't be far from my thoughts.

The rain had let up a little, but I covered my head with the hood of my jacket. The temperature was cooler, and

I shivered. The weather already reflected my mood, and I wondered if it would improve at all.

I walked a few feet before I heard my name. Hearing the correct name coming from that voice made me freeze in place.

I slowly turned to see Jake. He jogged over to me, holding a black umbrella over his head. With my obsession over Ali and her mom, I'd forgotten an umbrella. Even though I had a hood on, the rain still managed to seep through. "Hey, Casey. I called a few times, but you mustn't have heard me?" he smiled.

"Hi, Jake," I said. "Sorry, I'm a little distracted today."

He nodded and his smile widened. He had been super friendly with me all week. While I normally would have been shy with him while screaming with joy on the inside, since Ali's mom had died he had become the least of my concerns. I couldn't believe I'd been so obsessed with a boy, when Ali and her mom should have been my priority. And now that I had the opportunity in front of me, my old fluttery feelings over the good-looking boy beside me seemed to have disappeared.

"Here," he said, offering for me to stand under his umbrella.

I mustered a grateful smile. "Thank you."

We walked together to the front doors. "I guess practices are canceled, huh?" he said.

"I guess," I replied listlessly. Which was fine. I was in no mood to be a peppy cheerleader.

When we got inside, I shed my soaked jacket, and Jake shook out his umbrella, the rain droplets falling to the floor in the front foyer. We walked up the stairs together. A few girls noticed us and began whispering to each other. If this had been a week ago, I would have been in heaven. But the excitement of my crush seemed to have been pushed to the rear of my mind. And of course, now Jake seemed more interested than ever, whereas my feelings were almost non-existent. How could things have changed so much? His awkward manner towards both Ali and I the previous week was gone. And in its place was the smiling face of the boy I'd been seriously crushing over, way before Ali ever walked into my life.

When we reached Mrs. Halliday's classroom, Jake stopped in front of the doorway and turned to face me. "Maybe one night after practice we can get pizza or something?"

I tucked a strand of damp hair behind my ear. "Sure."

He smiled and then hooked his thumb behind him, indicating the area down the hallway. "Cool. I'm going to get my books from my locker. I'll see you in class."

"Okay," I said.

I watched him walk away, and my shoulders sagged. I didn't want to fall back into a place where Jake had no idea I existed, but I couldn't think of him right now. I wanted everything to be right again with Ali. That was my only priority and I was unable to think of much else, even Jake.

The warning bell for first period rang just as I was about to text Ali again. I glanced inside the room and Mrs. Halliday caught my eye from the doorway. She looked at my phone and gave me a disapproving look. I put it in my bag out of sight. I'd text Ali later.

CHAPTER TWO

Casey

I barely paid any attention to that morning's lessons. Instead, I stared out the window, thinking about Ali and her dad. What were they doing right now? Were they packing up their belongings, getting ready to head out of town, or even the state?

An empty pit grew in my stomach, and all I wanted was Ali to tell me what she was thinking. I tried a few times to close my eyes and access our psychic connection. But I didn't feel anything. Most of the time, to feel it we needed to be in close proximity to each other. I had no idea how it worked at all, so my attempt was silly, and I stopped trying soon after starting.

After lunch, Brie and I came back to class before the bell rang. I appreciated having such a close friend, one who didn't hound me about Ali like everyone else in the class did. There were a ton of questions about Ali during lunch from the other kids. Now that they all knew we were sisters, they expected me to know everything about how she was feeling or when she was coming back. I felt bad when I said I didn't know. I should know more about my own sister's future plans. A few of them made remarks that I was keeping Ali's life private. I let them think that. I supposed it was better than them knowing that Ali had shut me out too.

Brie and I returned to an empty classroom. The sun had peeked through the clouds, and most of our classmates remained outside for the rest of the break. We were the only two people in the room and it felt good to have space to ourselves for a few minutes.

"You should try texting Ali again," Brie said.

"Good idea." I nodded, and unzipped my bag to pull out my phone.

*Thinking about you...*was all I wrote.

Minutes later, a few of the other kids trickled into the room, followed by Mrs. Halliday. I quickly switched the ringer to vibrate and hid my phone in my bag. But my stomach flip-flopped, knowing what was about to happen next.

"Alright, everyone, take your seats," Mrs. Halliday instructed, as the end of break bell sounded. "I mentioned before recess that I'd be handing back the exams from last week. I have them right here and will pass them out once everyone is seated."

Clasping my hands nervously together on top of my desk, I glanced behind me at Brie. She gave me a thumbs up. Until Mrs. Halliday's earlier announcement about the test, I'd almost forgotten about the most recent swap between Ali and I. But the memory of the day she'd taken the History test while pretending to be me, came flooding back. We'd been so close to getting caught, and the fear I'd felt at the time was still fresh in my mind.

Holly and Ronnie's accusations of the swap were driven from my thoughts after Ali's mom died. Though they continued to make snide remarks and continually asked, "Are you Casey or Ali today?" I tried to ignore them. But it was hard. Having Ali around always boosted my confidence, and without her at school, it was more difficult to defend myself against those girls.

Mrs. Halliday grabbed the stack of papers from her desk. The top paper had her signature red pen scrawled across parts of it. Her method of grading was all over the place. Sometimes a lot of red markings meant she gave encouragements, and other times she noted the papers with bad marks. I hoped for at least a passing grade. I needed a passing grade or the swap would have been for nothing, and I would be grounded for the entire summer.

A rush of anxiety clamped around my throat and I found it hard to swallow. Mrs. Halliday walked down the first row, dropping the tests on each desk, making random comments:

"Great work, Alec."

"Good try, Nic."

"Your answers in the final section were what let you down, Sarah."

"Greta, maybe you need to be paying more attention in class?"

She tapped the test paper on Ronnie's desk, "See me after the lesson!"

I saw Ronnie stare down at the test on her desk, her face flushing a bright shade of red as she took in the comments.

As each of my classmates checked out their tests, some turned in their seats to mutter to their friends about the results. Some were happy and looked relieved. But several were disappointed, and the expressions on their faces went from hopeful to miserable.

I tapped my toes on the floor, anxiously waiting for my results.

Glancing over my shoulder, I looked at Brie, whose expression was as anxious as mine.

Mrs. Halliday continued up and down the aisles until she was one over from me. She clicked her tongue as she turned Holly's paper and faced it downwards on her desk.

Holly flipped it over, and from my seat, I could easily see Mrs. Halliday's red pen had prominently marked a large D at the top of the page. Holly dropped her head to her chin before whipping her head in my direction, as if she could sense I was looking at her results. She locked eyes with me and grimaced, slapping a hand over the D to hide it from view. She was unaware that I had already seen her grade.

My stomach churned and I sucked in a nervous breath as Mrs. Halliday approached my desk.

Holly made a point of staring in my direction, to see what grade I'd received. I worried that if Ali had come through for me, then Holly would have more of a reason to accuse me and Ali of the swap. I wished her and Ronnie would stop bothering me. I had enough worries in my life.

Mrs. Halliday passed my desk without giving me my paper. I turned around, wondering if she'd stacked the tests out of order, but she had handed papers to everyone else.

I looked down at Brie's desk. She had managed a B+.

"I can't believe it," she said with a huge smile. "This is my highest grade ever in History."

"I'm so happy for you," I said. Even though I was, I couldn't help but notice the lack of result on my own desk.

"Where's yours?" she asked, looking over my shoulder.

"She didn't give it back," I whispered.

Did Mrs. Halliday know that Ali and I had cheated? Did she tear up the test that day and plan on humiliating me in front of the class?

Mrs. Halliday stood at the front of the room, holding one exam in her hands. I glanced around, and everyone had a test except for me.

Oh no…

"Class, I wanted to hand out this paper last because it's a prime example of what can be achieved if you listen in class and take the time to study before an exam!" She smiled and looked right at me. "Casey Wrigley, Congratulations. You've managed the highest mark of all. What an outstanding effort. Well done!"

Brie patted my shoulder, but my entire body stiffened as everyone looked at me. There were only a few smiling—those who had managed good grades themselves—the others didn't look happy at all. I knew how they felt. I would have been one of them if it hadn't been for my twin sister.

I tuned Mrs. Halliday out as she opened the test and started going over the answers that Ali had written. I hoped she didn't ask me questions about it since I hadn't even studied for the test, and I had no idea what Ali had put down on the paper.

I wanted to shrivel up and melt into the floor. My cheeks and the tops of my ears flushed bright red as heat moved through my body. I felt as though I were being baked in a hot oven.

"If you'd completed the final question, the hardest one, you would have received an A+," Mrs. Halliday said. "But there was barely an error anywhere else, so you earned a solid A. And on the most difficult test of the year. Congratulations, Casey!"

I gulped, and if I could have blushed any redder, I would have. I wished Mrs. Halliday would move on from the test so everyone would return to looking elsewhere, rather than at me.

I glanced at Holly who still sat facing me. Her eyes were narrowed, and a wicked smile crossed her lips. I looked away from her, but not for long.

"Wow! That's amazing, Casey!" Holly said with fake enthusiasm. "I've never known you to do well in History before. How did you manage to do that? Please, tell us your secret!"

I stared at Holly, wishing she'd stop being so mean to me. She flicked her gaze to Ronnie as if they intended to continue the torment.

I ground my teeth together, wishing for all of this to be over. The other kids in the class began talking to each other, ignoring the silent battle going on between Holly and myself.

Mrs. Halliday frowned and then walked towards me, dropping my test on my desk. "Alright, class, we're moving on now."

My awareness of the other kids and their whisperings made my skin prickle. I glanced around and saw Ronnie glaring at me. I couldn't see the result on her test, but I knew part of the reason that she and Holly were doing this was because of their poor grades. Even though I didn't take the test, they had no reason to suspect me of cheating. They should focus on their own lives.

I sank into my chair and stared at the clock, wishing for the bell to ring. But we had a while until the class was over.

Sitting quietly through the lesson, my focus constantly flicked between Mrs. Halliday and the hands of the clock. Holding my breath for the last minute of class, it whooshed out of me when the bell finally rang.

Springing up from my chair, I turned around to Brie. "Let's go." I wanted to avoid Holly and Ronnie at all costs.

"Okay," Brie said, scooting in front of me. I shoved my test in my bag and zipped it up, following along behind her.

Holly's snooty voice made me freeze in my tracks. "Mrs. Halliday, can I speak to you about something, please?"

I glanced over my shoulder to see Holly leaning over the teacher's desk so she could talk to her privately. What if Holly told Mrs. Halliday about the swap? What was I going to do?

"Casey?" Brie called from the door.

I shuffled out of the room, "Holly is talking to Mrs. Halliday."

"She got a D on her test," Brie said. "She's probably hoping to get her mark changed.

"What if she tells Mrs. Halliday about the swap?" I hissed quietly. Even though Holly and Ronnie suspected something, we didn't want anyone else to hear us talking about what Ali and I had done.

Brie patted my shoulder and leaned close to me. "Holly and Ronnie have no proof. The test was over a week ago. If they were going to say something they would have already. Don't worry about it."

I nodded, but I wasn't so sure. My stomach twisted into knots and I had a sinking feeling that something bad was going to come of this.

"It's hard," I said. "They keep saying mean things to me."

"Ignore them. They're just jealous that you and Ali have been so popular since everyone found out that you're twins."

I shrugged. "I guess."

Brie and I walked to the buses together, and I waved to her when she hopped onto hers.

I headed past the line of buses, looking for Grandma Ann's car. Even though we didn't have practice, that morning she'd said she would pick me up as she had things to do and would be passing by the school. I didn't bother to ask her about it. I had too much on my mind.

Threads of guilt weaved through my body. Evidence of the swap was in my bag, and while I wanted to brag about my grade to my family, I didn't feel proud about it at all.

The satisfaction of seeing the A on my paper was not what I previously anticipated it would feel like. Instead, I felt terribly guilty, and worried that I would get caught out, then both Ali and I would suffer big time.

I could not remove the nauseous sensation from my stomach, nor the terrible thought from my head.

Sighing heavily, I wished that I had just done the test myself, even if it did mean a D. Getting Ali into trouble was the worst part of all.

CHAPTER THREE

Ali

My eyes sprung open when I heard movement outside my bedroom door. The clock on my bedside table read three-thirty. Since my room was somewhat lit from outside, even though the blinds were drawn, I knew it was the afternoon instead of three-thirty in the morning. I didn't remember when I'd fallen back to sleep again, but it was more than twelve hours ago.

Today was no different than any other since my mom's funeral. It had been the first and last place I had been, other than my bedroom, in the past week. The sadness that had engulfed me since she died, seemed to get worse every day. I had not been prepared for it to increase. I had expected to feel a tiny bit better with each passing day, knowing that she was no longer in pain. But that wasn't the case at all. I began to think that I'd never feel better again.

Going into my mom's bedroom, or any other room in the house, reminded me of her. So I locked myself in my room and buried myself under the covers, never wanting to come out.

Each morning, from the moment I woke and remembered that Mom was gone, tears sprung to my eyes and pressed against the corners for almost every minute of every hour. I didn't see the point in getting out of bed and witnessing the same sadness on my dad's face.

Sighing, I realized that it was my dad who had made the noise outside my door. He tried to coax me from my room several times each day, but apart from meal times, where I only picked at my food, I preferred to stay tucked away on my own. Deep down, I knew I was acting childish, but I didn't know any other way to deal with my feelings. Talking to Dad reminded me of her, and I was sure that talking with me, reminded him of her as well. It was better to be separated, for a little while at least, until I could get a hold of my emotions.

I'd distanced myself from Casey too, and although I thought about my sister a lot, I could not bring myself to speak with anyone. I didn't know what to say, and I was afraid of crying in front of them and making them feel sorry for me. But the last thing I wanted was their pity. I really didn't know how I'd ever recover.

I reached for my phone under the pillow.

There were a bunch of texts from different people telling me how sorry they were. I marked them as read so I wouldn't have to see the notifications anymore.

I stopped when I reached the thread for Casey. As I scrolled through her messages, I knew I should make an effort to respond, but I didn't have the energy.

How are you?

I'm so worried about you!

Are you okay?

Let me know if I can do anything.

I miss you!

I'm thinking of you.

When are you coming back to school?

I focused on that one.

I typed *Never* in the next box; but quickly deleted it. I didn't want Casey to see that I was replying when I didn't plan on saying anything. But it was true. I never wanted to go back to school. How could I ever go back to my normal life without my mom around? I knew that she would have eventually died from the terrible disease, but I wasn't prepared for it to happen so suddenly. I was stupid to think that the treatment was working. From what Dad told me, it prolonged her life a little while, but the disease was too much for her body to cope with. Mom and I had planned to do so much together, and now none of those things would ever take place.

I struggled terribly with the sense of loss inside of me. I felt as though I were missing a huge chunk of myself. I knew I had to move forward, but I had no idea how.

Pulling the covers over my head, I went to the photo app on my phone. I scrolled through pictures from last year when Mom was doing okay. She looked so different than she had at the hospital. The photos and my real-life Mom could have been two separate women. A year had made such a huge difference.

Tears filled my eyes and the pictures blurred. I wiped them away and continued to scroll through the photos. Near the end, there were only pictures of me and Casey. Casey was wearing my clothes and making silly faces. We looked so happy together.

And once again, I felt bad about shutting Casey out.

I put my phone under my pillow and pulled the covers tightly around me so no light came through.

My eyes began to close again, when the sound of the doorbell interrupted my thoughts.

I wondered who it was this time. Probably another neighbor dropping off a casserole or another home-baked pie so that Dad and I would have something to eat. Or perhaps someone passing on their sympathy and condolences. It was the same every time. I hated the pity in their voices and expressions.

I took a breath. I wasn't being fair. I knew our visitors meant well, but I wished that everyone would leave us alone. I'd answered the door only a few times before I gave up completely. I didn't know what to say. So I let Dad answer the door from then on. He was the strongest man I knew. I had no idea how he was so polite to everyone, while I'm sure on the inside he wanted to curl up in bed like me.

We'd only lived in this house for a short time, but it seemed as though the entire neighborhood knew about Mom's death, and they all wanted to help in some way. That was in large part because of Mom's friendly nature. She often spent time in the front garden and taking leisurely walks when she felt well enough. At dinner, she would talk about all the lovely neighbors we had. And this was their way of paying her back for her kindness. They all appeared to have been taken in by what a wonderful person she was.

Was.

I grew to dread and despise that word, yet I knew I would have to say it in reference to my mom for the rest of my life.

Kicking the covers off me, I took in a gulp of fresh air, my body so flushed with frustration and sadness that I could barely breathe.

I heard Dad and someone else's muffled voice from downstairs. He was at the door speaking with whoever had arrived. I hoped they would leave quickly.

Sitting up hurt my back. My muscles were weak from lack of movement. I was about to lay down again when I heard footsteps on the stairs. They didn't sound like Dad's heavy footsteps, but I still heard them.

I glanced toward the door. Why would Dad send someone up here? If I barely talked to him, he should have known I didn't want to talk to anyone else. Especially not one of the neighbors. I hardly knew them. My bedroom was my sacred space. Who had convinced Dad to let them upstairs? Why couldn't everyone just go away and leave us alone?

CHAPTER FOUR

Casey

I walked down the sidewalk outside of the school, looking for Grandma Ann's car. I thought it was a little strange that she'd asked Lucas to take the bus home and not me. I hoped she wasn't taking me to a surprise doctor's appointment or expecting me to go shopping with her. She always took so much time looking for anything at the store, which was why I never went along. If I wanted to be bored, I'd rather do my homework.

I spotted her car further down the bus line. She waved me over, and I slowly made my way down the sidewalk toward her. With each step, dread filled my stomach and weighed it down. My feet propelled me forward, while my brain tried to slow my pace. Though seeing her was inevitable at that point. I pictured getting into the car and Grandma Ann turning to me to ask, "So how did you do on your History exam?"

When I reached the car I grasped hold of the door handle, but was unwilling to open it.

Why had I said something about my test that morning? Stupidly, at breakfast I'd mentioned that we'd get our results today. Mom was skeptical, as usual, and she appeared ready to ground me, forcing me to stay home the entire summer due to my grades. This test was my last shot at freedom for the summer, which was why the initial idea for the swap was perfect.

For once though, Grandma Ann was on my side and encouraged me by saying she thought I'd do great. She and

Mom were usually on the same page when it came to me, but I had a feeling this was one of those moments where Grandma Ann wanted to prove Mom wrong. Or at least show me some support.

The results had been the one thing over the past week to give me some hope. The thought of an A on a History test was definitely something to look forward to. I'd pictured a big red A on the paper with my name beside it. Something that I rarely saw on any of my work, even subjects I enjoyed.

But now that I'd achieved the impossible, I didn't want it. I was a cheater. Both Holly and Ronnie knew about it, and now Mrs. Halliday would also know. To make matters worse, soon the whole class would probably find out, since Holly and Ronnie were major gossipers. Ali and I would be labeled cheaters for the rest of our years in school. I didn't want that reputation for me or my twin.

I imagined the consequences of Mrs. Halliday believing whatever Holly told her. I bet Mrs. Halliday would call Mom and I'd be grounded for more than just the summer, probably for the rest of my life. I'd be lucky to ever live this down with anyone in my family. Would it show up on my permanent record when I tried to apply for colleges?

The window rolled down, breaking me from my thoughts.

"Casey, what are you doing?" Grandma Ann asked.

"I uh—thought I saw something," I said, opening the door and sliding into the passenger seat.

I held my breath, expecting her to ask me about the test at any moment.

"How was school?" she asked.

I buckled my seatbelt, avoiding her eyes. "Okay."

"Did you learn anything new?" she asked.

"I guess," I said. Why didn't she just come out and ask me? I was bursting for this part of the conversation to be over.

"I have a surprise for you this afternoon, Casey," she

said.

I turned to her, wondering what she could be talking about.

Grandma Ann pulled the car out of the pick-up line and drove in the opposite direction to the one we usually took when heading home.

"Where are we going?" I asked.

Grandma Ann's eyes sparkled with mischief, a look I'd never seen from her before.

"Like I said. It's a surprise," she said.

What could it be? She seemed so excited about it. "A surprise? Really? What is it, Grandma Ann? Please tell me!" I insisted.

"You'll see." She turned towards me with a smile before returning her attention to the road.

"You know I hate surprises," I frowned. As much as I wanted to avoid talking to her about my test or my day at school, I really wanted to know this secret. "What is it?" I asked again.

"Are you going to do this the whole way there?" she asked, glancing over at me.

"Where is there?" I asked, a grin slowly creeping across my face.

Maybe today would turn out better than I thought. Even though I felt guilty about cheating, Holly and Ronnie had no proof, so I should just let it go. I wanted to enjoy whatever Grandma Ann had planned for me.

Grandma Ann sighed. "I'm taking you to Ali's house," she said.

I clamped my hands over my mouth and heat prickled at my eyes. I wanted to see Ali so much. The worries of the afternoon suddenly washed away. "Did Ali call you? Did she ask if I could come over?"

Grandma Ann glanced at me before focusing on the road again. "No, not exactly."

I rubbed at my chin. "So she doesn't know I'm

coming over?"

With Ali ignoring or at least not responding to my texts, I didn't have a good feeling about this. Ali had made it clear by her silence that she didn't want to talk to me. So why would Grandma Ann think that she'd want to see me?

Grandma Ann's hands nervously shifted over the steering wheel. "Ali's father called the house and asked if you could visit her."

I frowned. "I don't understand."

"He's very worried about Ali," Grandma Ann said. "She won't leave her room. Most of the time he has to take meals up to her, as she refuses to come out to eat. He thinks that you might be the only one to help her."

"So she doesn't know I'm coming?" I repeated, wanting to be sure of what was going on.

"No," Grandma Ann said.

"What if she doesn't want to see me?" I asked. "She's not replying to my texts, and she doesn't talk much when I call her. She might not want me to barge into her house. It seems like she wants to be alone."

"You're not barging in," Grandma Ann said. "Her father invited you."

"But what if she needs more time?" If Ali didn't want me there, this could be really awkward. She might be upset that her dad had planned all of this, but even more upset with me because I'd turned up without her knowing.

A quivering sensation settled in my stomach as Grandma Ann pulled down the familiar street. I was surprised that she could find her way there; until I noticed a slip of paper in the cup holder with Grandma Ann's handwriting on it. Ali's dad must have given her the address and directions. I wished they would have included me in this plan. But Grandma Ann probably knew that I wouldn't have gone without a direct invitation from Ali.

"I think I should text her," I said, pulling out my phone.

"We're already here," Grandma Ann said.

When the car turned into Ali's driveway, and the large house loomed over us, I leaned forward, glancing toward the top floor windows where I knew Ali's bedroom was situated. The curtains were drawn, so unless she heard the car pull into the driveway, she'd have no idea I was coming in. How would she react?

Even though I knew this wasn't a good idea, we were already there. And if I sat stubbornly in the car, I might disappoint Ali's dad. He'd called me to help Ali, and I didn't want to hurt him too. It was worth a shot. At the very least, I could leave right away if Ali really didn't want to see me.

I got out of the car, slung my bag over my shoulder, and started for the front door.

Then Grandma Ann began to pull out of the driveway.

I gave her a curious look. Wasn't she coming in too?

I jogged over to the car. "What are you doing? Aren't you coming in as well?"

"I have a few errands to run," she said. "I'll pick you up in an hour or so."

"Oh okay," I said, a slight tremor in my voice. I wasn't nervous to see Ali, but having Grandma Ann there might have helped calm me a little.

"You're going to be fine," she said, patting my arm. "Your sister needs you. You can be brave for her."

I nodded, and she backed down the driveway. Her car paused for a moment at the end, and she motioned for me to go to the door.

I turned toward the house and made my way along the pavement and up the steps. I stood at the door and knocked; lightly at first, but then harder. I didn't want to ring the doorbell and wake Ali if she was sleeping or resting.

Maybe her dad wouldn't hear me, and I could sit outside on the patio until Grandma Ann returned.

But no such luck.

The door opened, and I came face to face with Ali's dad. I offered him a small smile and turned to wave to Grandma Ann. She continued out of the driveway and her car disappeared down the road, leaving me to face my twin and her father.

"Thank you for coming, Casey," he said and moved aside, letting me inside the house.

I wanted to be honest with him, but I also wanted some information before I saw Ali. "Are you sure Ali wants me here? My grandmother told me she has no idea I'm coming."

"I'm really not sure what Ali wants," he sighed, and closed the door, "but she needs you, Casey. I can't get through to her. She will barely eat anything, and all she does is lay in bed. I know this is part of the grieving process, but I think she could use a friend. Or a sister." A very sad and concerned expression crossed his face.

"There's only so much I can do for her. And since you've become so close, I hope this will work.

I glanced at the stairs. Because of our connection, I kind of expected Ali to realize I'd arrived. Maybe she would run down the stairs to greet me and tell me how much she missed me too.

But I knew I only imagined that reaction. She was probably completely unaware that I had arrived to comfort her.

"You can go up," he said.

I nodded and forced myself to move toward the stairs.

CHAPTER FIVE

Ali

Whoever Dad had let upstairs stood outside my door. Then the person knocked. The knocking was light enough that I barely heard it. Maybe if I didn't make any noise, they would think I was sleeping and go away.

I held my breath and closed my eyes, wishing for them to leave me alone.

Then another set of knocking began. Louder this time; enough that it would have woken me even if I was sleeping. I could not pretend any longer. I glared at the door, and gripped the sheets in my hands. Letting out the breath I'd been holding, I silently groaned. Why did Dad let some random person upstairs? Who in the world would he think I wanted to see right then?

I'd have a talk with him later about invading my privacy. Didn't he realize I wanted to be alone? I didn't know how to make it any clearer to him. He didn't approve of locking doors, but maybe if I put a DO NOT DISTURB sign on the door, he would get the hint.

I sighed slowly and called out, "Come in!" My voice was hoarse from not using it for a while. I had no idea when I last talked to anyone, other than single words of agreement or disagreement to Dad about whether or not I wanted to eat. I cleared my throat and swallowed a few times. It ached. I hoped I wasn't coming down with something.

I prayed this would be a quick visit from whoever was interrupting my grieving time. I had no urge to want to do anything at all, especially talk with people about Mom.

Instead of coming face to face with the person in the hallway, he or she kept knocking. I stared at the closed door, more frustrated than ever.

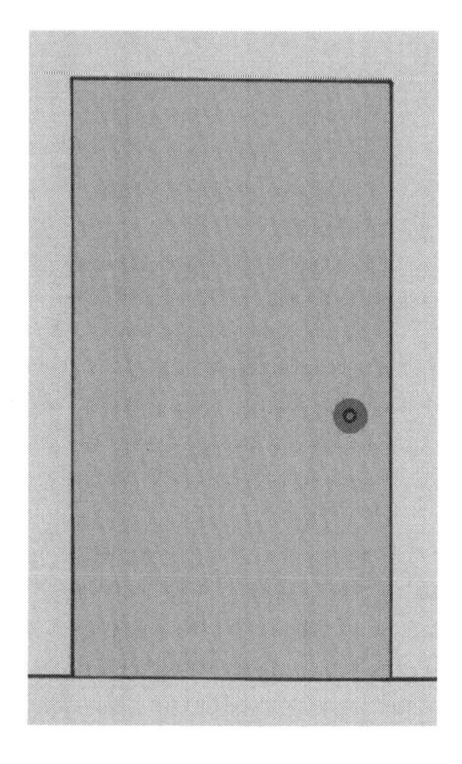

"I said—" my voice cracked and caught in my throat.

I shook my head in frustration and shoved the covers off my body. Sliding off my bed, I crossed the room to the door. My legs prickled with pins and needles. Why would Dad do this to me? Why would he send some stranger up to my room when clearly I wasn't in a state or appearance to see anyone? I tried to smooth my hair down but thought better of it. If this person wanted to see me, they could see the real me. I wouldn't give into the need to have a perfect appearance. Somehow, that idea made me feel a little better. I didn't have to pretend to be anything right now. I could just be me. Maybe it would make this person leave quicker.

Sighing with annoyance, loud enough that I knew the person behind the door would hear, I hoped they'd be embarrassed for barging in on me.

I placed my hand on the knob and turned, pulling the door open. And came face to face with the person who thought today would be a good day to annoy someone who just wanted to be left alone.

CHAPTER SIX

Casey

My feet felt like they had bricks attached to them as I slowly walked up to Ali's room. At the landing, I turned around to her dad for support. Before I'd climbed the stairs, he had winked at me reassuringly. I knew he had faith that I'd be able to help his daughter and I didn't want to disappoint him.

But instead, he was nowhere to be found. I guessed he wanted me to do this on my own. Now, I had to focus on

Ali. I'd never felt so alone in my life. But this wasn't about me. It was about my twin. And maybe I really was the only one to help her.

I licked my dry lips and took a deep breath before heading in the direction of her room.

When I reached her closed door, I hesitated. I shifted the weight of my feet and clasped my sweaty hands together. I was more uncertain than ever as to whether Ali would even want to see me.

Ali's dad's face popped into my mind. I had to act like the person he thought I was, even though every part of my body wanted to run back down the stairs and out of the house to safety.

I lifted my hand, curled my fingers into a fist, and softly knocked on the door.

I listened for her response. I didn't hear any movement from the inside. Was she sleeping?

The doors in Ali's house *were* thicker than the paper thin ones at my house. I guessed that went with having a really expensive home. At the very least, when I had pretended to be Ali, the thicker doors helped give me some privacy. Thinking of that time reminded me of Ali's mom, and the whole reason I had come here today.

I waited another minute, then knocked again, not wanting to barge into Ali's room uninvited.

The door abruptly opened, and I stepped back, sucking in a deep breath.

Ali stood there. Her hair hung untidily on her shoulders and appeared to have been uncombed for days. She looked different than she had at the funeral. The skin under her eyes was dark, and her cheekbones were more prominent than before. She wore a matching set of pajamas, an outfit I'd seen before in her dresser drawers. The clothing hung loosely on her body. Ali and I were thin, to begin with, but lack of food had made Ali look unwell and very pale.

My heart went out to her. Why hadn't I forced myself

to come sooner? She was in pain, and I hadn't been there when she needed me.

Her jaw dropped open as she stared, a blank expression apparent on her face.

My breathing roared in my ears. I had no idea how to respond. We stood there awkwardly, neither of us speaking. My mind began to race. She didn't want me there at all.

Ali's dad had been mistaken to think that I could help her.

CHAPTER SEVEN

Ali

The person standing at my door was the most familiar face I'd ever seen. My own.

I blinked a few times to make sure I wasn't dreaming. I stared at Casey, utterly bewildered. My mouth dropped open while a fluttering sensation bloomed in my stomach. What was Casey doing there? How did my twin come to be standing at my bedroom door?

I felt horrible for not answering her texts, but somehow she'd known I needed her. Had our psychic connection worked over a long distance? My whole body slumped, and I felt the pent-up tension immediately drift away. For the first time since my mother's death, I noticed a sense of relief. It was as though I had been saved.

Casey's eyes locked with mine, and although she did not utter a word, she didn't have to. Then something clicked. I wasn't sure if it was Casey's expression or our connection, but I lunged for her. Throwing my arms around her, I began sobbing against her shoulder.

Her arms squeezed around my body and we stood there locked together. The connection tingled between us, and I noticed Casey's voice in the depths of my mind.

It's okay, Ali.

I nodded against her shoulder, unable to stop the sobs that poured from my throat. Tears streamed down my face and onto her shirt. The damp fabric clung to my cheek.

Casey was the first person to break through the emotions I'd been trapped inside of. And a tiny glimmer of hope for my future peeked through the darkness.

Was it possible that I would be okay?

CHAPTER EIGHT

Ali

I moved away from Casey, and her arms dropped to her sides, her backpack fell to the floor at our feet. She was the first person in a week who did not give me a pitying look. No explanation was needed, she understood exactly how I was feeling. And a tiny flash of hope filled my chest that someday I might be able to feel somewhat normal again. The very sight of her had helped to release my most repressed emotions. I had my twin to thank for that. With one hug, she had the ability to break through my grief. Now at least, I was able to breathe without the choking tightness in my chest.

"I hope you don't mind me coming," Casey said, her words breaking the silence. "Your dad called and asked me to."

I took her hand and pulled her into my room. "Casey…I'm so glad you came."

She scooped up her school bag and placed it next to the wall by the door.

I closed the door behind her and brought her over to my bed. "I can't believe you're here."

My head seemed to spin as the whirlwind of relief and endless other emotions swirled around in my head.

Then the words burst forth in a rush. Every single thing I'd felt since my mom had died, poured from my mouth in an unstoppable flow. "Casey, I'm so sorry I haven't been a good sister to you. I should have answered your texts. But I just couldn't talk to anyone, not even you. It was so unfair to treat you that way."

"Ali, it's okay, I understand," Casey's reassuring tone eased my guilt. "You've been through so much. It's all so sad and I'm so sorry." She stared at me in a way that only Casey could, and the connection between us felt stronger than ever.

"I just miss her so much." Tears welled in my eyes as I sobbed the words. I wondered if I'd ever get to a point where I could think about my mom without bursting into tears.

Casey took my hands in hers. "I'm here for you Ali. Anytime you want to talk, I'm here."

"Thank you," I said, squeezing her hands in return. It felt so good to have her alongside me. I never imagined how good it would be to have a sister to confide in. Especially after my mother, the one person I felt closest to, was gone.

I rubbed my eyes, brushing the tears away. I suddenly felt incredibly tired but I didn't want Casey to go. I wondered if she would stay over. Maybe having her close to me would help to keep the nightmares away. But would it be too much to ask of her?

My thoughts were interrupted by a knock on the door.

"Come in," I said.

The door opened, and Dad's head peeked around it.

His eyebrows were raised questioningly. But the moment he saw Casey and I sitting alongside each other on the bed, his expression relaxed. I gave him a small apologetic smile. He'd been so patient over the past week. I made a silent promise to open up to him more. I knew that he was hurting as well.

"Is everything okay?" he asked, a hopeful smile appearing on his face.

"The best," I said. Hopping off the bed and crossing the room, I hugged him as tightly as I could.

He patted my back and ruffled my hair. "That's so

good to hear, Ali." I could see the relief in his eyes as he glanced towards Casey. "Can I make you girls something to eat?"

"Sure," I said, looking back at Casey.

She grinned and nodded her head. She'd made it clear after the first swap that she loved my parents' cooking. Even though she'd only be able to get Dad's cooking from now on, I was sure that would be okay with her.

"Can Casey stay the night?" I asked Dad. Then turned to Casey. "That is if you want to, Casey?"

She nodded. "Oh yes, I'd love to. But I just need to check with Mom first."

The mention of our mother struck something inside me. I'd grown up knowing I was adopted, but the woman who gave birth to us was still practically a stranger to me. When I was a little better, I'd make an effort to get closer to her. She was the only mother I'd have from now on.

"I'll call your mom to check if it's okay," Dad said. "But that's fine with me."

"And tomorrow we can go to school together," Casey grinned, a hopeful expression on her face.

I nodded eagerly towards her. With Casey by my side, I knew I could do that. And I also knew it was what my mom would have wanted.

"I'll come back up and let you know when dinner is ready," Dad smiled once more.

"Thanks!" Casey and I replied at the same time. We looked at each other and giggled.

Dad gave us another smile before closing the door.

I sighed and looked around my room. It was a mess! I pulled the curtains open so the room wouldn't look like such a cave, and the bright afternoon sunlight shone through the window. This brightened my mood even further.

"Do you want to help me clean up?" I asked Casey.

She hopped off the bed and rubbed her hands together. "Where do we start?"

CHAPTER NINE

Casey

Ali and I stripped her bed of her sheets and duvet. We took all the pillowcases off the pillows and tossed them into a pile by the door.

"I'll take these down to the laundry room before dinner," Ali said. "Let's get some new sheets."

Inside of Ali's private bathroom was a small linen closet. She picked out a new set of sheets and a fresh cover for her quilt. They were neatly folded in the closet, and I hesitated, not wanting to disturb how precisely they were stacked.

I imagined Ali's mom taking her time to make sure all of the sheets were perfect squares, before gently sliding them onto the shelves. I sighed thinking of her. Although I was careful not to show my regret to Ali.

We went back into the bedroom and took the two corners of the new sheet and threw our arms into the air, creating a parachute-like shape with the fabric. We laughed and did that a few times before tucking the sheet under the corners of the mattress.

It was so wonderful to see a smile on Ali's face again. We did the same thing with the top sheet, and then inserted the quilt into the freshly laundered pink cover before tossing it over the bed. Ali had a lot of pillows, so it took us some time to replace all the covers.

While we were at it, I wanted to fill our silence with all the drama that had been happening in my life, but I decided against it. Ali was just beginning to feel better. I didn't want to make her feel worse by sharing all my problems.

She clapped her hands together when we were finished. "That's so much better."

She then looked around the room. There were plates and glasses on the side tables, along with a heap of used tissues.

I watched her chew on her lower lip, and could see she was embarrassed by the mess.

"I'll get the dishes," I said.

Ali went into the bathroom and got the small trash can that normally sat under the sink. She picked up the tissues and shoved them inside the bin.

I stacked all of the dishes and put them by the door. I'd take them to the kitchen when we went down for dinner. Thinking of food made my stomach growl.

"I think I'm going to shower before we eat," Ali said.

"Go ahead," I said. "I need to get some homework done, anyway." I smiled.

"Can you make a list of the homework assignments that I missed?" Ali asked, as she looked through her dresser for clean pajamas.

"Sure," I said.

"Thanks," she said. "I'm sure I'll have a lot to catch up on, but at least it'll keep my mind busy for a while."

She went into the bathroom and closed the door.

I heard the shower turn on and sighed. In the short amount of time since I'd arrived, Ali had already transformed. If I hadn't seen the difference with my own eyes, I would not have believed it. It was so rewarding to know that I had helped that transformation to happen.

I went over to my bag and opened up a notebook, making a list of everything that Ali had missed. I knew she would catch up with schoolwork in no time. In any case, I was so happy to have my sister back. Although, I hadn't had the courage to ask her if she and her dad were leaving town. The question was at the forefront of my mind, but I didn't dare to ask it. For now, I had to make the best of our time together. She needed me, and I wanted to do all I could to help her.

After Ali had showered, she came out of the bathroom with her signature braid and dressed in a pretty set of polka dot pajamas. The top was sleeveless, which showed off the heart-shaped birthmark on her shoulder, the only physical difference between us. Ever since we'd told our classmates that we were twins, Ali hadn't been afraid to show it off.

"Okay, I'm ready to work," she said, sitting beside me.

We spread out my books across Ali's bedroom floor and started on our homework.

Every few minutes I looked over at Ali, who was deep in concentration. I'd considered telling her about the History exam and congratulating her on the A that she managed to achieve. But once again, I decided against it. I felt good inside, knowing that my visit had helped her. And I didn't want to spoil that with my fears over what had happened when the test papers were handed out.

I reveled in the connection we shared. It was a special feeling to be so close to a sibling. This was something I'd never had with my brother, Lucas, but with Ali, it was different. As twins, we'd created a special bond.

Ali's dad knocked on the door a little while later. "Casey, your mom said it was okay to stay over tonight."

"Yay!" I said, as Ali and I high-fived each other.

"You two have to go to bed at the regular weeknight time, though." He looked at each of us firmly.

"That's fine, Dad," Ali grinned, batting her eyelashes.

I giggled at seeing her playful nature again. The Ali that I had come to know so well had begun to shine through once more.

"Okay girls, it's time to eat," Ali's dad said, beckoning us towards the door. Ali and I both jumped up from the bed, and when we reached the top of the stairs, an unusual scent wafted up from the kitchen.

"Oh, my gosh," Ali said. "You're going to love Dad's tacos."

The only tacos I'd ever eaten before were from a fast food restaurant, and I had not enjoyed them at all. I wrinkled my nose but didn't comment. I knew that Ali's dad was a great cook, but I couldn't help feeling hesitant about the food we were about to eat.

Boy, was I wrong! After eating fish, beef, and chicken tacos, I added seconds to my plate. These did not taste like any tacos I'd ever eaten before. I was reminded of the incredible meals that Ali ate each night. And I was so grateful to have enjoyed her mom's cooking while she was still alive.

"Have as many as you want, Casey," Ali's dad said.

"Thank you, I will!" I said, eagerly reaching for

another.

Ali smiled. "This is nice."

"It is nice," her Dad repeated.

"Mom would have loved having you over," Ali said to me.

"She loved when we took seconds," Ali's dad said.

"Yes, she did!" Ali agreed.

I watched for Ali's reaction to the comments about her mom. She appeared to be okay for the moment. Maybe my sudden arrival at her bedroom door really had helped her to open up. It was so good to see her smiling face again. And perhaps I could encourage her to share more happy stories about her mother. That might even bring me closer to both her and her dad. If that helped them to feel better about staying, then I would be overjoyed.

After dinner, Ali's dad announced that he had the fixings for ice cream sundaes. I think I was the most excited of the three of us. Even though I'd eaten five tacos, there was always room for ice cream.

I helped Ali put sprinkles, chocolate chips, and fresh strawberries on the table, while her dad heated up the hot fudge sauce.

Then Ali and I scooped vanilla ice cream into the glass bowls. The ice cream was the expensive kind, with little flecks of vanilla beans throughout. I couldn't help taking an extra scoop for myself.

"Alright, here comes the fudge," Ali's dad said, carrying over the pot of hot sauce from the stove top.

Ali and I moved away from the bowls to give him room. My mouth watered as the rivulets of fudge trickled down the sides of the ice cream mounds.

"Ta-da!" he said. "Dig in before the ice cream melts."

He didn't need to tell me twice. I added all the fixings and placed a fresh strawberry on top.

I admired my creation for a moment and then took the first mouthful. It was delicious, and I quickly dug into the rest.

"This is so good!" I said. "I never get dessert after dinner."

"Really?" Ali asked, licking her spoon clean.

I shook my head.

"Mom loved everything sweet," Ali said. "Cookies, cake, pie, and all that."

I interacted as much as I could for the rest of the conversation about Ali's mom, but mostly I listened. The love that these two had for her was breathtaking. A few times, I was forced to hold back my tears at the sight of Ali's tear-soaked eyes. It wouldn't do any good for both of us to cry.

When we finished our sundaes, Ali jumped into her dad's arms for a hug. He rocked her a few times with his eyes tightly closed.

I turned away from them, feeling a little embarrassed about intruding on the moment they were sharing.

But when I turned back around, Ali's dad was right next to me with his arms opened wide. "Good night, Casey."

I hesitantly stepped into his one-armed embrace. His arms were very strong around me. Growing up with Mom and Grandma Ann, I'd never experienced a good night hug like that before. It felt nice having a father-figure in my life, even if he wasn't mine. "Thank you for coming over today," he said into my ear.

I nodded. "Thank you for asking me."

He let go of me and gave me a small smile. His eyes were teary, but he didn't cry.

Ali and I walked up the stairs. And with each step I took, I couldn't help but realize what I'd been missing all of these years without a dad of my own.

CHAPTER TEN

Casey

For the rest of the evening, Ali and I worked on homework. Normally, I was distracted by television or Lucas, but since Ali was so studious, I kept my focus on my work. After almost failing the History exam, I made a promise to myself to work harder. If Ali hadn't been there for me, I would have failed. Now I wanted to be more conscientious so she'd be proud of me for getting better grades on my own.

Ali had no problem digging into the work, so we happily completed the assignments in silence. Eventually, her dad had to remind us it was bedtime, since we'd lost track of time. He left us to get organized while he searched for an air mattress for me to sleep on. But Ali had other plans.

"Want to sleep in my bed tonight?" she asked, as we brushed our teeth. "It's big enough. And it's much more comfortable than the air bed."

"If you don't mind," I said.

I loved Ali's bed. It was so roomy and so soft, and I remembered feeling like I'd slept on a cloud when I stayed there for the swap.

"Not at all!" Ali said. "What's mine is yours."

"And what's mine is yours as well," I laughed.

The next morning, Ali and I woke from her alarm, which she'd set to wake us early so we'd have plenty of time to get ready. She allowed me to use the bathroom first, and I quickly showered and brushed my hair before skipping back into her room. I couldn't wait to look through her closet for something to wear. She had so many pretty things to choose from.

"This was my favorite part during the first swap," I said gleefully.

Ali was already in front of her closet, picking out her shoes for the day. She wore a pair of little ankle socks and had chosen a black and white patterned skirt that flared out at the hem. Her blue top had long sleeves and was studded with little sequins around the wrists and on the pockets. The fabric was silky and soft, it looked softer than anything I'd ever worn before.

"I was thinking of wearing boots with this," she said, holding up a pair of black lace-up ankle boots.

I nodded in agreement, "Those will be perfect with your outfit, Ali."

I picked through her clothes. Since I hadn't known I was staying the night, I had no spare clothes of my own. But being twins and practically the same size, it made our swaps and borrowing clothes that much easier. Besides, I wouldn't have wanted to wear anything I'd brought from home when I had her collection of beautiful clothes to sort through. Her closet was so organized that it made it super easy to choose an outfit.

I thought for a moment of my own messy cupboard at home, where I had sweaters and tops and jeans all shoved together onto various shelves, which made it so difficult every time I tried to find a particular piece of clothing.

But Ali's closet was a dream to search through, the only hard part was deciding on what I wanted to wear. Eventually, I selected a dark pink tank top with thin straps and looked for the pale pink knitted sweater that I'd eyed the last time I was at her house. I knew that would look great with Ali's black skinny jeans and her black Converse sneakers. Glancing quickly at the frayed sneakers I'd been wearing the day before, it was such a treat to wear something that was not old and faded, and worn out. I could just imagine the reaction from Holly and Ronnie when I saw them at school. At least I'd feel more confident about standing up for myself when they made their usual mean remarks.

Thinking of the two trouble-makers, I decided it was time to recap Ali on what had happened at school since she left for the hospital that day. Starting off with something positive, I focused on the test result first of all.

"By the way, you got an A on the History test!" I said

excitedly.

Ali blinked for a moment as if she'd completely forgotten about taking the test. Then she smiled. "What? Only an A? Not an A+?" She grinned at me mischievously.

I matched her smile. "Well, Mrs. Halliday said you would have had a higher score if you answered the last question."

I opened my mouth to tell her about Holly and Ronnie suspecting that we'd swapped places, but decided against it. A smiling Ali was a happy Ali. And I wanted her to stay happy for as long as she could. Worrying her with that extra detail would crush her mood, and I wanted to avoid that at all costs.

"Oh that's right, I left out the last question," she frowned.

"An A is fine with me," I said quickly. I didn't want her to feel bad about not getting an even higher grade. "I would have been happy with a B-."

"You should strive for better grades, Casey. I know you can do it," Ali said, standing in front of the mirror and tucking a stray chunk of hair into her braid.

"I'm not smart like you, Ali," I said, pulling on the jeans in my hand. "I'm okay with getting by with average grades."

"You shouldn't be," she said, turning to me with crossed arms. "What about college? Don't you want to get good grades so you can go to a good college?"

I laughed. Mom would never be able to afford anything but local community colleges. She didn't get her degree, and whenever anyone brought up college, she told me I'd have to settle with what we could afford.

Though with Ali's confidence in me and her help, I had a few years to make up my grades. I knew Ali's dad would be able to afford to send her anywhere. Maybe if I worked hard, we'd be able to go to the same college, far away from here. I'd have to get a scholarship of course. But that was a goal I would happily work for, as long as I stayed with my sister.

"We can work on it," I said.

"It'll be hard work and maybe a bit stressful, but it'll be worth it," she smiled encouragingly.

"Speaking of stressful," I said. "The day of the test was crazy, right?"

"It sure was," Ali said, shaking her head at the memory.

"And we were so close to being caught out," I said.

"Too close," Ali agreed. "I don't think I've ever felt that stressed in my life. But not about the test. I was so worried about getting to my mom in time."

I waited for her to continue. Any topic of her mother was sensitive, and I didn't want to push it.

"I'm glad it worked out though," Ali said with a brave smile. "I can't believe we pulled it off without a problem."

She'd given me another perfect opportunity to talk about Holly and Ronnie, but I couldn't make myself say the words. I hated the way they made me feel, but would they do the same to Ali when she got to school? Ali had just lost her mother, could those girls be that cruel? I wasn't sure, but I wanted to wait and see what would happen before saying anything to Ali. I hoped to ease her into school again, not scare her off. But if Ronnie and Holly were the ones to make Ali want to move away, I would never forgive them.

I decided to see what happened at school, then tell Ali all the details. I promised myself that. I didn't want any secrets between us.

While Ali went into the bathroom to finish getting ready, I packed all my books into my school bag.

All the while, I tried to calm my breathing.

Everything would work out.

As long as Ali and I were together.

CHAPTER ELEVEN

Ali

I didn't want to talk about the day of the swap anymore. And going to the bathroom to get ready was the perfect excuse to avoid it. That day *had* been a close call, and we were so close to being caught. It had been the worst day of my life. The swap itself had been really stressful but it was also the day that my mother died. However, for the first time since she passed, I felt *okay*. And I didn't want anything to send me back into that emotional turmoil. If I did, I just knew that I'd struggle to return.

As I finished braiding my hair, I thought about the conversation with Casey. I sensed she had something to tell me, but I didn't know what it was.

There was something I wanted to talk about too, but bringing up Jake to Casey might not work out my way. Casey hadn't spoken of him at all, so maybe he was still annoyed with us. I wondered if he knew that my mom had died. I was pretty sure everyone else at school would know, so he must be aware of it as well. I wasn't sure what I should have expected from him. A text? Were we close enough friends that he would send me a message like everyone else?

I shook the thoughts from my head and decided to ask Casey outright.

"How's Jake?" I called from the bathroom.

Casey appeared in the doorway, a wide smile lighting up her features. My stomach twisted into knots.

"Well..." she grinned. "Everything is actually really good now. He's been super friendly and really nice to me."

"That's so great," I replied, not meeting her eyes. "See, I knew he didn't think we'd swapped. I'm sure he was just uncomfortable because Matt said something about him liking me."

Casey gave me a strange look.

"Which is totally untrue," I added quickly. "Obviously, Matt made a mistake about that, especially since he's been nice to you. Whatever his problem was that day, he must have got over it."

"Even if he was suspicious about us swapping, he hasn't asked about you. So I guess you're right." Casey nodded.

A tweak of envy pinched at me, with the thought of Jake being interested in Casey rather than me. But I knew it was for the best. I had just lost my mom and could not be focusing on boys at a time like this. And besides, Casey liked him. She was my twin and I cared about her. I did not want to cause any trouble between us over a silly boy.

Casey went on to tell me about each occasion Jake had approached her during the last week. She filled me in on every detail and was bubbling over with excitement. I listened to each word, all the while, forcing a smile. But at the same time, I felt terrible for secretly liking him. What kind of sister was I?

I hoped I could be distracted enough with everything else in my life to get over him for good. I didn't want to feel worse than I already did.

In an effort to change the subject, I decided to ask about something else entirely. "How is cheerleading going?"

Since making the team, I hadn't been to one practice due to my mom being taken to the hospital. I felt bad about missing so many sessions, but Mom was more important to me than some random after school activity. Although I still felt a little guilty, especially as I was on track to be the leader.

Some leader I was…

"I forgot to tell you, I made leader of the squad," Casey said proudly.

"Oh really?" I paused for a moment to catch my breath. "That's so great, Casey."

Underneath, however, I felt my stomach churn enviously. Mrs. Caldwell said from the start that I was in the running for that role, and I struggled to mask my disappointment. But in reality, I knew that holding the position for me would not be fair for the other girls. Other than the tryouts, I hadn't been at practice, so it was only fair to replace me. And if it was going to be anyone, I was glad it was Casey.

"Thanks," Casey said. "I really like it, it's a lot of fun."

Casey finished packing her bag, but I sensed that she wanted to say something else.

"Did something else happen, Casey?" I glanced at her curiously.

She hesitated for a moment before replying. "Well," she sighed, "Mrs. Caldwell told me to tell you that if you miss one more practice, she's going to have to offer your spot to one of the reserves."

"Oh really?" I frowned.

"She knows about your Mom, so she understands why you've been away," Casey said. "But don't feel pressured to come back if you aren't ready. I might be able to convince her to hold the spot a little longer. It's not like you've been skipping them on purpose."

"No, that's okay," I said, shaking my head. "There's no need for that. I'll be there today."

Casey's eyebrows shot up. "Are you sure?"

"Yes, it'll take my mind off everything," I said. "And I want to see you in the lead spot! I'm sure I have a lot to catch up on and you can help me."

"Of course I will," Casey smiled, grabbing her bag from its spot on the floor.

I could see that everything was working out really

well for Casey. I knew I should be really happy for her. She had everything she'd hoped for.

I didn't mind too much about the lead cheer spot, but I still struggled a little about Jake. I couldn't help feeling jealous that he was talking to Casey more than he ever did before. When I'd spent time with him during our swaps, I sometimes forgot that I was meant to be "playing" Casey. And in that time, I discovered how much I liked him. I hated myself for being jealous, and I wished I could get him out of my head. But it wasn't that easy.

"Girls?" Dad called from the hallway.

"Yes?" Casey and I said at the same time. We looked at each other and smiled.

"Let's get going," he said.

Casey turned to me. "Are you sure you want to go back today?"

"Yes. I'm sure." I grinned as we locked arms and left the room.

I took a rather large, silent breath, hoping that today would be okay.

A vision of my mom's beautiful face came to mind and I held onto the idea that she was always with me, and she would help me get through.

I knew that she'd always be with me.

CHAPTER TWELVE

Casey

Ali and I sat together in the back of her dad's car, excitedly working on our cheers for practice. Just like with everything she tried, Ali caught on quickly, and after the short ride, she could recite them perfectly. I knew that would help her chances of staying on the team. Although there was no reason for Ali to miss practices anymore, I wanted her to be prepared. I'd work with her on the moves during recess and lunch break. But the phrases were the hard part. Mrs. Caldwell would have no reason to kick Ali off the team if she saw how hard she'd worked. And since she caught on quicker than most of the other girls, I hoped Mrs. Caldwell would feature her in the solo sections as well.

"Thanks, Dad!" Ali said, after he parked the car by the front entrance. "Love you."

Since he had to go into work early, he always dropped Ali off before the buses arrived, so we were able to pull right up to the school entrance. Anytime Mom or Grandma Ann dropped me off, they were always late, and we were stuck behind the long line of buses that wound down the driveway, so I usually just got out and walked.

"Love you too, Ali," her dad said, turning around in his seat. "I hope you both have a great day."

"Bye, Mr. Jackson. Thanks so much for having me!" I said, hopping out of the car behind Ali.

It was quite cold that morning, so Ali and I sprinted inside the building to stay warm. We then headed upstairs to our lockers to exchange our books for the ones we would need that morning.

I noticed Ali staring into her locker with her bag by her side.

I went over to her and gently touched her shoulder. But she flinched as though I had hurt her.

"Sorry," she said. "I zoned out for a minute."

"Are you okay?" I asked quietly.

"I know it's only been a week, but I feel so strange being back here. And I know that when I get home, Mom isn't going to be there to greet me the way she always did."

Her eyes filled with tears and I pulled her to me, hugging her tight. "I know it's hard, Ali. But everything will be okay. I promise."

Ali sniffed and nodded her head. "Thanks, Casey."

I'm sure if you need some time to yourself, Mrs. Halliday will understand," I reassured her, as I pulled away.

I leaned against the locker next to Ali's and waited for her to finish with her things.

"Oh my gosh!" she said, reaching into the dark space. She pulled out a white greeting card.

"What's that?" I asked.

A huge smile appeared on her face, yet at the same time, her eyes welled up once again. It seemed like an odd reaction.

"Are you okay?" I asked for the second time.

"Mom gave me this card on my first day of school, when we first moved here," Ali said.

I looked over her shoulder. Her mom's perfect handwriting filled the card from top to bottom on both sides.

I waited for her to read it. And when she finished and closed it, I grabbed one of the fuzzy neon pink magnets that she kept inside her locker.

"Put it here," I said, pointing to the inner locker door. "So you can always see it."

Ali wiped at her cheeks and smiled gratefully. "Good

idea. Thanks, Casey."

While she did that, I turned around to look for Brie. Instead of my best friend, however, I locked eyes with Holly, who was just passing by. I stood there, frozen to the spot. Ronnie was next to her. Holly bumped Ronnie's arm to bring her attention to me as well.

Ali turned around and was faced with the evil death stare that was being directed towards us both. What were Holly and Ronnie going to say now? Would they tell everyone their suspicions about the swap, right there in the hallway?

"Hi, Holly," Ali said. "Hi, Ronnie."

But instead of replying, they said nothing, and continued walking until they reached their lockers further down the row.

"What's their problem?" Ali asked, her eyebrows drawn together.

While I had tried to avoid the topic of Holly and Ronnie earlier, I knew I wasn't going to be able to keep it quiet any longer.

"Ali!" Brie interrupted, running up to us. "Oh my gosh. How are you? How are you feeling? I can't believe you're back at school so soon—"

I stood by as Brie gave Ali a gentle hug. At the same time, I was aware of Holly and Ronnie who were staring at us from down the hallway. From where we stood, I could hear them muttering to each other and it was obvious who they were talking about

Grabbing both Brie and Ali by the arms, I discreetly indicated towards Holly and Ronnie, and whispered urgently. "We need to go to our spot. Now!"

The two girls followed me to the second-floor bathroom, our regular meeting spot for any secret conversation we needed to have. And as we hurried along, Brie hissed, "What's wrong?"

"I'll tell you in a minute," I replied to her. We didn't

have much time to talk, but we had to find some privacy.

When we entered the bathroom, I closed the door firmly behind us. "What's going on?" Ali asked. "Why were Holly and Ronnie looking at us like that?"

"You didn't tell her?" Brie asked me.

"I'm telling her now," I said sharply.

"Tell me what?" Ali asked, her face filling with concern.

"Holly and Ronnie somehow know about the swap from last week," I said.

"What?" Ali exclaimed. "How?"

"I don't know," I said. "But they said something last week after cheer practice, and they've been saying other things about it since."

"Oh, no!" Ali said.

"But I keep telling Casey that it's fine because they have no proof," Brie's determined voice cut in. "They're probably jealous that you two are the center of attention right now. And with Casey as the leader of the squad, I'm sure they're even more jealous."

"Do you think they'll tell anyone else?" Ali asked.

"It's been a week and no one else has said anything," I stared worriedly towards her.

"Which means they haven't told anyone," Brie said. "They love to gossip. They would have told the whole school by now if they were sure."

"Yeah, but yesterday after school, after we got the tests back, Holly went up to Mrs. Halliday," I said.

"What did she say to her?" Ali asked. "Did she tell on us?"

"I don't know," I said, shaking my head.

"I think we should go to class and pretend that everything is normal," Brie looked at both of us, waiting for us to agree.

Ali's face paled. I knew that I should have warned her in advance. But would she have come to school if I had? I desperately wanted my twin back at school with me, selfish as that was.

"I'm sorry I didn't tell you, Ali," I said. "I was hoping that by coming back to school, you wouldn't leave town and that you'd want to stay."

"What are you talking about, Casey?" she shook her head at me. "Of course I'm staying. Dad and I aren't going anywhere. This is our home now."

I smiled. I couldn't believe I'd worried that she was leaving.

Her promise to stay filled me with relief. But that relief quickly faded away when I thought once more of what was going to happen when we went into class.

"I'm not sure what Holly told Mrs. Halliday, but I promise I will own up to everything," I said.

I was determined that I would take all the blame. Even so, my heart was thumping anxiously in my chest, and a black pool of dread had made its way into the pit of my stomach.

Sucking in a huge breath, I tried to find the courage I would need to enter our classroom.

CHAPTER THIRTEEN

Ali

I squeezed Casey's arm the moment we entered the room. Daring to glance quickly at Mrs. Halliday, I waited for her reaction. But she was working through a stack of papers on her desk and not paying any attention to the kids arriving right then. If Holly had told her about the swap, then wouldn't she be wanting to speak with us right away?

At one point during the history exam, I realized that Holly had noticed my headband, the one that I'd been wearing all day before swapping. At the time, I was so worried about my mom, that I totally overlooked that small detail when we exchanged clothes. Had I ruined this for Casey?

I decided that I couldn't let Casey take all the blame for this. After all, she was my sister, and I had agreed to do the swap. We were both to blame and would share the consequences equally. But as Brie had said, Holly didn't have any proof. If she and Ronnie were jealous of us, then that was their problem. As long as they kept their suspicions to themselves, then we'd be okay.

When I first came to school, they were nice to me, but I could tell that they liked to gossip, so I had never shared any more than I needed to with them. I just wished Casey had told me they were bullying her. I could have said something to them in the hallway. Although, I wasn't really sure what.

As we headed towards our seats, we passed Mrs. Halliday's desk and she looked up at us.

I gasped lightly, and Casey picked up her pace, quickly going to her seat. Since mine was at the back of the room, I had a few more feet to go before I heard my name being called.

I spun around to face Mrs. Halliday. "Ali, I'd like to speak with you, please."

I glanced at Casey, and her wide eyes mirrored the nervousness that unsettled my stomach.

Holly smirked at me as I passed her seat. I lifted my chin and focused on slowly breathing in and out, in an attempt to steady my racing pulse. I had to act as though everything was normal, while on the inside I was freaking out. This was it. We were caught! I knew Casey would defend me, but this wasn't something I wanted to face on my first day back at school. My dad was going to be so disappointed!

I felt Casey watching me, and I turned to her for support. Instead of seeing her cowering in her chair, Casey was making her way to the front of the classroom. That little show of support made me feel the tiniest bit better that I wouldn't go through this alone.

One thing I didn't understand, was why had Mrs. Halliday brought this up in front of the class? Even though we hadn't begun the lesson, everyone was curious about what was going on at the front of the classroom. Did Mrs. Halliday intend to make us an example? I knew she sometimes embarrassed kids who did things wrong, but when it came to cheating like this, I thought she'd be the type of teacher to talk privately first.

I had to explain our side of the story, before Holly's accusations were taken as the complete truth. Even though we were wrong to do the swap in the first place, I wanted Mrs. Halliday to know the whole story before punishing us.

When I arrived at her desk, I opened my mouth to speak, relieved to finally get it off my chest.

"Mrs. Halliday," someone said from behind me. I

turned to see Everett standing there. "Sorry, Ali. Can I ask Mrs. Halliday a question first?"

Mrs. Halliday looked from me to him. "Yes, Everett, what's wrong?"

Casey came to my side and gave me a look that said, "We're in this together."

I nodded, and we patiently listened while Everett asked Mrs. Halliday a question about last night's assignment.

Mrs. Halliday talked him through the problem, and he thanked her before heading back to his desk.

"Ali, I'm so sorry to hear about your mom," Mrs. Halliday said, turning her attention to us.

Casey moved closer to me, her hand brushing against mine. I felt her support, and tried to keep myself together. It was still hard to talk about my mother, but I managed to hold back the tears that threatened to spill over.

I gulped and nodded my head. "Thank you."

Mrs. Halliday looked to Casey then back to me. "I'm glad to see you have support from Casey. It's obvious you two have become very close."

"Yes, we have," Casey smiled at me.

"You're so identical," our teacher said, leaning forward and propping her chin on her folded hands. "It's amazing, really. The only difference is how you wear your hair. Apart from that, I wouldn't have a clue who is who. Though I've noticed you like to braid your hair, Ali. And you often wear a headband, whereas Casey doesn't. That's the only way I can tell you apart."

I stiffened. Holly had told her! What a snake!

"Casey," Mrs. Halliday said. "If you were to wear a headband, you could easily pass as Ali."

Why didn't she just tell us that she knew about the swap? The headband had been the only thing that could have revealed our identities. And with her commenting on it, she had to know.

"Okay, you two should return to your seats, we need to get started shortly," she said.

I stood there for a moment, and Mrs. Halliday gave me a strange look. Casey bumped my arm, and we turned around at the same time, the two of us heading in the direction of our desks.

My legs moved me forward on their own, while my mind raced. Did Mrs. Halliday only want to offer her condolences and comment on us being twins? Unless Holly had said something, it seemed a strange coincidence that Mrs. Halliday had mentioned hairstyles at all. But if she knew, wouldn't she have scolded us for cheating?

She had no problem calling out troublemakers in front of the whole class. I knew that first-hand. So had we read too much into this? Had Holly talked to Mrs. Halliday yesterday afternoon about something completely unrelated to the swap and Casey was mistaken? It appeared to look that way, at least for now.

The wild thumping of my heart had begun to settle by the time I reached my seat. But my thoughts were interrupted by the sound of a familiar voice.

"Hi, Ali," Jake said, his smiling face staring at mine.

"Hi, Jake," I mumbled, still thinking about what had just happened with our teacher.

"Sorry to hear about your mom," he said.

"Thank you." His eyes were full of pity, in the same way everyone else's had been, but I knew he meant to wish me well.

I had to get over people looking at me like that. I knew everyone was only trying to be kind.

"Alright, class, pull out your assignments from last night and swap them with the person next to you," Mrs. Halliday said.

While everyone else reached into their bags, I looked at Casey, and she turned in her seat and shrugged at me. I noticed Holly giving Casey a knowing look, and I wished that I sat closer so I could tell her off. Though, that might have made everything worse. I hated the fact that these girls had bullied my sister when I wasn't there; and also threatened to tell on us for something they couldn't prove.

I was still struggling to breathe and it took some time for the feeling of relief to really wash over me. While it appeared we were once again in the clear. I remained on high alert for the rest of the morning.

After morning classes, Casey, Brie, and I met at the front of the classroom and headed out to recess together. We said nothing to each other until we were outside. We went straight to the benches at the other end of the paved courtyard so we could talk about what had happened in private.

"Did we really just get away with that?" Casey asked.

"I think so," I said, shaking my head in disbelief. I still found it difficult to accept the fact that we had not been caught out after all. Well, not by Mrs. Halliday at least.

When we filled Brie in on the conversation with our teacher, she looked at us in surprise. "So, she mentioned the headband?"

"That was the only strange part," I said. "Then she told us to go back to our seats."

"Wow! So lucky!" Brie exclaimed. "Maybe she just made a comment because you wore a headband the last time she saw you?"

"Or…" Casey added slowly. I could almost feel her brain ticking over.

"Or what?" I asked.

Casey chewed on her lip. "What if she did suspect something? But because of your mom, she was reluctant to make an issue of it and decided to let it go? Maybe the headband remark was her way of warning us?"

"Would she do that?" I asked. I didn't know Mrs. Halliday that well, but Casey and Brie did.

"Maybe," Brie said. "But unless you two ask her

about it, we have no way of knowing."

"There's no way I'm asking her!" Casey furiously shook her head at that idea.

I shook my head as well. "Me neither. That was too close."

"How about we never do a swap ever again," Casey declared adamantly. "Well, at least not for a test." She laughed, and I joined in, relieved that the drama was finally over with.

"Deal," I said.

"You two have someone watching over you," Brie said. "You're the luckiest people I know."

I looked up at the sky. "I think my mom is by my side."

As I said the words, I felt her presence within me. Even before she died, she seemed to tune into what was going on in my life. And now that she was gone, I still felt her alongside me. She was my guardian angel and always would be. The card I'd found in my locker that morning had proved it. She wanted me to find it, to remind me that she would be with me at all times.

The sudden sound of loud laughter broke through my thoughts, and I looked in the direction that it had come from. Holly and Ronnie had claimed a bench seat nearby and were laughing hysterically. They whispered to each other as they stared towards us, making it completely obvious that they were laughing about us.

"Ugh, ignore them," Brie said.

"We will," I replied, focusing on Brie and Casey instead of the mean girls in our midst. Holly and Ronnie could keep laughing, but they wouldn't get us into trouble. So the best thing was to simply ignore them as Brie had said.

"Casey," Brie hissed abruptly, nodding her head in the opposite direction.

Casey and I turned to see what Brie was referring to, and spotted Jake and his friends walking in our direction. I had a flashback of the last day I was at school, when he did the same thing. But then at the last moment, he completely ignored us.

This time, however, he kept walking, but he looked right at Casey and smiled before continuing on his way.

The moment he was out of earshot, Brie nudged Casey and grinned. "Did you see the way he looked at you?"

Casey beamed back at her. "How cute is he! Oh my gosh, everything is falling into place."

I tried to feel happy for Casey, but the twinge of envy came back. Even though I did my best to push it away, it continued to linger and then settled heavily in my stomach.

Holly and Ronnie were being a problem but everything was working out with Jake.

I glanced at the beaming grin on my sister's face and sighed.

CHAPTER FOURTEEN

Ali

For the rest of the school day, I buried my head in my books and tried my hardest to focus on schoolwork. Casey hadn't fully prepared me for all the work I'd missed from only one week away from school.

While I had caught up a little last night, I knew this weekend would be spent working, so I could get back to where the rest of my classmates were. Although I didn't mind too much. I just hoped I'd be able to keep my emotions about my mom deep inside me, while I tried to get my life back on track.

Mom always believed in me when it came to my schooling. She used to call me her Ivy-league daughter, even though I had a long way to go until college.

When the final bell rang, I sat back in my seat and tilted my head back. The muscles in my shoulders and back were stiff from being hunched over my desk the entire day. I wanted nothing more than to have Dad pick me up, so I could go home and fall asleep for the rest of the afternoon. It wasn't easy going from entire days in bed, to sitting in an uncomfortable chair for the day.

But I promised Casey I'd go to cheerleading practice. And since Mrs. Caldwell had warned Casey about replacing me, I wanted to show her I was dedicated, even though my life wasn't in the best shape at the moment.

"Are you ready?" Casey asked. She stood in front of my desk. The rest of the class had already cleared out, except for Casey and Brie.

"Yeah," I said, shoving my books into my bag.

"Are you sure?" Brie asked. "You look a little pale."

I forced a smile to my lips. It was the one I used for all the guests who had come to the house after the funeral. I hoped it fooled Casey and Brie as much as it had those people. "I'm fine. I'm worried about catching up, that's all."

"You'll be fine," Casey said. "I'm sure Mrs. Halliday won't push you. You've already proved to her you're a good student. You get all the highest grades."

I smiled at Casey. She sure knew how to make me feel better.

The three of us went to our lockers so Casey and Brie could empty their bags of some books. I decided to take all of mine home, and by the time I reached the locker room, I was happy to take the heavy bag off my shoulders.

Most of the girls were already changed by the time we arrived there. Casey changed the quickest, reminding me that she had to be first at the field, as she was the leader.

I encouraged Casey to go on ahead of us while Brie waited for me to get changed. Then we jogged to the field together.

When we arrived, the girls were stretching or chatting in small groups. I went straight to Mrs. Caldwell and apologized for being absent from practice.

"Ali!" Mrs. Caldwell said, patting my shoulder. "It's so good to see you back. And I'm so terribly sorry to hear about your Mom."

I pressed my lips together. I wished people would stop with their sympathy. Everyone wanted me to move on, but how could I, when everyone was constantly telling me how sorry they were?

I gritted my teeth, not saying a word. I knew that she meant well. Even though I wanted nothing more than to turn away from the sympathetic expression on her face. It had been the same thing all day. Kids who I barely knew, had approached me with sympathetic comments and gestures. I had thought that by coming to school I could escape all of this, but it happened wherever I went!

"Well, we're about to get started," Mrs. Caldwell said, as if sensing my unease. "Ali, how about you stand toward the back until you get all of the moves down."

"Okay," I said, pleased to have something else to focus on.

"But take your time, Ali," Mrs. Caldwell added with a reassuring smile. "The girls have had a whole week to learn these steps. Once we go through the routine a few times, I'll work with smaller groups and help the girls who need it, so don't be discouraged if you don't catch on right away."

I nodded, and Mrs. Caldwell blew her whistle. "Get into formation, girls!"

After a few minutes into practice, my mood had improved. While focusing on the steps, I was distracted enough that it helped to clear all the negative thoughts and some of the sadness from my head, for the time being at least. And I was glad that I had decided to come.

Because Casey had taught me the words to the cheers earlier that day, I was able to concentrate on perfecting the moves. And I couldn't help but smile at Casey who was at the front of the group, expertly running through all the steps of the routine. I felt so proud of her.

After she'd led the group through the routine three times, Mrs. Caldwell blew her whistle and called myself and three other girls to the side. "The rest of you can continue to work with Casey. You need to keep practicing those moves."

Casey waved at me as I left the group. I gave her two thumbs up and headed towards Mrs. Caldwell. She walked through the moves slowly, and being in a smaller group helped me to make sense of them. Working with those who already had it down was tough, since they moved so quickly as a unit. But I would catch up with them soon enough. Even though I wasn't going to be the leader, I wanted to be one of the strongest cheerleaders on the team. That would show

Mrs. Caldwell and everyone else that they didn't have to feel bad for me anymore.

We were halfway through the routine for a second time, when something caught my eye.

Mrs. Caldwell hadn't noticed, but Holly had moved right next to Casey, completely out of place, and seemed to be mimicking everything that Casey did.

Casey's eyes were wide. She continued with the routine but at the same time was telling Holly to move back into place. I couldn't hear her words but it was clear to me what was going on through her gestures.

I kept my eyes on Holly as the other girls came into formation again across the way. Holly said something to Ronnie, leaning close to her friend and whispering something. I felt sure that it was probably something about Casey.

As the girls moved around Casey for the ending, I watched Holly slide her foot under Casey's. Casey's toe connected with Holly's leg and her hands shot out in front of her as she fell heavily to the ground.

"Mrs. Caldwell!" I called, rushing towards Casey who was hunched over and grasping hold of her ankle.

"Casey, are you alright?" Mrs. Caldwell moved quickly to Casey's side.

"I'm not sure," Casey said, holding back the tears. "It really hurts."

Mrs. Caldwell turned to me. "Ali, there's an ice pack in the first aid kit over there. Can you please get it for me?"

I went to the kit and grabbed the ice pack. Gripping it tightly in my hands, I raced back to Casey. I couldn't believe that Holly had tripped Casey on purpose! That was so mean. I glared at her in disgust.

Meanwhile, Ronnie stared back and grinned, as though the whole incident was a joke.

I helped Casey to the nearby bench and handed her the ice pack. Her lower lip trembled, but she didn't cry. Although, I could tell by her expression that her ankle was really hurting.

Mrs. Caldwell positioned the ice pack on Casey's ankle and told her to keep it in place.

"You'll have to sit out for the rest of practice," Mrs. Caldwell said to her.

Without skipping a beat, Holly quickly spoke up. "I'll take her place!"

I narrowed my eyes at her.

"Just for today, Holly," Mrs. Caldwell said, then instructed everyone to resume their places on the field.

"I saw her trip you," I said to Casey. "I'm going to tell Mrs. Caldwell."

"No, Ali," Casey hissed. "I don't want to make a big deal of it."

"Why not? She hurt you. On purpose! And it looks like she just wanted to take your place as leader."

"If she gets into trouble because of me, she might try and say something else about our swap. Just let it go, Ali."

I couldn't believe what Casey was saying.

When I glanced over at Ronnie and Holly, I could see them both smirking at Casey. Those girls were jerks! I held my tongue about it this time, but next time they wouldn't be so lucky. No one was going to hurt my sister and get away with it.

I patted Casey's shoulder and headed off onto the field, keeping both eyes on the troublemakers.

After the last few rounds, I managed to master most of the routine. Holly was a terrible leader though, and she even messed up on the steps and some of the phrases. I couldn't help but smile at that. Mrs. Caldwell would never let Holly take Casey's place, at least I knew that much.

At the end of practice, I headed quickly back to Casey.

Mrs. Caldwell removed the ice pack and we could see that the swelling had subsided a little.

"Stay off of it as much as you can," Mrs. Caldwell said.

Casey nodded and began to gather her things.

Then we heard the sound of Holly's voice. "Jake!" she called out loudly. "Hey, Jake! Jake!"

Casey and I looked over. The boys who had been running laps across the field had stopped for a break. Some of the girls from our squad jogged over to them, and we watched as Holly and Ronnie headed straight for Jake. At that distance, I couldn't hear what they were saying, but they constantly glanced back at us as they continued giggling and flirting with Jake.

Casey frowned.

"They're just trying to make you jealous," I said, feeling the same way that Casey did. Although I tried not to let that emotion show, I could not help my annoyed expression.

Casey said nothing. Instead, she gently rubbed her foot, wincing slightly with the pain.

"Girls!" Mrs. Caldwell called, waving her hands to bring Holly, Ronnie, and a few others back to our group. "I have one more announcement before you go today. For the game this weekend, we'll be leaving early on the bus on Saturday morning. We're competing against our main rival team, so this is a very important football game for our school. There will be large crowds, so you girls really need to be prepared, and be able to project your voices to be heard."

She paused for a moment to make sure we were listening and understood the importance of what she was saying. "Here are your permission slips for the bus ride with all the information for your parents. Please have this back to me by tomorrow afternoon."

From there, everyone grabbed their bags and headed up to the locker rooms. Brie and I stayed with Casey, helping her to make her way.

She seemed much stronger on her foot than before, and I silently hoped she'd be okay on Saturday. There was no way I wanted Holly to be given a chance as leader, especially for such an important game.

She and Ronnie skipped passed us on the way to the locker room. They were talking about Jake and making sure that we could hear every word. I completely ignored them. But I couldn't say the same for Casey.

In an effort to cheer her up, I said, "How about you stay over at my house again tonight? I need to work on the routine, and since you're the leader, who better to help me?"

"I can try and help you from a chair," Casey said with a small smile. "I probably need to rest my ankle, so I don't have to sit out on Saturday."

"That sounds like a good plan," I grinned, happy to

see the smile returning to my twin's face.

Although I really did want Casey to feel better about what had happened, I had another reason for asking her to stay over again. When she was around, I found it so much easier to cope with my mom's death. I dreaded going home to a quiet house with just my dad and me. Without Mom to greet me as soon as I walked in the door, I knew I'd struggle to cope. But with Casey alongside me, I felt so much stronger. And I was sure my dad would agree to her staying another night.

I had no doubt that my mom would also approve.

Her smiling face flashed through my thoughts and I was sure I could even hear her voice in my head.

I'm here with you, Ali.

I'll always be with you.

CHAPTER FIFTEEN

Casey

I sat down on the locker room bench. My ankle was sore again from walking up the hill to the school. "I'll have to check with Mom first." I smiled at Ali hopefully. I really wanted to stay at her house for another night. I could imagine her dad taking care of me, and with Ali's bed being so comfortable, it was hard to resist. I had to be better for the game on Saturday. And I had to prove to Holly and Ronnie that I wasn't someone to be messed with.

Grabbing my phone from my bag, I went straight to my favorites list so I could call my mom. I hated that I'd let my guard down around those horrible girls. Even though I'd had a feeling they were planning something, I never thought that Holly would do something so mean. I used to think of her as a friend, but I guess that I never really knew her at all, not the real Holly, anyway.

Mom picked up on the fourth ring. "Casey, is everything okay? I'm on my way to get you, I'm just about to head out the door."

"Everything is fine, Mom," I said.

I wanted to avoid all the details of hurting my ankle. If she worried too much, she might refuse to let me have another sleepover. "Can I stay at Ali's again tonight?"

"Another night?" she asked. "I don't know, Casey."

"There's a big game on Saturday and I need to catch Ali up on the steps so she's ready for it. And then we plan to do homework the rest of the time. I promise. Mom. I'll get heaps of work done if I'm with Ali."

Mom knew my grades weren't great, which was why I was in this whole mess, to begin with. If I had never freaked out about the test in the first place, and let Ali swap places again, then I wouldn't be faced with Holly and Ronnie being so mean.

After a long pause, she replied, "Okay. As long as you get your schoolwork done, I guess it's alright." I nodded to Ali, silently telling her that Mom had agreed.

"Can I bring you some clothes?" Mom asked.

"No, that's okay," I said. "I'll just borrow them from Ali. But since you were already on your way, would you mind bringing a toothbrush and my history notebook? I left it on my desk and I need it to get some homework done for tomorrow."

"Yeah, that's fine," Mom replied. "I'll grab them now and see you outside the school in about fifteen minutes."

Since Mom had found out about Ali's existence in my life, she had tried to make more of an effort with me. And because I hadn't seen her in over a day, I had a feeling that she might actually miss me. I realized that I missed her too.

Brie stood up and slung her bag over her shoulder. "I have to go, guys," she said. "My mom is waiting. But I'll see you both tomorrow. I hope your ankle gets better, Casey!"

I smiled gratefully at my friend. "See you tomorrow, Brie."

"See you tomorrow," Ali chimed in.

We both waved to her as she left the room.

Ali held my bag for me while I slowly made my way out of the locker room, keeping most of my weight on my good ankle. With each step, I thought more about Holly and Ronnie, and soon tears of frustration were spilling from my eyes.

"Casey," Ali frowned. "What's wrong?"

"This has gone too far," I said. "They're being so mean to me. When will it all stop?"

Ali sighed. "I don't know. But I think you should tell

Ms. Caldwell that Holly tripped you on purpose."

I shook my head. "I don't want to do that."

Ali sighed. "Well, let's just stick together and keep an eye on them. If they try anything else we need to stand up to them."

"Yes, you're right," I said, wiping at my cheeks. I knew that I had to be stronger and not let them get away with their bullying.

At the end of the hallway, the doors opened and the entire football team entered, heading our way.

I wiped my cheeks a few more times, trying to brush away all evidence of tears. Ali and I moved out of the way while the boys passed us, their boots stomping loudly on the wooden floor as they made their way toward the locker room.

I spotted Jake in the middle of the group.

"We're going to kick their butts this weekend!" someone shouted, and then the rest of the boys whooped and hollered. I watched Jake as he laughed with his friends.

Jake's eyes suddenly connected with mine, and he left the group to stop and talk to us.

"Hi, Casey. Hi, Ali," Jake said, his eyes sparkling.

"Hey," I smiled.

"Hey Jake," Ali said

You guys looked great out there," Jake grinned.

"Thanks, you too," I beamed back at him.

Ali moved a step away from us, and I pretended not to notice. She was giving me space to talk to Jake, and I appreciated it. But with her nearby, I was able to channel more confidence from her.

"So, the big game Saturday, huh?" I said.

"Yeah," Jake nodded. "I think we have a good chance this year. Coach said we all get new equipment if we win."

"Wow, that's cool," I said. I wasn't sure I would care about football equipment, but he seemed excited about it.

We locked eyes for a minute, before he chuckled a

little and then rubbed his hand through his hair. "Well, I should go shower and head home."

"See you tomorrow," I said.

"Definitely," he said, nodding his head.

He waved to Ali and then made his way down the hall.

I couldn't move from my spot until he had disappeared into the locker room.

I turned to Ali and covered my mouth. A giggle burst from my lips.

"Wow!" Ali said. "You were right about Jake. What a change since last week."

"I know!" Casey said. "He actually left his friends to talk to me. He's never done that before."

"Well, he definitely likes you," Ali said. "It's so obvious."

My insides warmed, thinking of Jake. He was clearly interested. And I was too. I decided to take him up on his offer to go out for pizza. Butterflies fluttered in my stomach at the thought of his smile, and I was unable to remove the wide grin that was fixed to my face. All thoughts of Holly and Ronnie had disappeared.

We waited outside for almost ten minutes before Moms' car pulled into the parking lot. And right behind her was Ali's dad.

"That's really weird," Ali said. "Dad usually arrives earlier."

When they pulled up, Ali's dad was the first one out of his car. He came over to us and grabbed my sister's bag from her. "Sorry I'm late, sweetheart. I got stuck on a phone call."

Ali hugged him. "It's fine. We were waiting for my—er—Casey's mom."

Ali looked at me with wide eyes. Technically we shared the same biological mother, but I was sure it was strange for Ali to call our mom *her* mom after her adopted mother had recently died.

"Can Casey stay over again?" Ali asked, skipping past the awkwardness.

"Is it okay with Casey's mom?" Ali's dad asked.

Mom came up behind him. "It's fine with me."

Ali's dad turned around and nodded at her. "Then it's settled. It's good to see you again, Jackie."

"You too," Mom said. "And if you need anything from my family, or if we can help in any way, please let me know. We'd love Ali to stay over again, anytime she feels ready."

Ali's dad smiled, and Mom did as well.

For a crazy moment, the idea popped into my head that it would be amazing if Ali's dad and our mom ended up together. I mean, Ali and I were twin sisters, we had the same biological mother. It would make perfect sense. But then I silently reprimanded myself for thinking that way. It just wouldn't be right. Ali's adopted mom had just passed away. And I wondered if her dad would ever recover from the loss.

Although I pushed the thought to the back of my mind, I kept it there for safe keeping. If they ever did end up together, then Ali and I would have a full family. Something we both wanted.

It was a wild kind of fairy tale thought.

But maybe someday in the future, it could happen!

CHAPTER SIXTEEN

Ali

After Casey and I hugged our mom goodbye, Dad took us home. Dad had asked Casey about her foot, since he saw her limping on the way to the car. But our mom hadn't even noticed. I knew Casey hadn't said anything to her, and she probably didn't have too much of an opportunity, but I had hoped she would at least notice. As much as I hated to believe it, I wondered if some of Casey's accusations about her not caring enough, might actually be true. I knew she was trying harder, I just hoped that would continue so things between Casey and her would improve.

Once Dad pulled into the driveway, he turned to us and said, "I'm going to go and start dinner, now. It will be ready in about an hour."

"Okay, we'll be in the backyard," I replied. "It's still nice out, and I really need to get this cheerleader routine down. Casey can sit on one of the garden chairs and help me."

"What about homework?" he asked.

"We'll do it after dinner, Dad, I promise."

He nodded. "Okay, girls. Just be careful with your ankle, Casey, you really need to stay off it as much as possible."

Casey and I took the side gate to the back of the house. We passed through Mom's garden. Even in one week, the flowers at the edge were starting to turn brown. I would have to remember to water them each day after school, so they'd continue to grow. Mom would be so disappointed if I didn't do that.

We put our bags down by the side of the house.

"Casey, sit here," I said, pulling over one of the lounge chairs to the edge of the patio.

Then I stood in front of her on the grass. "Okay, please tell me what I'm doing wrong."

She sat down and propped her leg up on the side of the chair. Her limp had improved in the short car ride home. I was so glad that it wasn't as bad as we'd originally thought.

I did the routine for her.

"Good," she said. "You're better than a few of the other girls who have already had a week's worth of practice."

I smiled.

She stood up and walked over to me. The limp wasn't even noticeable now. "You need to be sharper on this move."

Casey and I went through the routine, slower this time, and she corrected me as needed. By the time Dad called us in for dinner, we'd already run through it three times without any mistakes.

I was grinning broadly when we entered the kitchen. It felt good to be caught up in one part of my life. Now, I needed to tackle my schoolwork. But that would have to wait until after dinner.

The next day at school was much better than my first day back. Holly and Ronnie seemed really disappointed that Casey had fully recovered. And I smiled smugly towards them when I noticed their annoyed reactions. For the entire day, I didn't leave my twin's side. I was ready to stand up for her if those girls tried anything more. Whether it was me by Casey's side, or the girls had given up on bullying her, I had no idea, but they didn't bother either of us at all.

Practice that afternoon was much better, and it seemed like we were going to be prepared for the game the following day. Mrs. Caldwell even complimented me on how quickly I'd learned the steps. I made sure she knew that Casey had been responsible for helping me to learn so quickly. Mrs. Caldwell seemed pleased about that, and so did Casey.

Casey had done so much for me in just a couple of days. It was such a small gesture to show my gratitude. Just having her nearby made me feel as though I could cope. And without much convincing, she stayed over again on Friday night.

I liked to think I was a good influence on her as well. Because we were prepared for the game the next day, after dinner I suggested we get stuck into our homework for the weekend, and get it out of the way.

At first, she wasn't too thrilled at the idea, but when we were done, and she realized we had the whole weekend free from schoolwork, she was over the moon.

After we had packed up our books, Casey went upstairs to shower. I wanted to say goodnight to Dad and found him in his office at the other end of the house.

As I approached the door, I heard him laugh.

Laugh!

I hadn't heard that sound in a while. It warmed my heart.

I slowly and quietly approached the door. I could clearly hear his conversation and realized that he must be on the phone.

The door was slightly ajar, and I turned my head to listen.

"Jackie, your daughter is amazing!" he said.

Jackie?? There was only one person we knew who had a daughter and was named Jackie! I realized instantly that he was talking to our mom.

"It's been wonderful having her at our house. She's been such a tremendous support to Ali, and it's made all the difference. Ali and Casey get along so well, and it's so nice to see them reunited."

For some reason, I didn't want to interrupt their conversation. I heard the smile in Dad's voice and didn't want it to end. We had both lost someone. That person was my adopted mother, but she was also my dad's wife, and I knew that he had loved her very much. He was hurting and he needed me as much as I needed him, perhaps even more. I made a silent promise to myself to try harder, and to think of him as much as he thought of me.

Casey and I woke bright and early the next morning, and Dad drove us to the school parking lot where all the cheerleaders and football players had been asked to meet. There was a large yellow school bus waiting for everyone to board, so we could travel to our rival school. By the time we climbed the steps, we found that the bus was mostly full.

Brie had saved us a seat in front of her so we could be together for the ride.

Even though I tried not to have feelings for Jake, out of habit, before sitting down I looked for him. And I watched Casey do the same thing.

He was at the back of the bus with the other football players, and we were a few seats in front of them.

Just as the bus began to move from its parked position onto the road, Holly and Ronnie rushed down the aisle toward the back of the bus, giggling and laughing as they passed us. I turned in their direction, and saw them squeeze into a seat in between Jake and his friend. I could hardly believe what I saw. There was no stopping those girls.

"Should we move away from them?" Brie asked, knowing how annoying Holly and Ronnie would be for the rest of the ride.

The only available seats were at the front of the bus.

I turned to Casey to see what she wanted to do.

"Yeah," Casey said. "Let's move."

Even at the front, Holly and Ronnie's voices carried

up to us. A few times Mrs. Caldwell had to tell them to quieten down, but their silence only lasted a few seconds.

Mrs. Caldwell eventually gave up, and instead, ignored the noise at the back and continued to chat with the football coach, who sat next to her.

I tried to lift Casey's spirits, but she mostly stared out the window. I didn't remember Holly and Ronnie being like this when I first came to the school. It was as if they had purposely tried to become a part of Jake's group just to make Casey upset.

And their plan was working.

CHAPTER SEVENTEEN

Casey

When we arrived at our rival school, there was already a huge line of people waiting to get onto the field. After helping to get the equipment off the bus, we headed down a separate entrance where we set up in preparation for the game.

"Okay, let's warm up!" I called to the group, once we were settled in our place.

I glanced over at the cheerleaders on the other team. They were sitting on their bench chatting with each other, and several were on their phones.

That wasn't going to happen for my team. We were going to be focused and show off our routines perfectly.

We all sat in a circle and went over our stretches together before heading out onto the field and quickly running through all our steps.

Before I knew it, the buzzer had sounded and the game had begun. We stood on the sideline with the buzz of the cheering crowd surrounding us. The exciting atmosphere helped add to the excitement of our team. And when it was time for us to run onto the field and perform one of our main routines, all of the girls were smiling and bursting with energy.

The girls performed to perfection and I smiled proudly at our group. One of the girls, a dark-haired girl named Amy, seemed the most enthusiastic of all.

When we reached the point of the pyramid, all of the girls on the bottom row took formation. I walked over to my bases, Holly and Ronnie. I couldn't believe that of all the girls on our team, Mrs. Caldwell had assigned them to me. And since Ali had missed too many practices, I wasn't able to have her as one of my bases instead.

I stood in front of Holly and Ronnie, with three other girls who were also to be lifted, and we prepared to perform the last of the cheer before heading to the back of the group.

"Don't fall, Casey," Ronnie snickered. "It's a big crowd."

"It would be sooo embarrassing," Holly added.

My palms broke out into a sweat. Would Holly do something to make me fall? She'd already tried to hurt me once, but that was during practice. Would she do that at a big game with everyone watching? Though if I did fall, Holly would look bad too, since she was supposed to hold my weight. But Holly had made it clear that she didn't like me and was capable of anything, even openly mocking me in front of everyone else.

My stomach twisted, and I could feel the thumping of my heartbeat against my chest.

I tried to pay attention to the second group of girls, Ali and Brie included, as they did somersaults before the big lift.

The seconds flew by, and before I knew it, I had to step up onto Holly and Ronnie's hands. I held onto their shoulders and gathered my balance.

The crowd grew excited, especially those who were cheering for our team. I swallowed hard and let go of a big breath.

You can do this.

Holly and Ronnie lifted me. But Holly was a few seconds behind. I wobbled for a moment before regaining my balance.

Standing up, I held my arms high above my head. The crowd went wild.

We held steady for about ten seconds, before the girls lowered me to the ground so we could finish the routine. I avoided their eyes, but felt them staring at me, almost as a warning.

With the hard part over, I was able to concentrate on the game going on in front of us. But still my pulse raced after the routine we'd just completed. I felt proud that we'd pulled it off, but at the same time, the nervous sensation and my fear of falling remained.

I sat anxiously watching the rest of the game, partly ill at ease over what could have been the most embarrassing moment of my life, and partly because of the close score between the two teams on the field in front of us

But when the buzzer finally sounded, every ounce of anxiety quickly faded away. The game was over and our team had won by a touchdown! Everyone on our side of the field cheered so loudly that I thought my ears would burst.

Jake threw off his helmet and joined his team, each of

the boys jumping in the air and grabbing hold of one another ecstatically.

Ali, Brie, and I jumped up and down together, shaking our pom-poms in the air above us.

I couldn't believe we had won!

Jake caught my eye and gave me a big smile. I smiled back at him. The boys had played a really good game, and none of the cheerleaders had messed up even once! All my concerns over Holly and Ronnie were forgotten. It was the perfect day.

None of us could stop talking about the game on the way back to the bus. The other team—who had jeered at us for most of the game—hung their heads as they went back into their school.

It served them right!

I wasn't sure how it happened, but I found Jake directly in front of me when we boarded the bus. He was talking to one of his teammates and then sat alone in one of the seats.

Looking up at me as I neared his seat, he smiled, "Hey Casey, do you want to sit next to me?"

"Thanks, Jake—" my words were cut short when someone bumped into my arm.

Holly squeezed past me and plopped down in the seat alongside Jake.

"Oh, my gosh, Jake! What an awesome game. You did so well. I watched you the whole time. It was such a close game, I was freaking out!" She kept going on in her over the top friendly manner.

Jake looked up at me and shrugged. I pretended that I wasn't bothered, as I continued down the aisle towards the back where Ali and Brie were already sitting together. I found the closest empty seat and scooted in, propping my arm up next to the window.

Grabbing hold of my phone, I turned it on.

Immediately, a text came in from Ali.

I saw what Holly did to you.

I turned in my seat and rolled my eyes then typed back: *I'm glad U saw it 2. Jake is 2 nice to say anything.*

Do you want to stay over at my house again tonight?

I should probably stay at home tonight. But I'd love for U to stay with us! Mom doesn't mind. I already asked her.

That sounds so good! Let me check with my dad.

When we got off the bus, Ali's father was waiting for us next to my mom and Grandma Ann. I spotted Lucas playing with Jake's brother, Matt, in the adjoining parking lot.

"Dad said it was okay for me to stay," Ali said. "But he came here anyway, so he could bring me a few things and see me before I went to your house."

I nodded my head in understanding.

"But I'm worried about leaving him on his own tonight. He'll be all by himself in the house. It's the first time since Mom…" Casey trailed off.

"Will he mind if you're not at home?" I asked.

Ali shook her head. "He says it's fine and that it'll be 'good for me'."

"Then I'm sure it's okay with him," I smiled, trying to reassure her.

Ali smiled back but I could see that she was not convinced.

We said goodbye to Brie and headed towards our families. It was strange seeing Mom and Grandma Ann speaking with Ali's dad. This was the new normal for us. It seemed that our families had finally been brought together, though definitely not in the way we'd anticipated.

Mom came over to us and gave me a hug. It was an unexpected surprise.

"Congratulations," Mom said to Ali and me. "From the excitement of your classmates, it looks like everything went well?"

"We won," Ali said.

"Were you able to do your routine?" Ali's dad asked her.

"Yes," she said, putting her hand on my shoulder. "Thanks to Casey for helping me."

"Your mom invited me for dinner," Ali's dad said to her.

For a moment, Ali didn't move. An uncomfortable expression crossed her face and I felt a surge of emotion coming from within her. Her dad had said, "Your mom", which indicated "our mom". He didn't seem bothered by it at all, even though Ali did.

"If that's okay with you?" he smiled.

There was only a moment's hesitation while Ali processed the meaning of his words, and then her face lit up excitedly.

"Yes!" she beamed.

She grinned at me and I knew exactly what was going through her head. She was just as excited as I was to finally have our families together.

The kitchen table was more cramped than I'd ever experienced. With two extra guests, we were all squashed next to each other. But I loved it. Everyone was smiling while they talked. After eating two slices of pizza, I was hungry for more. Leaving my seat, I moved to the counter top where the open boxes of pizza had been placed. After choosing another slice I turned back to the table, but stood for a moment and took in the scene in front of me.

Ali's dad was talking about their trip to Maine some years before, and everyone, including Lucas, was watching him. The image was of the perfect family, the type of family I had always wanted and had always dreamed of having.

As bizarre as the thought was, I could not remove it from my mind, and for the rest of the evening, I watched how our mom and Ali's dad interacted with each other.

They appeared to get on very well and for the second time, I contemplated the fairy tale idea of our two families becoming one.

A wide smile formed on my face as I considered the thought further.

Could it be possible?

CHAPTER EIGHTEEN

Ali

The opportunity to have my dad and Casey's family together at the one table created the strangest sensation of peace within me.

To see my dad distracted, for a short time at least, from the terrible heartache that I knew existed deep inside him, warmed my heart. I knew that both he and I may never fully recover from my mother's death, but I was convinced that having Casey in our lives would help us both to heal and to live again.

I watched my birth mother as she chatted to Dad, and took in her beautiful smile.

For a fleeting second, I considered how wonderful it would be for us all to become a real family together.

I dwelled in that perfect picture for just a moment, and then shoved it quickly away. Right then, I could not even contemplate replacing my adopted mom. That thought was way too painful. I knew it would also take time before I could think of my dad with anyone else.

But possibly in the future.

Focusing on the sound of Lucas' laughter alongside me, I tuned back into the dinner time chatter as I munched on the pizza in front of me. It was so wonderful to be part of a large family and to have my sister and brother alongside me.

Accepting Casey's offer of more pizza, I locked eyes with her and smiled. I could sense the happiness she was feeling right then. I could also sense that once again, my adopted mother would approve. All she had ever wanted was for her family to be happy.

And in time, I knew that my dad and I would find true happiness again.

I ended up staying at Casey's house for the remainder of the weekend and as it turned out, into the following week as well. Dad had a work trip organized and it was necessary for him to leave early on Monday morning. Without the offer to stay at Casey's, I would have been forced to go along with him. But there was no reason for that since Casey and her family were happy to take me.

Once again, I was reminded of the fact that Casey was always there for me when I needed her.

Because Sunday was a gloomy, rainy day and we'd already completed our homework, we spent Sunday on the couch watching most of the Harry Potter movies. Lucas joined us, while Grandma Ann flitted in and out of the room constantly making sure we had enough to eat.

Even though we'd seen each of the movies before, we

were all so engrossed in them and the time passed quickly. I loved the feeling of having a brother and a sister, and Lucas was always at my side.

Casey and I spent Sunday evening in her room and I laughed at Lucas' constant attempts to be included.

"Get out of my room!" Casey yelled at him more than once.

When I saw his face fall with disappointment, I felt sorry for him. It was obvious to me that he simply wanted our attention. This was something I didn't mind at all, but as Casey explained, it became very annoying after a while.

I could understand her point of view, although for me it was a treat to have siblings to spend time with. This was something I had begun to treasure, especially after being an only child my entire life, until now.

After Lucas was finally dragged away by our mom, and instructed to leave us in peace, Casey and I had the chance to plan our outfits for the following day.

Although she complained about having too few clothes to choose from, I loved her sense of style and the variety of cool clothes that she owned. She commented that she didn't own anything of quality and that her clothes could never compare to mine. But I didn't care about that. It was just fun to have a sister to share with.

The weekend was over much too quickly, however, and before we knew it, Monday morning had arrived.

But as soon as I opened my eyes, I knew that something was wrong.

A nauseous sensation sat in my stomach, but I had no idea why.

I hadn't eaten anything out of the ordinary, so I knew that couldn't be it.

My head pounded and my fingers and toes tingled.

Even though I'd had a full night's rest, I felt drained and exhausted.

"Morning, Ali," Casey said from above me. I'd slept

on the trundle bed next to her, since her bed was only a single-sized one.

"I don't feel right, Casey," I said.

She sat up and dropped down to the bed next to me. "What's wrong?"

I told her, and she got Grandma Ann right away.

Grandma Ann felt my head and checked me out for a few moments before she said anything. "You don't have a fever, but you're very pale. How about you stand up?"

I stood, but then the whole room tilted, and I began to fall backward. Grandma Ann caught me by the arms and slowly brought me back down toward the bed.

"I don't think you should go to school today," she said.

I was not going to argue. All I wanted to do was go back to sleep.

She checked the clock on Casey's nightstand. "I have to take Lucas to school early, and I promised I'd be a parent helper on his field trip. But if you're unwell, then I don't think I should leave you on your own."

"I don't have a fever," I said. "So it can't be too serious. Maybe I should just get some more rest. I'm sure I'll be fine. You don't have to miss the field trip. Lucas was looking forward to you going."

It was all he could talk about the night before so I did not want to be responsible for keeping his grandmother at home.

"It's no big deal," I assured her. "Really. I'll be fine on my own."

Grandma Ann narrowed her eyes, but I gave her a small smile. A shooting pain ripped through my head, and I tried not to flinch. I did not want her to notice. I'd hate for Lucas to miss out on having her with him today.

"Call me if you feel any worse," Grandma Ann said. "Your mom is in meetings all day, a few towns over, so I'll be able to get home quicker than she can. I'll be home around lunch time since the field trip is just for the morning."

"Okay, I will," I gave her another small smile.

"Lucas and I need to go in a few minutes," she said. "Casey, can you please keep an eye on Ali until it's time for you leave for the bus."

"Yes, Grandma Ann. Don't worry, I will," Casey said.

I laid back down while Casey got ready.

After a few minutes, the room became sweltering and I pushed the covers aside. Grandma Ann said I didn't have a fever, but I felt much worse now than I did when she was home. Maybe a cold shower would help?

I got out of bed, and held onto Casey's dresser for balance, then walked out of the bedroom and into the hallway.

Casey was in the kitchen eating breakfast as I made my way into the bathroom. I turned on the shower and got in. The cold temperature of the water stung at first, but then it felt good. I stood there for a few minutes, hoping the water would cool me down.

But when I eventually turned off the spray, I knew it wasn't going to be that easy.

After dressing back into my pajamas, I went straight to Casey's room. She was in there, gathering her books. She turned around, and her face fell.

"Ali, you don't look well at all."

"I don't feel any better. Actually, I feel worse."

All of a sudden, I began to shiver. I just wished my body would make up its mind. Was I hot or was I cold?

Casey covered me with the quilt. "I think I should stay with you. Just in case."

"No," I said. "I'll be okay. Go to school. I'm just going to try and sleep. There's no reason for you to miss school because of me."

She chewed on her lip, deciding.

"Grandma Ann will be back soon," I said. "I'll be

fine."

"Okay, but make sure you call either me or Grandma Ann if you feel any worse, okay?"

"I will," I promised, closing my eyes.

Casey hesitated, but then I heard her leaving the room, followed by the sound of the front door closing behind her.

I tried to fall asleep, hoping that when I woke up I would feel better.

I could only hope that would be the case.

Sharp bolts of pain suddenly shot through my temples, like a sudden strike of lightning. My eyes glazed over and the room began to spin.

CHAPTER NINETEEN

Casey

I'd almost reached the bus stop when I sensed something was terribly wrong. I felt it deep within, in that special place where all my fears lay. The tremors had begun only moments earlier, but already they were working their way to the surface. And I knew beyond doubt, it had something to do with Ali.

I shouldn't have left her by herself when she was so sick. Like every other time, I was able to connect with her emotions, and I felt certain that she was in trouble.

The bus pulled up to the curb in front of me. If I missed it, I'd be late for school, the third time in less than a month which meant a week's detention. Why had Mrs. Jensen enforced that rule anyway? The new principal was way too strict! I couldn't miss cheerleading practice either. I would have to fight to keep my spot away from Holly.

But the threat of those issues, even a week's detention, was overpowered by the chilling sensation that I must turn back. Ignoring everything else, I spun quickly around and raced down the street. The breaths whooshed out of me as I ran. My house was so close, the brightly colored mailbox stood like a sentry at the edge of the pavement. But my heavy school bag weighed me down. I shrugged it off and dropped it onto the grass at my feet, then rushed ahead, across the lawn towards the front door.

I searched desperately for the key that was tucked away in its hiding place, behind the leafy bush by the door. I grabbed hold of it and fumbled with the lock.

"Come on! Come on!" I said to myself, my fingers fighting to get the key into the knob so I could turn it and release the latch.

Bursting through the front door, there was only silence. My feeling of dread worsened. In my rush, I tripped over Lucas's pile of stupid action figures that he'd left in the hallway and I stumbled and fell, banging my knee heavily on the floor.

Adrenaline pumped through my veins and spurred me on toward my bedroom.

That was where I had left Ali only a short time earlier. Grandma Ann said to call her if Ali felt any worse, but I knew there was no time for that. By the time she returned home, it would be too late.

Swinging the bedroom door open, I found the room empty, the covers of my sister's bed lying in an untidy heap on the floor. Turning quickly back in the direction I came from, I raced along the hallway towards the bathroom. It was as though a magnetic pull drew me in that direction and I was positive that's where Ali would be. But when I turned the handle, the door wouldn't budge. It was securely locked!

The fear in my belly intensified as I frantically jiggled the circular knob on the door.

"Ali? Ali?" I called my twin's name but there was no response. And in desperation, I pushed fiercely on the door with my shoulder, shoving it with every ounce of strength I had.

"Ali!" I cried.

But the door still wouldn't move.

And just as I was about to give up, the door burst open and I fell forward.

***

Find out what happens next in Twins Book 7

Available NOW!!

You can also choose to read the final 4 books in the Twins series as a collection in a combined set at a

DISCOUNTED PRICE!

(This is much cheaper than buying the next 4 books individually).

TWINS - Part Three: Books 7, 8, 9 & 10

***

Thank you so much for reading this book. I hope that you really enjoyed it. If you did, would you mind leaving a review? I'd be so grateful!

Thanks so much,

Katrina x

Like us on Facebook
https://www.facebook.com/JuliaJonesDiary/

And follow us on Instagram

@juliajonesdiary

@freebooksforkids

Here is another great book that I hope you enjoy…

THE SECRET

Mind Magic

When Tess meets her neighbor and discovers his secret, she finds that her life will never be the same again.

And I'm sure you'll enjoy these books as well…

JULIA JONES'
DIARY
BOOK
1
MY
Worst
DAY
EVER!
Katrina Kahler

Witch
School
Book 1
Katrina Kahler

DIARY OF AN
ALMOST COOL GIRL
Where it all started..
Meet Maddi
"Ooops!"
Book
1
B. CAMPBELL

DIARY OF
MR TDH
AKA
MR
TALL
DARK
AND
HANDSOME
Book
1
KAZ CAMPBELL
ALMOST COOL SERIES

I SHRUNK
MY
BEST
FRIEND
BOOK 1
OOOPS!
KATRINA KAHLER & JOHN SAKOUR

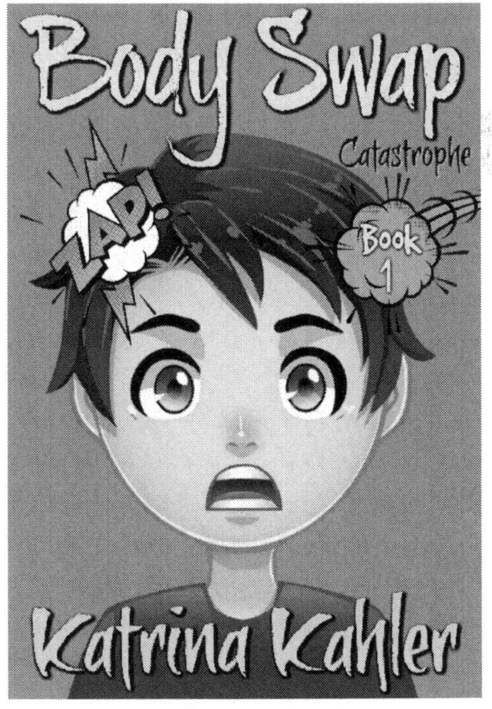
Body Swap
Catastrophe
ZAP!
Book
1
Katrina Kahler

41813216R00173

Made in the USA
Lexington, KY
11 June 2019